# BLINDFOLD

Other Scholastic titles
you will enjoy:

*Dance of Death*
Jo Gibson

*Homecoming Queen*
John Hall

*Prom Date*
Diane Hoh

*The Stalker*
Carol Ellis

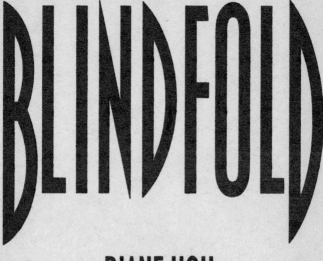

# BLINDFOLD

## DIANE HOH

SCHOLASTIC INC.
New York Toronto London Auckland Sydney

ISBN 0-590-98842-5

Text copyright © 1997 by Diane Hoh. All rights reserved. Published by Scholastic Inc.

12 11 10 9 8 7 6 5 4 3 2 1          7 8 9/9 0 1 2/0

Printed in the U.S.A.                    01
First Scholastic printing, October 1997

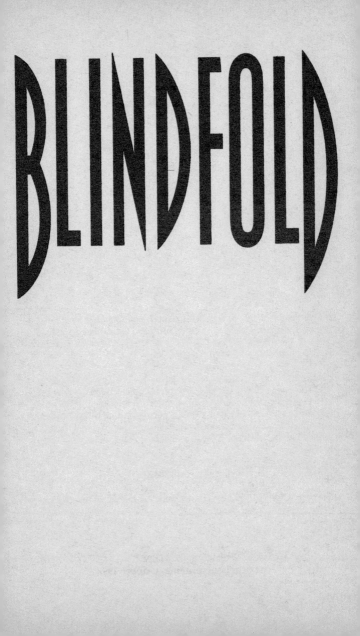

# Prologue

A Friday morning in early October begins like any other morning in Felicity, Ohio.

But in the basement of the old courthouse at Fourth and Market Streets in the heart of the downtown area, the cold, hard-packed, earthen floor seems suddenly to shift, to recoil, as if something has frightened it, and the scurrying sounds of small creatures within the rough, white stone walls stop, as if the animals are listening intently, trying to figure out what the oncoming, unknown danger might be.

The six jail cells, three on each side of a narrow corridor, are empty. The small, filthy windows high on the back wall of each cell are blank and unseeing, the black metal iron-barred doors standing wide open.

In other places, an open door means welcome. But not here. Not in this dark, damp, dismal place. Here, an open door is an invitation to danger, to despair, perhaps even to death.

# Chapter 1

There it sits. The oldest building in town, once a mansion, now nothing but a tired, disgusting old structure used as a courthouse and jail. Once upon a time, it was an impressive home, glossy white, with shiny black shutters and parklike grounds. But that was a very long time ago.

Every time I pass it now, my jaw clenches so tight my teeth ache. I think I'm afraid that if I don't clench my jaw, my mouth will open and I'll start screaming, *"Tear it down, tear it down, bury it under a ton of cement!"* And people will think I'm crazy.

But it's a constant reminder. They have got to get rid of it.

That stupid Women of Heritage group! With their silly prattle about "history" and "preserving tradition," blah, blah, blah. Wanting to save that ugly old building as if it were an orphaned child or a sick animal. Nothing should be allowed to last so long. Nothing.

It's ancient and tired and ugly now, an old hound too stubborn to give up. Why can't they let it die a decent death? And let all of its secrets die with it.

Restore it to its "former glory"? *Why?* What is wrong with that Keene woman that she can't let things stay in their natural state? Always fixing up, restoring, preserving, like it's her mission in life. If she has her way, they'll have crews in there any day now, digging and poking and prodding, ripping out doors and walls and flooring . . . and uncovering secrets.

Why should that building survive? It doesn't deserve to.

I have to come up with something.

I never meant to hurt anyone. Especially Christy. We were friends.

But when we were thirteen, she started experimenting with makeup and hairstyles and clothes she saw in magazines, while I was still all knees and elbows. She looked sixteen years old. I was still an awkward, uncertain thirteen, and she didn't want to be seen with me, because she was afraid everyone would guess she was the same age as me.

I didn't understand what was happening. I only knew I didn't like it. I hated it. I missed her. Friends were so hard to come by way out there in the country, where the farms were spread so far apart.

We all went to half a dozen different elementary schools scattered along rural roads while we waited for high school to come along and rescue us. Going to different schools didn't matter if we were close enough to hike or bike to one another's houses.

That was true for Christy and Dante and me. He was three years older than us, but out there, that didn't matter, either. He had other friends, too, friends his own age. People liked Dante. But he still spent time with Christy and me.

On weekends, if we got to go into Felicity together, we liked to sneak in through the coal chute window of the old courthouse, slide down the chute, and play in the basement passageways. We weren't supposed to, but the town kids did it all the time. It was creepy down there, but fun. Someone told me once that all those gloomy subterranean passageways had been used to hide slaves who'd escaped from the South through the Underground Railroad.

We were careful to stay away from the one corridor that housed the six basement cells. Not that there was ever anyone dangerous in those cells. A drunk or two, maybe, sometimes a transient who'd stolen something from one of the stores in town. I heard there was a murderer there once, some guy who'd killed his cousin over a prize pig. But mostly, the prisoners were harmless.

Still, we avoided that corridor.

Then Dante outgrew those fun escapades. And soon after Christy did, too. It wasn't any fun by myself.

Everything else changed then, too. Things changed forever for all three of us when Dante looked at Christy one day and saw just how much she had changed. We were just thirteen and looking forward to high school the following fall. He was sixteen.

I saw the look he gave her that one autumn day. I didn't like it a bit. My stomach felt hollow inside. I knew it meant that nothing would ever be the same again.

Nothing was.

From then on, it was Dante and Christy, Christy and Dante, together all the time. With me on the outside, looking in.

# Chapter 2

"Maggie! Can you run these plans over to the old courthouse before school? They need them over there, and I'm not going to have a free second today."

Maggie Keene, dressed in a short denim skirt, a white T-shirt, and red boots, was sprawled on her stomach across her unmade bed amid a jumble of pine-green sheets, open textbooks, and papers. In spite of the din created by her CD player, she heard her mother's shouted request from the foot of the stairs outside her bedroom. She let out a deep, heartfelt groan. She had peer jury hearings before classes began, and a second-period geometry test, for which she was not the least bit prepared. And she hadn't had a chance to do anything with her hair, which she had shampooed last night before bed and slept on damp, always a gruesome mistake with naturally wavy hair. And now her mother wanted her to run an errand?

She jumped off the bed and stomped to the door, glancing into her dresser mirror as she passed it. The sight of the tall, slender figure in the glass brought forth another groan. "Great!" she muttered, yanking open the door. "I look like a Raggedy Ann doll! Just shoot me *now*." A disgusted expression on her angular, fair-skinned face, she ran a self-conscious hand through the short, bronze-colored waves and called down the stairs, "Mom, no can do! Get Dog-face to do it!" Dog-face was her older brother, Darren.

"Your brother has already left. Maggie, please! I've got that bazaar tonight, and I'm way behind schedule."

Dog-face had split already, probably knowing what was coming. Jerk! Why wasn't she an only child? What would it take to make her one? Nothing legal, unfortunately.

"It will only take you five minutes. You go right by the courthouse on your way to school." Maggie's mother stood at the foot of the stairs, looking upward with expectancy in her face, an older version of her daughter's. Wearing worn jeans and an oversized white sweatshirt that read SAVE OUR ANTIQUITIES, YOU'LL BE ONE SOMEDAY, she smiled up at Maggie. "I've got tons of other stuff to do today if we're going to be ready on time tonight." Sheila Keene was president of the Women of Heritage Society in Felicity and was spearheading the drive to save the old courthouse. To that end, she had organized a bazaar being held on the courthouse grounds that evening.

Maggie felt a twinge of guilt. What with the start of school and the renewal of peer jury activities, she had helped her mother very little with what had to be an overwhelming task. "Okay, okay. I'll go! Give me a sec." Heaving a sigh, she returned to her dresser, where she stabbed at her hair repeatedly with a pink plastic pick. "It wasn't *my* idea to save the stupid courthouse," she muttered as she struggled with the chaotic waves. "If you want *my* opinion, that old wreck of a building should be put to rest. And everyone on the peer jury thinks the same thing, so it's not just me. This whole bazaar thing is a huge waste of time."

Snatching up her suede shoulder bag from its usual resting place on the cluttered floor, Maggie turned away from the dresser.

Her mother, holding out a sheaf of papers, was standing in the doorway. She looked hurt, which told Maggie that she'd overheard the last comment.

"Oh. I didn't know you were there," Maggie said, embarrassed.

"That's obvious."

"Mom . . ." Maggie began.

Sheila Keene waved a hand. "Never mind. Your father feels the same way. So does your brother. So does half the *town*! I don't even know that we're going to win this battle. But," a grin spread across her face, "if we lose the battle, and the building *is* torn down, the money we raise tonight will go toward that rec center you and your friends want built in its place. So if I were you, I'd try to muster up a little more enthusiasm."

Maggie relented and returned the grin. She took the papers and the car keys her mother handed her. "Who do I give these to?"

"Anyone. It doesn't matter. They're the plans for the renovation." The hurt look was gone. "And thanks, Maggie. I know your schedule is pretty full. I should have delivered them myself yesterday."

Shrugging, Maggie said, "Nobody's perfect. That old dump is right across the street from school anyway. I guess a few extra steps won't kill me. But do I have to go inside? Can't I just slip these into the mail slot? I hate that place! Every time I go in there, I think the floors are going to collapse or the ceiling's going to land on me."

"You're exaggerating. If it were that bad, it would have been condemned long ago. People are still working in that building, Maggie, and nothing's fallen on them. And no, you can't drop them in the mail slot. I want them hand-delivered, so I know someone got them. Please? Tell you what, as a reward for helping me out this morning, you can keep the van all day. Trudy's picking me up later for the errands we have to run."

Maggie pocketed the keys. Passing her mother in the doorway, she said, "Bribery works every time. See you later."

"Don't forget, you're helping out tonight. You're on the kitchen schedule for eight P.M. sharp!"

"I won't forget. Not that you'd let me."

It was a beautiful early autumn morning. The air was warm and sweet, almost like summer, and the leaves were beginning to turn, hinting of the deep purples and scarlets, and the brilliant, blazing oranges and yellows they would soon become. Maggie hadn't been in the van more than a minute when she found herself relaxing and enjoying the drive down their hill toward the center of town.

The welcoming signs posted at the city limits boasted, FIFTEEN THOUSAND FRIENDLY PEOPLE. Maggie always viewed those signs with a cynical eye. The town itself contained far fewer residents. Reaching fifteen thousand required adding up all of the people in the surrounding rural communities: Arcadia, Muleshoe, Updown, Sugar Hill, Nestegg, and Thompson. Rural students made up half the population at Otis Bransom High School, an ugly, old, gray-stone, three-story structure just around the corner from the supermarket and the ancient courthouse.

Half of Maggie's classmates in her junior year and all of her closest friends were kids she had never even met until ninth grade. The rural schools included grades kindergarten through eighth. It wasn't until they were ready for ninth grade that the farm kids piled into big yellow buses and rode into the heart of Felicity, where the high school would be their daytime home for four years.

Freshman year had to be hard for the newcomers, Maggie thought, not for the first time, as she drove down Main Street toward the courthouse and the high school. First, because the rural kids entered a school where the town kids already knew each other. Cliques had already been formed, allegiances sworn, teams established. Second, since ninth-graders weren't old enough yet to drive, they could only enroll in extracurricular activities if one of the few "late buses" traveled close enough to their homes, most of which, but not all, were farms. For many of them, a high school social life couldn't really begin until junior year, when they had driver's licenses. And then only if they had access to wheels to carry them along the dusty farm roads and onto the paved highway into town for practices and games, rehearsals and dances and parties.

Maggie had always been grateful that her family lived in town. If nothing ever happened inside the city limits, even less had to be happening outside them, where there wasn't even a theater.

When she arrived in the heart of town, quiet this early in the morning, she hesitated. Could the plans wait? Which was more important, being on time for the peer jury hearings, or delivering the plans? It wasn't as if the renovations were going to begin that day. She could take the plans over later, between classes or even after school. What difference did it make?

She hit a red light at the intersection of Market and Fourth. Otis Bransom High School occupied one corner. The old courthouse, which had actually once been the Bransom family home, occupied another. Everyone called it "the old courthouse" now because a new one was in the process of being built just a block away and was, in fact, almost finished. Soon the old building, a huge, white-pillared pre-Civil War structure, would be emptied, stripped of everything but dust and memories.

Her mother wanted it preserved. Some people agreed with her. Others wanted it torn down. Her mother would probably win. Preserving Felicity's history was her "cause," and she almost always overcame any objections.

"That is a *really* creepy-looking building, even in daylight, even with the sun shining," Maggie muttered. "Hard to believe a family ever lived in that rotting old place."

Of course, she knew it hadn't looked that bad way back then. It was, now, a weary, decrepit structure of peeling paint, sagging shutters, and dying ivy. But old photos of the Bransom House on display at the Women of Heritage offices on Third Street showed a very different image. The pictures reflected a pristine, pillared, white mansion with immaculate grounds and shiny black shutters.

"Can you believe the courthouse ever looked like that?" Maggie's best friend, Helen Morgan, had said, awestruck, when they saw the photos. "It looks so awful now!"

The shutters were tilting on their hinges. Most of the lawn, except for a long, narrow strip near the kitchen wing, had become a paved parking lot. The lush gardens, front and back, had been mowed down. The mansion itself, seriously in need of a fresh coat of paint, sagged more with every passing year.

Maggie couldn't have cared less what happened to the ugly old building. But everyone on the peer jury, and just about every other teen in town, wanted it torn down and a rec center built on the site. She had to admit a rec center sounded cool, considering the fact that teen social life in Felicity was sorely lacking. The new mall had only four movie screens instead of eight or twelve like malls she'd read about. Summers were deadly unless you had a pool or the kind of cool parents who let you drive to Cleveland for some fun. From June through August, there was never a single dance held in all of Greene County, unless you counted Friday night square dancing at Jimmy's Barbecue.

With all of that to deal with, a rec center sounded like a really great idea.

Of course she couldn't talk about that much at home, because her mother got *that* look on her face, and Maggie ended up feeling like a traitor.

But if *she* were running Felicity, a recreation center for teens would already be on the drawing board and the old courthouse would be . . . well . . . *history*.

Conscious of passing time, Maggie tapped her fingers impatiently on the steering wheel and glanced sideways at the old courthouse one more time. And shuddered. She couldn't help it. Maybe it had been beautiful once, when there was a happy family living there, but now it just looked like somebody's bad memory, and if you asked *her*, it *should* be torn down.

The light turned green. Maggie pressed down on the gas, glad to get away from the building, with its tall, narrow windows staring back at her as if daring her to come inside. She shuddered again, realizing that she would have to do just that when the peer jury began assisting in the transfer of supplies from the old building to the new. That bright idea had come from the principal, Gail Marsh. Something about "taking responsibility in your community as well as here at Otis Bransom High." Whatever. Maggie was foreperson of the peer jury. No way could she opt out of the chore.

Glancing in her side mirror as she rounded the corner, she noticed only one car behind her, a navy-blue sedan so nondescript she immediately dismissed it. No one she knew would drive such a boring car, so there was no need to wave to the driver, whoever it might be. She pulled into the high school parking lot with one minute to spare before the peer jury hearings were scheduled to begin.

In her rush, she never noticed that the blue car had pulled into a space near her.

In spite of her anxiety about being late, she took the time to stuff into her backpack the roll of plans her mother had given her. Then she jumped out of the van and rushed into the gray stone building.

If she hadn't done that . . . if she had instead left the plans in the van and locked the doors, that Friday would have been no different from any other Friday.

But she took the plans with her.

After a brief interval, the driver's door of the blue sedan opened, and, a moment later, closed again. Footsteps followed Maggie into the high school.

# Chapter 3

Maggie hefted the gavel, loving its smooth, comforting feel. It was solid wood and heavy. A genuine antique. It had belonged to Scout Redfern's great-grandfather, a judge. Most of Scout's ancestors were lawyers and judges. Maggie didn't really need a gavel. She only got to use it when deliberations in the jury room got out of hand. But it was nice to have one. She was touched that Scout had given it to her to prove he harbored no bad feelings when she'd been selected jury foreperson instead of him.

She wouldn't have blamed him if he'd been ticked. After all, he'd been appointed to the peer jury because of his good grades and his demonstrated leadership abilities (he was an officer of practically every organization at Bransom High). She, on the other hand, had been *assigned*, not appointed, to jury duty because Ms. Gross, an English lit teacher who was her counselor, couldn't think of any other way to keep her busy (meaning, Maggie knew, keep her out of trouble).

"What are we going to do with you, Magdalene?" the slim, dark-haired teacher had said in her office at the end of first semester last year. She had sounded exasperated. "You tried drama, and hated it. Then you worked on the school paper with Scout for what, all of six weeks? And quit. He said you were bored. Big surprise. The same thing happened with chorus. It's a good thing you like sports, but sporting events are not enough to keep your mind occupied. We need something else. Frankly, Maggie," the teacher added, "the only thing left for you to try is the peer jury."

"Oh, lovely." Maggie, slumped in a leather chair opposite Ms. Gross's desk, her long, jeaned legs stretched out in front of her, had made a face. "Like I really want to be one of those geeky people who smacks a classmate's hand when he's been naughty. Now *there's* a super way to make friends!"

"You already have plenty of friends," the teacher had responded sharply. "And if you were interested in collecting more of them, you'd have stayed in drama or on the newspaper or campaigned for an office. What gets me is, your peers don't seem to mind your inability to stick to anything for very long."

"That's because they know I'm a loyal and faithful and true friend," Maggie joked, realizing she was straining the counselor's patience. She liked Ms. Gross. But the woman had deliberately returned to Felicity after college and taken a job *here*, when she could have moved to a big city to teach. Which meant she didn't mind being bored, so how could she possibly understand why Maggie hated it?

And Maggie *did* hate it. Very much. She still faced two and a half long, dreary years in Felicity, where nothing much ever happened. They stretched out ahead of her like a jail term. Then she was out of here! On her way to college somewhere far, far away, then to a job in a huge, exciting city. She'd come home on holidays, of course, because it wasn't as if she didn't like her family. Her dad had a great sense of humor and was very generous with allowances, and her mother, when she wasn't so busy reshaping Felicity, was a lot of fun. Dog-face would come home from college, too, and maybe he'd have been magically transformed into a real human being by then.

But it would *take* a holiday to drag her back to Felicity.

"There are ten members of the jury, not twelve," Ms. Gross had continued, apparently unaware that Maggie wasn't really listening. "Sessions are held as often as necessary. They take place either in the morning before classes begin, or after school, whichever time is most convenient for jury members, and last anywhere from an hour to two hours, depending upon the problems presented."

Maggie lifted her head. "You mean, depending upon the *crimes* presented. Horrendous offenses like stealing a candy bar from the vending machine or putting feet up on a desk or mouthing off to a teacher." She twirled an index finger in the air. "I don't know if I can stand the excitement, Ms. Gross."

Ignoring the gesture, the counselor continued, "I must caution you, you'll be dealing with some students who are repeat offenders. They don't like being disciplined, and they especially don't like being disciplined by their peers. If anyone gives you any trouble, you must report it to this office or the principal."

"This office"? Maggie hid a smile. Ms. Gross thought of herself as "this office"? That's what came of settling in Felicity. The woman didn't even see herself as a person anymore.

"Many of the students who get into trouble are simply, like yourself, bored." The counselor's tone deepened, became stern. "I wouldn't want to see that happen to you, Maggie."

"It won't," Maggie answered confidently. It wouldn't. Not because she was afraid of breaking the rules. She wasn't. But getting out of Felicity required going to college and going to college required a relatively unblemished transcript, no matter how screamingly, achingly bored she got. She wasn't taking any chances with that transcript. "Okay, so I'll take a shot at this peer jury thing. Might be fun."

"It isn't supposed to be fun." Ms. Gross frowned as she stood up. "I hope I'm not making a mistake here. The majority of the other nine members are straight-A students, which you could be, too, if you'd apply yourself. I've seen your PSATs. And most of your fellow jurors hold office. Two of them are *cheerleaders*."

"Oh, wow," Maggie breathed with what she hoped was the appropriate degree of awe. The teacher missed the sarcasm. Maggie knew the two girls, "Bennie" Sawyer and Tanya Frye, and liked them. But Ms. Gross couldn't possibly be including Bennie and Tanya in that "majority" of straight-A students. Fortunately for the two girls, good grades weren't essential for cheerleading duties at Bransom High.

"I expect you to take this seriously, Maggie," were Ms. Gross's parting words as Maggie left the office.

Maggie had done just that. She hadn't exactly planned to. She had thought of it more as a lark than anything else, something to pass the time. Four of her closest friends were already on the ten-member jury, so it wasn't as if she'd be walking into a group of strangers.

Helen, her hazel eyes wide, had cried, "No kidding? *You?*"

Alex threw an arm around her shoulders and cried, "Hey, great! I'd already decided we were going to hang out more together this year, now that I'm driving and can hang out in town more. It's like Ms. Gross read my mind."

Lane smiled and said, "Cool. We'll have our very own little club."

Scout gave Maggie an affectionate but cynical grin and said, "Yeah, well, we won't print your name on the roster in permanent ink until we see how long you last."

When she *did* last, Maggie had probably been

more surprised than Scout. Her enthusiasm for the business of debating first innocence and guilt, and then the appropriate disciplinary measures to be taken, had grown rapidly. She had actually begun toying with the idea of going into law someday. The dedication she began bringing to peer jury hearings earned the respect and admiration of her fellow jurors, and at the beginning of this year, she had been selected as foreperson for the first semester. She knew Scout had wanted it, and had expected him to be angry. But the next day he'd given her the antique gavel and told her to use it "in good health." He had sounded sincere.

When she was seated in the first row of folding chairs in the center of the gym, she pulled her gavel from her backpack, dropped the pack on the floor, and glanced around. "Everybody here?"

"Robert's not," Helen volunteered. Tall and broad-shouldered, with a wide, strong face completely devoid of makeup, and light brown hair cut short and straight, Helen looked very much like the athlete that she was. A champion soccer player, the keystone of the girls' basketball team, and a blue-ribbon swimmer, Helen had long since earned the respect of her classmates at Bransom High. With clear eyes, thickly lashed, and a full, upturned mouth, she could have been very pretty with very little effort. But she was adamant in her refusals of Maggie's offers to do a "makeover."

"I couldn't stand having all that goo on my face," Helen always demurred, "and I need to keep my hair short like this for sports."

Lane had told Maggie knowingly, "Helen's afraid of boys. Anyone can see that. She must have been deeply hurt by one, before we met her."

Maggie, who knew Helen better than Lane did, wasn't sure she agreed with Lane. Since when did a lack of makeup signify a fear of the opposite sex? And Helen had confided in her once that she hadn't had many friends, growing up out in the country. "My social skills," she had said, laughing lightly, "are practically nonexistent." But she got along fine with everyone on the peer jury.

"So?" Maggie glanced around the table. "Where *is* Robert?" Now that she was in place herself, she felt impatient with anyone who wasn't seated on time. They had three hearings scheduled for this morning. The "judge" and the "accused" and their "lawyers" would be here soon. The jury should be in place.

"Robert isn't coming," a deep, unfamiliar voice said from the doorway.

All heads turned.

The boy in the doorway, leaning against the frame as if he'd built it himself, was tall, with long legs in jeans, and wide shoulders in a navy-blue suede jacket over a white T-shirt.

"Oh, wow," Helen breathed, and Lane declared, "Omigod, it's John F. Kennedy, Junior! What's *he* doing here?" The two cheerleaders sat up very straight, their hands automatically flying to their hair.

He's a swimmer, Maggie thought, assessing the span of the newcomer's shoulders. She glanced Helen's way to see if there was recognition on her face. There wasn't, so the guy didn't swim at Bransom. Of course not. If he did, Maggie would have seen him when she went to Helen's meets. And if she'd seen him, she'd remember him, because that was definitely *not* a forgettable face. Nice bones. Nice skin, still tanned, although it was too late in the year to be swimming outside. Tennis, too, maybe? He had the shoulders for it. Nice eyes. Bright. Keen, as if they could see things ordinary eyes couldn't. Were they brown or hazel? His hair was brown, a little wavy around the edges, and recently combed, Maggie thought. Maybe right before he entered the gym? What was he smiling at? No one had said anything funny. No one had said anything at all. But he *was* smiling. Like he knew something they didn't.

Well, he *did*. He knew that Robert wasn't coming. And why.

"Okay, I'll bite," Maggie said coolly. Lane was wrong. This guy didn't look that much like John F. Kennedy, Jr. His hair was lighter. "Why *isn't* Robert coming?"

The boy didn't move. Four people arrived and passed him in the doorway, but he stayed where he was. Maggie recognized the quartet. It included Susan Blair, this semester's "judge." Behind her, his usual sullen expression present, walked James Keith, a sophomore; his girlfriend, Connie Fox; and James's student "lawyer," Ralph Santini, who looked like he would rather be taking a pop math quiz blindfolded.

This was James Keith's third appearance before the peer jury this semester, and it was only early October. He had the personality of a badger, the manners of a hyena, and was as sly and stealthy as a snake. We should just sentence him to the zoo, Maggie thought, feeling James's hostile glare. He was focusing it only on her. One of the prices she paid for being foreperson.

Susan took her seat behind the judge's desk, and the other three sat in front of her on folding chairs. James, short and dark and barrel-chested, stared at her arrogantly. Ralph looked far less confident than he usually did. He knew his "client" well. Everyone at Bransom did. No wonder Ralph looked nervous. Connie, a small, pretty girl, wore a bored expression on her face.

"Your friend Robert," the boy in the doorway said in answer to Maggie's question, "is waging a tough battle in calculus. He decided his time would be better spent by hitting the books than by meting out justice. He asked me if I'd be interested in taking his place, since I'd mentioned to him that I might be going into law someday. I thought about this jury thing, and it seemed like a good idea. So here I am. That my chair?" he finished, pointing to the empty chair on Maggie's left.

"You can't just take someone's place," Scout protested. "You have to talk to Mrs. Marsh, our principal, or one of the counselors. You have to be *picked*."

Maggie and Helen exchanged an amused look that said silently, *Boys!* Scout Redfern, who was almost as tall as the boy in the doorway and almost, but not quite, as good-looking, was used to being in charge of things. He obviously wasn't thrilled by the arrival of another great-looking guy in *his* territory. Bad enough that a *girl* had been selected as foreperson. Now, in the doorway, stood yet another threat to Scout's heretofore peaceful, unchallenged reign at Bransom.

Helen smiled and Maggie shrugged. *He'll get over it*, she signaled with her eyes.

"Gotcha," the new boy replied lazily. "I talked to your principal. She's okay. A lot friendlier than the headmaster at Cutler Day."

Phoebe Cutler Day School was a private high school on the outskirts of town, named for one of Otis Bransom's granddaughters. Very expensive. "Since you're standing in *our* doorway," Maggie said, "and joining *our* peer jury, isn't Mrs. Marsh *your* principal now, too?"

The boy laughed and entered the room. He moved with an easy, comfortable stride that announced a healthy dose of self-confidence. "You're right. You're absolutely right. But I've only been here two days. I haven't got used to the change yet. Still got jet lag." Dropping his books on the floor, he slid into his seat.

Maggie's eyebrows rose. "You *flew* here from Cutler Day?" she asked dryly. "Short trip. It's only thirty minutes from town."

This time, he didn't laugh. When she looked at him, he was gazing back coolly. His eyes were dark. Very dark brown, almost black. And not all that warm, come to think of it, at least not at this particular moment. Not while he was looking at *her*. "I meant, I'm still adjusting to the change," he said. His voice had lost its easy warmth, too. But it warmed again as he turned away from her and spoke to the others. "Thomas Aquinas Whittier," he said, smiling. "Dump the Thomas, call me Whit. So what should I know about this deal that I don't? Your . . . *our* principal filled me in some, but I've never done this gig before. We're supposed to judge whether or not the culprit is guilty, and then decide if he gets death by hanging or just a slap on the wrist?"

"That's pretty much it," Alex Goodman said, his voice friendly. Not as competitive as Scout, Alex seemed happy to have another guy on the panel. "You're a junior?"

"Yep." Thomas Whittier kept his face turned away from Maggie. Deliberately, she was sure. Giving new meaning to the expression "cold shoulder." It actually *did* feel chilly.

"How come you switched from Cutler Day?" Alex wore a friendly smile. While he wasn't as gorgeous as Scout, Alex was what most Bransom girls called "cute" or "adorable." Not that tall, with a face that would still look boyish when he was forty. He was always messing with his dark blond hair, trying, Maggie suspected, to make it lie flat like Scout's. It never did.

"Two reasons. One, I hated the place. Two, I'm interested in what's going on with your courthouse here. History in the making. Can't miss that."

"Courthouses, plural," Maggie couldn't resist correcting. "We have two. For right now, anyway."

"What I meant. Courthous*es*." He still wasn't looking at her. "I dig architecture. I know some of the history of the Bransom home, and I wanted to be around to see what happens to it. Have they decided yet? Stay . . . or go? Which is it?"

"I thought you said you were going into law, not architecture." Maggie saw Helen frowning at her, and knew what the frown meant. *Be nice*. Maggie ignored it.

Whittier kept his back to her. "I *am* going into law. Does that mean I can't be interested in architecture? Is there a rule here that says we're only allowed to be interested in one thing? Isn't that kind of limiting?"

Maggie noticed then that Scout looked happier. She couldn't remember the last time she'd seen him looking so smug. He's *glad* this guy doesn't like me, she told herself, annoyed with Scout. And he's glad the feeling seems to be mutual. Like he owns me or something.

She did date Scout sometimes. Often, actually. They'd gone to a lot of movies and picnics over the summer. But Scout had a lot of problems, and Maggie never knew what to say to him when he was feeling down. Then, too, she wasn't interested in getting serious, especially not with someone whose father owned a business in Felicity and would almost certainly offer his only son a very good job right here in town after college. The son would probably take it. And live here forever. Gross.

Scout had a lot of nerve relishing the cold shoulder the new boy was giving Maggie Keene.

Tossing her head in annoyance, she sat up very straight. "Before we start discussing the courthouses and the pros and cons of tearing that old monstrosity down or fixing it up, we have a hearing to conduct here. And two more after that. I suggest we get started if we don't want to miss our first period classes, okay, everybody?"

"Yes, *ma'am!*" Whit said, throwing a salute her way.

Of course he didn't look at Maggie when he said it.

And of course she pretended she didn't notice.

She nodded at Susan to signal they were all in place, and Susan called the hearing to order.

Throughout that hearing and the two that followed, Maggie had the uneasy feeling that there were eyes on her, targeting her like an X ray. She told herself she was imagining things, but her nerves began to sing a warning. It was hard to concentrate on the business at hand.

# Chapter 4

Ignoring the new boy on her left, Maggie studied her notes. James Keith's offense, his fourth of the semester, was his most serious to date. He had been caught stealing a set of keys from the maintenance room, where a careless janitor had left them lying on a desk. The keys would have allowed James access to classrooms, which would also have allowed him access to the school's computers. Aiming to change his grades, Maggie was convinced. As if no one would know.

Although Ralph Santini did his best, he was fighting a losing battle. "Ladies and gentlemen of the jury," he summed up, "let us not make one of our own the scapegoat here. The maintenance man lost those keys and wants to blame my client for his carelessness. We all know who was in the wrong here, and it wasn't James Keith."

*Oh, sure it was, Ralph,* Maggie retorted silently. *You know it, and everyone on this jury knows it.*

*Look up the word "innocent" in the dictionary. James's name won't be there.*

The jury retired to the jury room. Maggie knew it was an open-and-shut case, and didn't expect much argument from any of the peer jurors. Not even from the two cheerleaders. She knew for a fact that James had recently tried to steal Bennie's car; she was always leaving the keys in the ignition when she left her little red sportscar. Maggie also knew that when Tanya had seen him and screamed for help, he'd knocked her down as he ran past her. She'd scraped her elbow and broken her new sunglasses.

James had, of course, denied the episode, saying he was just checking to see who the car belonged to so he could take the keys to the owner. No one could prove otherwise.

Maggie was sure Bennie and Tanya hadn't forgotten, or forgiven, the incident. They wouldn't argue with any punishment handed down to James Keith on this fine October morning.

They didn't.

While ideas on what the guilty party's punishment might be were tossed around, Maggie noticed that Lane was coolly studying Thomas Whittier, openly and unself-consciously. Lane was leaning back in her chair, one finger lazily curling a lock of her long, sleek, ink black hair, the very hair that Maggie Keene had coveted since the very first day she saw Lane Bridgewater walking the halls of Bransom High. She had immediately thought wistfully of at least a dozen wonderful things you could do with hair that didn't frizz up when there was so much as one drop of moisture in the air, and had glared at the new, gorgeous girl, who wasn't really all that tall but walked as if she thought she were.

Up close, Maggie had realized with relief that Lane wasn't really beautiful. Lane herself had said laughingly, "I didn't always look like this. I was scrawny and my hair was short and straight, and I had braces and glasses. I am *so* grateful I grew up." Her olive skin was smooth and unblemished, and her eyes were nearly perfect, a deep, dark blue, with thick, smoky lashes, set exactly the right distance apart and topped by perfectly arched brows. But her mouth was too wide, her nose too thin.

Not that a single guy at Bransom High ever noticed those slight imperfections. Every adolescent male head turned when, in their freshman year, Lane Bridgewater arrived at Bransom High. Maggie and Helen always made a point of welcoming the kids who came in from outlying areas and didn't know anyone in Felicity. So Maggie had swallowed her envy and approached Lane. And discovered three surprising things. The first was, while Lane had been raised in one of the rural areas, she now lived in town. "My dad's no farmer," she had said ruefully. "He's just a construction worker who wanted to grow vegetables. Problem. He didn't know *how*. We lost everything we owned. Now he's a construction worker again, but this time he's working on the new courthouse instead of owning his own business like he used to." They were living in a rented house on the east side of town, which made Lane a "townie" now, and accessible for friendship, should anyone be interested.

Maggie was interested. Secretly, she was hoping some of Lane's cool sophistication would rub off on her. By the time she finally realized it probably wasn't going to, she liked Lane enough to continue the friendship anyway. That had been the second surprising thing.

Equally surprising was the fact that Helen and Lane got along. As different as they seemed to be at first glance, they had two things in common. Sports, which all three girls loved, and the fact that Helen had once lived in the country, too, although her parents had never farmed. When Helen reached adolescence, they felt she should have the advantages of town life, and had sold their country house to buy a condominium in Felicity. Currently, Dr. and Mrs. Morgan were in Egypt on an archaeological dig, and Helen was boarding with Ms. Gross.

"I love living in town," Lane said repeatedly. "God, I hated the country! Nothing to do but listen to the hay dry. My dad, the gentleman farmer! He's still brooding over losing the farm. Me and my mom, we couldn't be happier. Poor ... but happy."

Poor or not, Lane had a flair for dressing that the other girls envied. She could take a simple skirt and blouse and, by adding an inexpensive print scarf or belt, jazz up the outfit so that it looked like it had been sold to her that way ... at one of the better stores in town.

Today, she had dressed in white trousers that Maggie knew she'd bought at the Army-Navy surplus store, topping them with a red-striped boat-neck T-shirt and a matching scarf. Where on earth had she dug up the white yachting cap she was wearing low over her thick, dark bangs? She looked as if she had a date for sailing after school.

There was no body of water large enough for boating in all of Greene County.

Nevertheless, Lane made a *very* fetching picture, leaning back in her chair, her incredible eyes fixed on Thomas Whittier. If he glanced away from Alex, with whom he was discussing James Keith's punishment, and noticed Lane . . . *really* noticed her, Maggie was sure he'd be hers. Except, Lane already had a boyfriend. There *was* justice in the world. He was a college boy, of course. Maggie had seen his picture in Lane's wallet. Cute. Very cute. Almost as cute as the new guy.

Getting back to the business at hand, Maggie said briskly, "Okay, so what have we decided? Death by hanging or a slap on the wrist?" Instantly, she realized that she had stolen Thomas Whittier's line, and felt her cheeks burn again.

"After-school detention, four weeks," Alex announced. "Right, everyone?"

Heads nodded.

"Four weeks?" Helen looked dubious. "James will have a fit. That's the longest he's ever been given. He'll hate us all."

Scout laughed. "Like he doesn't already. He hates us, he hates school, James hates *life*. Giving him a lighter sentence won't change that. Come on, Morgan, peer jury is no place for gutless wonders.

James asked for it, and we're going to give it to him."

Helen's cheeks flushed. "I'm *not* a gutless wonder, Scout. I wasn't arguing. I was just saying . . . James can get pretty nasty. I've seen him slap trays of food out of people's hands in the cafeteria. And Tanya almost broke her arm when he knocked her down last week."

Tanya and Bennie nodded soberly.

"We can handle James," Scout insisted. "Relax. Let's go give him the good news."

Maggie banged her gavel to dismiss the session, and they all trooped out of the room. She didn't think Whit had noticed Lane. But she couldn't be sure.

James Keith went ballistic upon hearing his sentence. And he directed most of his fury at Maggie, who had stood up to read the verdict and the sentence.

"Four weeks?" he shouted, his beefy face red with rage. "Are you crazy? I got a job after school! No way can I sit in some stinking classroom for four weeks! You're supposed to give me a fine, that's what you did before. I can pay a fine. But I'll lose my job if I miss four weeks in a row."

They had given him fines in the past. He always paid them, but it never changed his behavior in the slightest. Which was why they'd decided against it this time.

"Four weeks," the judge repeated firmly. "From three P.M. to five, Ms. Gross's office. Be there, James. Or I'll up it to six weeks."

James kicked the chair he'd been sitting in, punched Ralph's arm angrily, and called Maggie names she had only heard in movies, but Susan, the judge, never gave an inch. She finally put an end to James's tantrum by banging her gavel on the desk and adding a hefty fine to the detention.

"Hey, that ain't fair!" James's blonde girlfriend shouted. "You already gave him detention, you can't fine him, too!"

"Sure I can," Susan answered, standing up. "I just did. Pay the bailiff, James."

The "bailiff," a thin, pale girl named Wendy, went even paler at the idea of being approached by the volatile defendant, but she needn't have worried. James threw the money at Ralph and ordered him to pay, then stalked out, dragging his girlfriend along with him. When he reached the doorway, he turned and snarled over his shoulder, "You all think you're so hot! You sit there in them chairs like you're something special. This ain't a real court. You're just pretendin', like brat kids playin' grown-up. I lose my job over this, you all better watch out, that's all I've got to say."

When James had gone, Thomas Whittier turned to Maggie and surprised her by asking, "You really think that's all he's got to say?"

"No way. I think James Keith has plenty to say, and I think we should take him seriously. Helen's right. He's a bomb waiting to go off. I wish we could have expelled him, but we don't have the power to do that. Only Mrs. Marsh can do that, and even then she has to let him have a hearing in front of the school board."

Surprised that she was actually talking to him, Maggie's lips clamped together. Then she relented. He'd been rude. But now he was being friendly. And she'd been rude, too. Time to make amends. She lifted her head to look straight at him and apologized, "If I was rude, I'm sorry."

He laughed. "*If?*"

"Okay, okay, I was rude. Like I said, I'm sorry."

"You're forgiven. So what's next?"

What was next was the case of two girls, best friends, who had cheated on an important test and been caught. They sat white-faced and silent during their hearing, and never opened their mouths, not even when the judge asked for comments from "the accused." The jury went easy on them. No one liked the idea of cheats at Bransom, but their lawyer insisted it was the first time they'd ever done anything like that, and both girls were so shaken, the jury felt they'd learned their lesson. They were ordered to take another test, a different one, and to write a one-thousand-word essay on the merits of honesty.

The third case was also a girl. Tall, thin, and bony, dressed entirely in shiny black leather, crew-cut hair dyed black, lips flaming red, the accused slid into her seat and slumped down in her chair, impatiently tapping the heels of her black boots on the hardwood floor as her name was announced. "Chantilly Beckwith."

Helen laughed. "Chantilly? As if. Her real name

is Alice Ann Beckwith. I went to grade school with her. She had blonde hair then and was real shy and quiet, just like me."

Alice Ann, a.k.a. "Chantilly" Beckwith had been accused of beating up another girl. Maggie was shocked by the crime. The closest they'd been to violent crime so far was the tossing of a frog out of a biology classroom window. And that had supposedly been a rescue mission, intent on saving the poor creature.

Like James Keith, Alice Ann did not take well to her punishment, which was a recommendation of suspension, the strongest the peer jury had to offer. The jury couldn't actually suspend anyone, but the administration would take their recommendation under advisement. In the meantime, Alice Ann still had her real court trial to deal with. The victim's parents had pressed charges. Alice Ann was not a happy camper when she stomped from the room. The expression on her face was similar to James Keith's, and a few of the words she directed at Maggie as she stomped from the gym were from the same vocabulary.

As Maggie stuffed the gavel into her backpack, Whit said, "Looks like you've got a few people ready to hang you in the town square. Maybe I should walk you to your first class. That Keith guy could be hanging around out in the hall, waiting for you."

"Hey, man, don't sweat it!" Scout interrupted, coming up behind them and reaching down to lift the backpack. "She's okay, man. *I'll* see that she's okay." To an embarrassed Maggie, he said, "Come on, let's go. We'll be late." And before she could protest, his hand was firmly on her left elbow and he was propelling her from the room.

"What's the *matter* with you?" she hissed. "*Stop it!* That was really rude, Scout."

When she managed to swivel her head to look over her shoulder, she saw Helen and Lane approaching a bewildered-looking Thomas Whittier, and heard Lane say, "Hi. I'm Lane Bridgewater and this is my friend, Helen Morgan. Anything you need to know about Bransom High? We'd be happy to give you the grand tour."

Scout was moving so rapidly across the gym floor, Maggie couldn't hear what the new boy said in return. Probably something like, "Hey, why not? You are totally gorgeous and you don't have a pushy boy attached to your elbow. Lead the way."

James was *not* waiting outside in the hall. There was no sign of him. Alice Ann, too, was nowhere to be seen.

But like Whit, Maggie was convinced she hadn't seen the last of either one.

# Chapter 5

Dante's parents weren't any happier about his sudden romance with Christy than I was. They didn't like the "new" Christy. Mrs. Guardino said, "That girl is trouble. I can see it in her eyes and in the way she walks, like she's hoping someone has a camera on her every second." Mr. Guardino tried to keep Dante so busy on the farm that he'd be too tired to go out at night. Dumb idea. It didn't work. Might as well try keeping a bee away from flowers. Dante was sixteen, with unlimited energy, not to mention a fierce desire to spend every waking moment with the girl of his dreams.

All Dante talked about was Christy, even though he knew it gave his parents fits. He raved on and on, about how "grown-up" she was, how pretty she was, how much fun, blah, blah, blah. And I had to sit there and listen.

I never warned Dante away from Christy. It wouldn't have done any good, and I knew how mad it would make him. I didn't want him mad at me, even though I hardly ever saw him anymore. Three's a crowd, that was the message the two of them sent me repeatedly. I didn't fight it. What good would it have done?

Mrs. Guardino warned Dante, over and over again. She told him to stay away from Christy. "That girl will bring you down, you mark my words," she said. "Might as well stick a knife in your own heart, save her the trouble."

I knew Dante wasn't listening.

He wasn't. He finally stopped talking about Christy at home, but I knew he was still seeing her. Everyone in the county knew. When Dante's parents did find out, there was constant fighting in their house, his mother pleading with him to, "Leave that girl alone!" Dante shouting back that his parents should butt out and let him live his own life.

I hated all of it. They'd been such a nice, ordinary, happy family until then. That was one of the reasons I spent so much time at their place. It felt like being around one of those families on television, where everybody talks things out calmly. Not like at my house.

As for Dante and Christy, at first it was all really rosy. They were nuts about each other and even I had to admit, although I hated to, that they looked really good together. Mr. and Ms. Teenage America.

But then they started fighting, which I could have predicted. I knew her so well. She was just beginning to realize how much power she had when it came to boys, and she wasn't ready to tie herself down to any one boy, not even one as cute and smart and popular as Dante.

The trouble was, *he* didn't want anyone else, only *her*. Her constant flirting with other guys made him nuts. They started fighting all the time, and everywhere. A lot of the arguments were public, and they never seemed to notice that there were tons of people around.

So, when Christy's body was found, lying underneath an old pickup truck on the Guardino property, her head smashed like a pumpkin, Dante was arrested.

I couldn't believe it at first. Dante hadn't done anything wrong. He could never have raised a hand to Christy. He loved her too much.

But no one knew that.

Except for the person who *had* done something wrong. Something really wrong. Something horrible.

Something they could never, ever take back.

# Chapter 6

In the hallway, Maggie finally managed to yank her elbow free of Scout's grip. At the same time, she yanked her backpack away from him. "*What* do you think you're doing?" she shouted, aware that people were staring at them, and not caring. "Don't *ever* do that again! You do *not* drag me out of a room as if I were a puppy who's peed on the new carpet. What's the matter with you?"

Scout's lips tightened. "Well, who does that guy think he is? He waltzes in here, says he's on our peer jury, just like that, and then makes a move on *you*."

"He didn't make a *move* on me, Scout. He was just being friendly." In spite of her anger, Maggie lowered her voice. She was afraid the new boy would come out of the gym at any moment and overhear. "And since when am I not allowed to make new friends?"

Scout shrugged. His eyes avoided hers. "I'm not very good at sharing," he muttered.

Maggie stared at him. "Sharing? I'm not a box of cookies, Scout. People don't *share* other people. And you are *not* my social secretary." She had never thought of herself and Scout as a "couple." Although she was aware that other people might. She had kissed him. And she'd liked it. Scout happened to be a great kisser. But they had never discussed seeing only each other. She wasn't interested in seeing only Scout. She didn't know who else she did want to see. No one in particular. She just didn't want to become Scout's *property*, which now seemed to be very much what he had in mind.

He had never acted like this before. Why was it suddenly so important to him to wrap and tag her as his?

"Don't tell me what to do, Scout," she said quietly but firmly. "You're not my keeper. And if that's a problem for you, then maybe we shouldn't spend so much time together."

Scout's deep blue eyes narrowed. "It's because of *him*, isn't it?" He flicked a hand over one shoulder, toward the gym. "Well, don't worry about that guy, because if I know Lane, and I *do*, she's already staked her claim. So you can forget it, Maggie. Three's a crowd, right? Three has *always* been a crowd."

Maggie didn't answer him. She knew he wasn't talking about Lane and Whit and Maggie creating a triangle. He was talking about Whit and Maggie and *himself*. Warning her away from Whit. Scout was *warning* her? What was wrong with him?

"Lane already has a boyfriend," Maggie said angrily.

Seeing the look in her eyes, Scout's face eased, and he forced a smile. "Hey, I'm sorry. Look, it's just . . . well, you know . . . we're starting a whole new year of school and we've got SATs ahead of us and now we've got this crazy business of emptying out the old courthouse. That's going to take time away from football practice and Coach is going to be ticked and my mom's really going off the deep end. I've been under a lot of stress lately."

Maggie hated that expression. "Under a lot of stress." People used it all the time, to excuse rotten behavior and bad manners. Who *wasn't* under stress? *Life* was stressful, period. Since when was that a good excuse for acting like a jerk? When she was feeling stressed-out, she ate chocolate doughnuts. The only damage that caused was to her waistline. It didn't hurt anybody else.

Still, Scout *had* had a hard time since his parents' divorce. "Are we clear about who's in charge of my life?" she asked, not ready to forgive Scout's heavy-handedness.

"I guess." He didn't sound convinced, but Maggie could see that he wasn't willing to argue.

He looked so downcast, she took pity on him and reached out to take his hand. She was about to say something cheerful like, "Relax, Scout, I'm not the love of your life," when the new boy, along with Helen, Lane, and Alex, emerged from the gym. They were all talking animatedly, but Whit did look up as they entered the hall, and his dark eyes focused on Maggie's hand in Scout's. He nodded, as if to say, That's what I thought, and then quickly turned his attention back to Lane.

As the trio approached Maggie and Scout, she heard Whit say, "So, if we're going to be moving stuff from the old courthouse to the new one next week, maybe we could go scope out the place this afternoon. I need to see what we're up against."

"What a great idea!" Lane responded quickly. "American history fascinates me. Personally, I think that eyesore should be torn down. But since it hasn't been, exploring it might be fun."

Maggie almost laughed aloud. The only American's history Lane Bridgewater was interested in was Thomas Whittier's. Hadn't *her* boyfriend ever told her three was a crowd? Apparently not.

"Good, we can all go," Maggie heard herself saying. "I have to take some renovation plans over there for my mother." She pulled the sheaf of papers from her backpack, waving them in the air.

"Count me in," Scout enjoined. He hadn't let go of Maggie's hand. "I still want it torn down, but if it's not gonna be, it'll be fun to see what it looks like before Maggie's mom and friends work their magic on it, turning it into a tourist attraction."

Maggie was surprised when Alex agreed to go, too. He'd avoided going near the old courthouse ever since his father, who had worked there for twenty years, died.

He was all for tearing the building down. When they talked about it, he had said, "Those beams have to be rotted through. They'll pour a fortune into that building, dressing it up with paint and paneling and new flooring, and then one day the whole thing will collapse anyway. It's stupid. Scout's right. A rec center would be just the thing. Even a parking garage for the new courthouse would make more sense."

But she suspected his attitude had more to do with what had happened to his father than with the building itself.

Although Maggie hadn't been inside the courthouse in a long time, she discovered that afternoon that with the evacuation process already begun, it was even more depressing than she'd remembered. So empty and desolate, as if it had already been abandoned.

They spent less than an hour exploring the upper floors, where there was little activity and few people. Only the larger pieces of furniture remained in many of the offices. Their footsteps echoed hollowly on the bare, worn, wooden floors, and their voices rang out in the staircases. "It's kind of like a haunted house already," Helen murmured nervously, and no one disagreed.

Maggie handed the renovation papers to a lone clerk on the second floor. Most of the staff was at the new courthouse, putting the finishing touches on their new offices. It wouldn't be long, Maggie was told by the clerk, before the peer jury would be put to work toting small supplies and books through the alleyway from the old building to the new. Moving vans would carry off the heavier things. Then the ancient, once-proud building would stand empty after almost a century and a half.

They moved from floor to floor, past deserted offices with peeling wallpaper and high ceilings with water stains, through wide but dim corridors, and up and down wide, curving, wooden staircases whose railings shook and whose treads creaked ominously beneath their feet.

Finished with the upper floors, Alex, who seemed surprisingly at home in the old courthouse, talked them into exploring the basement. Helen protested, but finally gave in because she was unwilling to remain upstairs alone.

When they opened the door to the cellarway, Maggie, repelled by the strong, musty smell, took a step backward, and narrowly missed bumping into James Keith, just entering the building. Alice Ann "Chantilly" Beckwith was with him, as were two other friends, both as sullen-looking as James.

"Oops, sorry!" Maggie apologizied. "I didn't see you."

"Like *that's* a surprise," the girl snarled. But to Maggie's relief, the four kept walking.

"She's here for her pretrial hearing," Lane said knowingly. "Phew," she said as she entered the enclosed, narrow stairway, "it stinks! Reminds me of the farm. That's practically the only thing I remember about the farm . . . all those disgusting smells. I don't *like* being reminded of the farm." But she began descending the shaky, wooden staircase anyway.

The others followed silently, heads bent against

the sloping ceiling, their feet feeling carefully for the next step.

Maggie was suddenly overwhelmed with the feeling that they were making a terrible mistake. Something about the basement — the smell? The darkness? — seemed to be warning them to stay away.

She opened her mouth to voice the feeling, but before any sound could come out, she was at the foot of the stairs, and it was too late.

The white limestone ceiling was so low, they had to walk with their heads down. Periodically, they had to step to one side to avoid floor-to-ceiling beams positioned in the middle of the corridors. Dank, dark water ran down the sides of the white walls, and scurrying noises sounded within them. There was no light at all and no one had thought to bring a flashlight. They had to feel their way.

Maggie was never sure exactly how she became separated from the others, but once they had passed through the jail cell corridor she could no longer even make out Lane's white yachting cap. And the depressing atmosphere of that corridor, where prisoners must have felt they'd been buried alive, however briefly, had stricken all of them silent, so she hadn't even voices to guide her. It was impossible to see anything, even her own feet.

The corridors twisted and turned in a dizzying maze. It had been so long since she'd been down here, she couldn't remember which passageway led where. She had never become lost as a child, playing in the basement, alone or with friends. But it all seemed different now.

However it happened, the moment came when she found herself bumping into the small, arched doorway that led to the coal bin. On an impulse, she decided to take a look around inside. The bin hadn't been used in years, not since the gas furnace had been installed upstairs. But she'd had fun as a child, crawling in through the little window at ground level, to slide down the metal coal chute and play with the round, hard, black nuggets of coal still nearly filling the bin.

"Hey!" she called over her shoulder as she lifted the wooden bar that acted as a lock. "C'mere, everybody! I want to check out the coal bin."

When no one answered, Maggie hesitated. Were they already that far ahead of her? She'd only stopped for a second. She shouted again, then, deciding that it really didn't matter since she could always exit through the chute and meet them all outside, she went into the coal bin, leaving the door open, and ducked her head to avoid striking it on the frame.

Inside, it looked the way she remembered it. Black as pitch but for a dingy glow emanating from the chute window, at the top of the front wall. Coal had been delivered through that window, spilling down the chute into the wooden bin at its base. The bin took up most of the space in the tiny room and an ancient black coal furnace sat in one corner.

There are probably spiders in here, Maggie thought uneasily. And climbing up that chute now that she was grown didn't look as easy as it had when she was small. Besides, the window was probably locked from the outside.

She turned to leave.

A sudden whoosh of air hit her as the door slammed shut in her face.

She heard the wooden bar on the outside of the door slam into place with a thud.

She was locked in.

After her initial surprise had passed, Maggie laughed uncertainly and called out, "Helen? Scout? Guys, this is not so funny! C'mon, let me out of here."

There was no answer from beyond the door. The only sound Maggie heard was the stealthy rustling of some small creature deep inside the walls.

She was alone in the coal bin and the door was locked.

# Chapter 7

The old red pickup under which Christy's body was found hadn't gone anywhere in a long time. Dante had fooled around with it a year or so earlier, hoping to get it going again. But the truck was too old and decrepit. He'd finally given up. Pushed it into the woods and left it there. On *his* property.

Which was one reason they arrested him. But that was only *one* reason.

The police said Christy had been hit over the head with a tire iron, which they found not too far from the body. The tire iron had Dante's fingerprints on it.

Well, of course it did. It was his father's truck, and Dante was the one who had worked on it.

As far as anyone *else's* fingerprints are concerned, people wear gloves in Ohio when it's cold. It was *very* cold that night.

They said that Christy lived for four or five hours after her skull was cracked. They said if she'd

*51*

been found sooner, she might have survived. When I heard that, I got this awful, metallic taste in my mouth. She had certainly looked dead to me, when I rolled her body under the truck.

She'd been lying there, alive, for hours? That gave me nightmares.

But then someone said that even if she'd lived, she never would have been the same again. Her brain had been pulverized. I think whoever said that actually used the word "vegetable." Then I didn't feel so bad, because I knew how Christy would have hated that. I did wonder, though, if she'd been cold that whole time, although she'd been wearing a heavy coat in her favorite color, red, and black leather gloves. But she hadn't had boots on her feet, so they were probably cold.

Not that it mattered. I mean, she was *dying*, right? Frozen toes were the least of her problems.

The truth is, I *have* wondered, sometimes, if she actually *knew* she was dying. And what that would feel like. It probably would have made her really, really mad, because she thought she had the world by the tail and that only wonderful things were going to happen to her. I mean, she was young, she was pretty, and I know she had big plans, because she'd told me so, more than once.

Well, you just never know, do you?

Christy was better off dead anyway. She'd have hated being stuck in a bed in some nursing home being fed by tubes and not knowing whether it was Monday or Friday. Not even knowing what a Monday or a Friday *was*. She would have especially hated never being able to dance again. That girl did love to dance.

She should have stuck to only one partner.

The thing is, I didn't mind so much that they had shut me out. I had other friends. What I really hated was what she was doing to Dante. She was totally ruining his life, and his family's life. It wasn't right. It just wasn't right.

Someone had to stop her.

So I did.

But now, Dante was being blamed for her murder.

I didn't know what to do about that.

# Chapter 8

It didn't take much to make Maggie lose her temper. But the person she was really angry with was herself. When I was little and played in here for hours, I was never scared, she told herself in disgust. Nothing's different about this place. It's just like it was then. But I'm scared now. So I'm the one who's changed.

She hated that. It made her feel that she had lost something, something useful, something she needed. "Bravery is wasted on the young," she said aloud. "They don't need it."

Over her head, footsteps trod the ancient wooden boards on the first floor. A thin veil of black dust filtered down upon Maggie, making her sneeze and cough and swipe at her eyes. "If I ever get out of here," she declared as she moved to the door to begin pounding on it with both fists, "I'm going to strangle the person who locked me in here!"

The darkness and the isolation, the confinement,

and the scurrying sounds in the walls got to her then. Her pounding became more frantic, her shouting more panicky, and she began kicking at the door, hoping its age would help her break it down.

Her hands were already sore and raw when she heard, over her own voice, Alex calling her name. She stopped pounding, shouting, and kicking, to listen.

"Maggie? Maggie, you in there?"

"Get me *out* of here! Hurry up, Alex!"

The door opened and Maggie stumbled out into Alex's arms. A moment later, Whit, Helen, Lane, and Scout came around a corner and joined them, all asking questions at the same time.

"What were you *doing* in there?" Alex asked when Maggie had calmed down. Her trembling had subsided, and, embarrassed now, she stepped away from him, careful to avoid the door to the coal bin.

"Trying on shoes," she answered caustically. Then, because it wasn't *his* fault, she added soberly, "I went in there to check it out and someone thought it would be funny to lock me in." She couldn't see anyone's face clearly, but she knew by their questions that they were all there. "Which one of you is the guilty party?" She managed a shaky laugh. "I think I'll just have to jail you in one of the cells for a while, show you how it feels."

One at a time, they all denied having any part in her confinement. And Scout, especially, didn't like being accused. "Like I would ever do that to you!" he said indignantly.

Maggie didn't know what to think. *Someone* had locked that door behind her. If it wasn't any of her friends, then who?

"I'm out of here," she said firmly. "I've seen more than enough. I need fresh air and sunshine. You guys coming? And can we please stay together this time?" she asked as they began walking.

They promised, but it was impossible to see them in the dark. All she could do was assume they were still with her.

They hadn't gone far when a veil of soot descended upon their heads and shoulders. Unable to see anything, Maggie stopped walking, clapping her hands protectively over her nose and mouth. She realized that everyone else must have stopped, too, because in place of footsteps padding along the passageway, all she heard was more coughing and sneezing.

They were so lost in the discomfort of the coughing fits, they didn't hear the faint groaning sound near them. They didn't notice as the groan gained strength, growing louder until it had become a full-fledged tearing, ripping sound.

By the time they did hear it, it was too late. The ground beneath their feet shook and shuddered as the upright, wooden beam stretching from the ground to the ceiling gave way, toppling to one side in a shower of wood chips and chunks, dirt, bugs, and dust.

Maggie was the first to realize what was happening. She screamed a warning, but her throat was so full of dust, the sound that came out was little more than a hoarse cry.

Still, the others heard her, and realized that something bad was taking place. Instinctively, they jumped backward.

Just in time.

There was a second, mightier shudder when the beam slammed into the ground. A thick spray of brown, musty-smelling dirt flew upward upon impact, spraying all of them as they stood frozen, mouths open, watching disaster strike. The floor above had no choice. It had to follow. It sank downward slowly in a thick shower of hardwood flooring, dust, more bugs, papers, dirt, and limestone. Even a desk chair made its way into the debris.

Everyone jumped backward further to avoid being struck. Their hands over their mouths for protection, they stared, speechless, for long moments after the shower came to a halt.

When the last thud had died and the dirt had settled beneath a hole in the ceiling the size of a bass drum, Alex was the first to speak, his voice hoarse. "Man," he breathed huskily, "what was *that*?"

All eyes were on the mess in front of them. The heavy beam was lying directly in their path. Piled atop it, as if someone were planning a large bonfire, lay a heap of remains from the first floor. Chunks and slices of hardwood flooring from above were crisscrossed in the heap like skis standing on end, their edges stabbing upward. Here and there, sheets of white paper dotted the debris. The towering mountain of rubble reached almost to the low ceiling. Some light shone faintly through the hole, and distant cries of alarm began to filter downward.

Lane and Whit echoed Alex's question. "What *happened*?"

When their breathing had finally slowed to some regularity and they had made certain that no one was injured, they stood silently for several more minutes.

Finally, Scout said, "The question is, what do we do *now*?"

Even in their shock and disbelief, they could all see very clearly why Scout had asked that particular question. Because although they were more than ready to leave the basement — *eager* to leave the basement of the old courthouse — they couldn't.

A pile of debris that reached from floor to ceiling and from one wall to the other was barring their path.

They weren't going anywhere.

# Chapter 9

They had come very close to being buried alive.

Dazed and disoriented, Maggie lifted her head to see an enormous hole above them. Had it spread into the coal bin? If she had still been locked in there, would the ceiling have collapsed upon her, burying her, a fear she had only this morning expressed to her mother?

That would teach her a lesson, Maggie thought foggily. She'd never ask me to run an errand again. Not that I'd be able to . . .

After what seemed a very long time, during which they all leaned against the wall staring silently at the pile of rubble barring their way, a voice called down through the ceiling hole. "Everyone okay?" A balding head, a pair of wire-rimmed eyeglasses, and a double chin, appeared cautiously at the edge of the hole. "You kids shouldn't even be down there."

Maggie heard the accusation in the man's voice,

and called in return, "We're not hurt. But we can't get out. There's a big mess blocking our way."

Pale eyebrows drew together in a frown and the shiny, pink scalp withdrew.

"That was Samuel Petersen," Alex said, his own voice not quite steady. "Town clerk. My dad always said Mr. Petersen never makes a decision until he's thought about it for a long time. He says hell could freeze over twice while Samuel Petersen thinks things through. We might be here for a while."

With some effort, Maggie pulled herself together. She was *not* waiting around in this horrible place. "No, we won't," she announced, side-stepping the fringes of the rubble and pushing aside broken pieces of flooring to clear her way to the coal bin door. As reluctant as she was to reenter the tiny room, she was even more reluctant to stay where she was. "We can climb up through the coal chute. If it's not filled to the ceiling with debris from upstairs." She lifted the bar and pulled the door open again. The hole *had* spread into the room, but there was no debris blocking the way to the metal chute.

"Oh, *there's* an idea," Lane said sarcastically. Recovered completely from shock, she was running fingers through her silky dark hair in an effort to dislodge as much dust as possible. She had removed the yachting cap and stuck it in the waistband of her slacks. The hat was now more gray than white. "I'm not going in there. That chute has to be filthy with coal dust. And cobwebs. Maybe bats and spiders live in there. It hasn't been used in years."

Maggie glanced down at her own denim skirt and white T-shirt. They were coated with a thick sheen of gray and brown dust and dirt. "You're worried about getting dirty? Lane, we're already filthy. Look at your hat!"

"Besides," Alex added, "by the time old Petersen figures out how to get us out of here, more than your cap will be gray, Lane. Your hair will be, too."

"We're not kids anymore," Lane argued, shaking the cap vigorously and plunking it back on her head. "Maybe we won't fit in the chute."

"There's only one way to find out. Come on." Maggie stepped into the place she had fought so hard to escape.

"I've never been in here," Alex commented over his shoulder.

"Then how did you get in and out of the basement?" Maggie asked as she moved cautiously through the blackness to the bottom of the chute. "When you played down here?"

"I never played down here." He sounded indignant. "When my mom brought me into town, I went upstairs to my dad's office to visit him, then I went to the movies." He frowned. "Why would I want to play down here?"

Helen, behind him, said, "Everyone did. When we came in from the country on Saturday, I couldn't wait to play down here."

Sirens sounded faintly in the distance. "They're sending help," Lane called from outside the coal room. "Why don't we just wait? They can put a ladder down through the hole in the ceiling for us."

But Whit argued, "A ladder won't do us any good. Leaning a heavy wooden ladder up against the edges of that jagged hole could make more of the floor up there collapse. No, thanks. I'm going up the chute, like Maggie."

Scout said hastily, "I'm with you," and after a moment of hesitation, Alex said the same thing. Helen and Lane were the last to agree.

Maggie could only hope that more of the ceiling didn't decide to give way while they were struggling up the chute to the window.

There was only enough space for two people to maneuver at a time. The others waited their turn out in the corridor.

Maggie approached the chute cautiously, without the reckless abandon she'd enjoyed as a child when she had scrambled up it as if she had suction cups on her feet. To Whit, behind her, she said, "It's a good thing this chute is here, or we'd be stuck! I just hope the window isn't latched from the outside."

Before the gas furnace had been installed in the courthouse, a truck had regularly backed up to the window, fastened it open with a latch that slipped into a hook on an outside wall of the building, and dumped a steady stream of the nuggets down the chute until the bin was heaped high. Pleased to be the first person in Felicity to be heating with coal instead of wood, Otis Bransom had built the chute himself.

As a child, Maggie had found sliding down it

great fun. Almost like a slide at the playground, except that the chute was narrower and had higher sides, to keep the coal from spilling over. She'd had little trouble going back up it, gripping the curving sides of the slippery metal chute with all her might to pull herself up and out. But . . . she'd been little then . . . and stupid. Climbing up the slippery metal chute looked just about impossible to her now.

Because the hole in the bin's ceiling was smaller than the one in the passageway, there was very little light pouring through it. Maggie had to feel the way with her hands. Her stomach twisted at the thought of inadvertently touching something gross. *Were* there bats down here? Hadn't someone said there were probably bats in the cupola perched on top of the building?

"We have to go up one at a time," she cautioned Whit. He was already close on her heels. She waved him backward. "The chute is slippery. We don't have to rush, anyway. It's not like the building's on fire."

Lane, waiting in the doorway, overheard. "Please don't mention that word," she warned. "Everyone knows the courthouse is the worst firetrap in town. My mother says even a heated argument could set this building ablaze. It'd be ashes in minutes."

"You weren't listening, Lane." Maggie climbed up onto the chute, sank to a crouching position, and gripped the sides with both hands. "I said there *wasn't* any fire. Relax!"

Maggie was thin and wiry, with the agility of an

athlete, but she had a hard time on the slick metal. Though it had been years since a load of fuel had been delivered, a fine sheen of coal dust remained on the surface. Even without it, the metal itself was slippery. Sneakers might have helped. Maggie was wearing boots with leather soles. Useless. Using her hands and her knees was her only hope. Her shoulders and back ached with the strain of pulling herself upward by gripping the side walls. Below her, Whit called out encouragement.

No one appeared at the edge of the small, semi-circular hole over the coal bin to see how they were doing. Don't they *care* that we're stuck down here? Maggie wondered resentfully. Why isn't someone doing something to help?

Alex called, "What if you get to the top and the window is latched from the outside?"

"I thought you never played down here." Maggie's voice was husky with exertion. "So how do you even know there *is* a window?" What if he was right? What if the window *was* locked from the outside? She couldn't very well undo an outside latch from in here.

"I saw it in the display at the Women of Heritage Society. Remember? They had a diagram of the basement before this place became the courthouse. We talked about how easy it would have been for a thief to crawl into the Bransom mansion by un-latching the coal chute window, until Mrs. Potter told us the chute window was always locked from the inside, too."

"Right." Maggie, breathing hard, had reached

the top of the chute. The window was filthy with cobwebs and grime. Kneeling, unable to loosen her grip for fear she'd slide right back down to the bottom, she had to twist her upper body to use her elbow against the webs. She shuddered involuntarily, but quickly reminded herself that cobwebs were harmless, and began seeking out the inside lock.

There it was, a sliding bolt on the bottom of the peeling, white frame. She hoped it hadn't rusted in place.

It hadn't. By locking one leg around the side rail and holding on firmly with her right hand, she was able to release her left hand to slip the bolt free. It moved easily. The window was unlocked from the inside.

But it was physically impossible to stay in place using only her leg and one hand. She was already beginning to slip backward. She *had* to use both hands. Reestablishing a two-handed grip on the chute's sides, she swung her left elbow again, this time to push against the window. It didn't budge.

"Try it again!" Whit urged. "It's probably just stuck!"

"Or locked on the outside!" Lane called, her voice grim.

Sirens screeched to a halt somewhere outside.

Maggie pushed on the window again, and then again, and then a third time. Nothing happened.

She sank back on her heels, still gripping the chute sides with her hands. "It's locked," she said heavily. "From the outside. We'll just have to wait for Petersen to do his rescue thing."

Just then, something soft and furry scurried past her along the windowsill, brushing against her bare elbow.

Maggie gasped. But instead of recoiling in revulsion, she involuntarily threw her elbow against the window again, harder this time. Too hard. One of the panes shattered with a sharp, tinkling sound. A thin shard of glass sliced the top of her arm in the fleshy part just below the elbow, and blood gushed forth.

Mindful of the furry creature, which just might decide to take another pass at her at any moment, Maggie recklessly thrust her injured arm through the new hole and reached up to undo the outside latch. She left thin streaks of bright red on the unbroken panes.

But she got the window open.

A minute or two later, she was lying on her back in the parking lot, surrounded by fresh air and sunshine. She automatically kept one hand on her injured arm to stop the bleeding. She lifted her head only when a fireman approached, calling out, "Hey, you okay?"

Maggie didn't answer. Couldn't. Because she really didn't *know* the answer.

# Chapter 10

Dante insisted that he hadn't seen Christy the night she died. He said he'd been sitting down by the pond (probably brooding about her, I figured). When the sheriff asked him, Dante said Christy had told him she couldn't see him that night because she had to wash her hair and do her nails (ha!). Which Dante, knowing her pretty well by that time, interpreted to mean she had a date with somebody else. He admitted that he'd even thought about driving over to her farm, maybe catch her leaving the house with some other guy. But he hadn't done it, because he was afraid of how he'd react if he did catch her in the act of two-timing him. He actually *said* he was afraid he'd strangle both of them. What a thing to tell the police when your girlfriend has just been murdered.

But see, the thing was, Dante *knew* he hadn't done anything wrong. So he wasn't worried about saying the wrong thing.

When the papers reported that remark of Dante's, like they reported every single word he uttered and every move he made, I couldn't believe he'd actually *said* something so stupid. That he was afraid of strangling his girlfriend? Idiot. The sheriff, who was in charge before they moved Dante to Felicity, must have thought he'd hit pay dirt. And Dante's lawyer, dumb old Milton Scruggs, must have just about fainted. Or maybe old Miltie was too stupid to even realize that his client was putting his own head in a noose, talking so much.

Of course, Christy *wasn't* strangled, so maybe Dante's comment wasn't so self-incriminating. No, that was *not* how she died. Death by tire iron was the fate that befell Christy Miller. Still, if I were a detective on the Greene County payroll, and I'd already made up my mind that a certain person had murdered someone, I guess I wouldn't quibble about the chosen method. I'd take whatever I could get, especially if it had just been handed to me like a birthday present by the person I'd already decided was guilty.

Dante never budged from his story that he'd been home all night long, down by the pond. The trouble was, no one could back up his story. His dad was away at a farm equipment exposition in Cincinnati, his mother at a neighbor's farm crying on her best friend's shoulder about how impossible it was to "raise a teenager these days" . . . that quote directly from the best friend, who had no qualms about talking to newspaper reporters.

As for me, I couldn't give him an alibi, that's for

sure. How could I testify that he really *had* been brooding down by the pond all evening when I wasn't anywhere around? Because I . . . well, I was elsewhere. With Christy, of course.

Like I said, I never meant to kill her. I just wanted her to dump Dante, really dump him, and make him know that she meant it. So that Dante could get back to being the Dante I'd known. So his family could get back to normal. Christy was destroying all of them with her flirting and her temper tantrums and her manipulating ways. It was because of her that the Guardinos fought all the time now, just like *my* family. It was her fault that Mrs. Guardino cried all the time, and Mr. Guardino looked ten years older than he used to.

She agreed to meet me that night. She actually believed me when I said Dante wanted to see her. Fool. But then when she showed up, she refused to do what I asked. She said she had no intention of dating only Dante, because she was young and there were too many other cute boys around . . . but she wasn't about to let Dante go, either. He was too good to her, she said, always buying her nice things, taking her out to dinner in decent restaurants instead of only to Dairy Queen. "So," she said coldly, *"I have every intention of hanging onto him, and there's not a thing you can do about it."*

First, she had ruined my life, going in a different direction without me. Then she'd ruined Dante's life, and his family life, too. Never mind that Dante had been stupid to get involved with her in the first place. People do dumb things when their hormones are running wild. But Dante was still a good guy. It wasn't too late to save him, it couldn't be. All she had to do was leave him alone, and everything would be fine again.

But she refused. She came strolling down the frozen, rutted dirt road that night like the sign had her name on it instead of "Lazy Dog Road." Wavy blonde hair bouncing around on her shoulders, makeup perfect, the collar of her red coat drawn up around her neck like it was a mink stole.

"Where's Dante?" she asked, looking around like she expected him to jump out from behind a tree. "You said Dante wanted to see me. So where is he?"

"I wanted to talk to you," I said, leading her into the woods to stand in the underbrush, the frozen creek on one side of us, Dante's old truck on the other, "and I figured you wouldn't come unless I said Dante wanted to see you."

All she had to do was promise to leave him alone, that was all. But she refused. She was determined to keep going, a human tornado, destroying everything in her path. I couldn't let that happen. She was only thirteen years old. Thirteen! She had no business ruining so many lives. I wanted to kill her for what she'd done.

So I did.

But I still didn't *mean* to do it.

It just happened.

And once it had, there was nothing I could do to change it. Nothing.

# Chapter 11

The fireman who had inquired about Maggie's state of health was quickly joined by two other firemen, then Mr. Petersen. They were joined by a rapidly increasing crowd of townspeople who had heard the sirens and rushed to see if the old courthouse was finally engulfed in flames. Lane's mother wasn't the only Felicity resident who thought of the ancient building as a firetrap.

The crowd gathered around Maggie, still lying on her back on the cement. Scout, then Alex, then Lane and Whit and Helen, filthy and breathing hard, crawled through the open window at the top of the chute and, avoiding the broken glass on the surface around them, collapsed on the parking lot beside Maggie.

"What were you people *doing* down there?" Petersen shouted. "Didn't you see the sign posted at the top of the stairs? No one is supposed to be down there. It's too dangerous."

"No kidding," Scout muttered, his face covered with coal dust.

Although Maggie hadn't noticed a NO ADMITTANCE sign posted near the basement door, she knew it wouldn't have stopped them. The third floor of the courthouse had been condemned for years, but kids still sneaked up there to play. Teenagers went up there for privacy. And so far, *that* floor hadn't collapsed.

One of the firemen returned to his truck to fetch a first aid kit for Maggie. Her arm was bleeding profusely. "Someone notify the Red Cross," she joked weakly. "This would be such a perfect time for me to donate blood. If I had any left by the time they got here."

"Does it hurt?" Lane asked. Her clothes were filthy, her sleek, dark hair no longer shining like patent leather.

"Does it *hurt?*" Helen echoed. "Of *course* it hurts." She knelt beside Maggie and handed her a clean, white handkerchief to wrap around the wound. The cloth bore her initials in delicate, pale blue stitching. "Ms. Gross got me these for Christmas. I'm the only person in town under eighty who carries a handkerchief, but she says tissues are disgusting. She thinks *anything* disposable is disgusting. She says we're becoming a totally disposable society, too lazy to take care of things. Maybe she's right."

"I can't use this," Maggie protested, holding up the fine, linen square. "It's too pretty. It'll get ruined!" She thrust the hankie back into Helen's hands. "Anyway, a fireman is bringing a first aid kit. But thanks, Helen."

While a fireman wound white gauze around the gash in Maggie's arm, speculation over the cause of the collapse began circulating in the crowd. Maggie heard, "Bound to happen, sooner or later" and "Beam must have given out. Wonder it didn't give years ago" and "Good thing there weren't any people on that floor when it went."

Something she heard sounded wrong. Something jarred, as if a word had been pronounced incorrectly. She couldn't put her finger on what it was.

The fireman was gentle, but his ministrations still hurt. "You'd best get yourself to the emergency room," he told her when he had finished. "Looks to me like that might need stitches."

"I'll take her," Scout said, standing up. His deep-set blue eyes looked owlish, surrounded by so much gray grime. He reached down to help Maggie to her feet. She reeled slightly as she stood, and he wrapped a protective arm around her. "You okay?"

"Yeah." She glanced around her. Her friends were getting to their feet, too, swiping in vain at their blackened jeans and shorts and shirts. "Helen, how about coming, too? Lane? Maybe you inhaled coal dust or something, and need to be checked out."

The truth was, she didn't want to go to the hospital with just Scout. He was being very considerate and helpful, but if she was going to need stitches, she wanted Helen alongside her, not Scout. He'd had stitches so many times as a result of athletic injuries, he'd think nothing of it. Magdalene Jaye Keene, on the other hand, had never once been sewed back together, and she wanted some-one there who would ooze sympathy. That would be Helen.

"Well, thanks a lot!" Alex declared with mock in-dignation. "I didn't hear you invite me and Whit along. You don't *care* if we inhaled coal dust, too?" He swiped at his eyes with the back of one hand.

"You guys can come, too," Maggie said. "I wasn't sure you'd want to. You hate hospitals, Alex. You've said so a thousand times."

Alex's father had died recently after a long bat-tle with cancer. During the last year, Alex had spent more time at the hospital than he had in school. While maintaining a vigil at his father's bed-side, he had tried hard to keep up with his school-work. Maggie, Helen, and Lane had helped as much as they could, bringing him assignments and notes from classes. Alex's mother had thanked them at the funeral, insisting they'd made it possible for Alex to pass.

Maggie was sure Alex would have passed any-way. His grade-point average was one of the high-est in their class, allowing him plenty of leeway.

He'd gone through a tough time, though. Alex's basic personality was easygoing and calm, but he'd been angry about the unfairness of the illness itself. "My father never hurt anyone in his life," he had railed to Maggie, "why does this have to happen to him?" She'd had no answer for him.

But what made matters so much worse and turned Alex's anger into rage, had been the firing of his dad by the city manager, for whom his father had worked for twenty years as an accountant. Although he'd still been well enough to work, he had been "let go" for losing time to radiation and chemotherapy treatments. In spite of a generous severance package and the extension of medical benefits, the loss of the salary had been hard on the family. They were forced to sell their country house and move into an apartment in Felicity. Alex's mother, trying to make the best of a bad situation, had insisted the move made sense because it eliminated the long round-trips to the hospital. Alex agreed reluctantly, but he told Maggie he didn't like living in town. He missed the country.

After his father's death, his anger grew when his mother was forced to go to work, at a time when her family needed her at home. And he was furious when the only job she could get was in the same courthouse where her husband had been employed for twenty years. Alex had protested that move, too, feeling she was being disloyal to Alex's father, but Mrs. Goodman had no choice.

She still worked there, but had received several promotions in the past year and would be moving into her own, modern office in the new building.

When Alex applied for his driver's license, six months after his father's death, Maggie had gone with him. As they emerged from the building into bright sunshine, angry tears shone in Alex's eyes. "That building just doesn't feel the same without my father in it," he had said quietly. "Whenever my mom and I came into town, I always liked going upstairs to his office to see him. Now all I can think about in there is how they treated him." He had added bitterly, "I'll bet that new accountant they hired doesn't know spit."

Maggie had never seen him so angry. He hadn't even stopped in to see his mother that day.

After a while, he got beyond all of that. Brooding wasn't Alex's style. Then, too, his mother's success had helped.

Still, Maggie had been surprised when Alex had joined the forces intent on razing the old courthouse. She'd have thought he would have wanted it left standing, not just because of his love of architecture, but to remind him of his father. And maybe he *would* have felt that way . . . if his father hadn't been fired. Now, he just wanted the building gone.

As they all began making their way across the parking lot to Scout's Jeep, Mr. Petersen called after them, "So, who's going to pay for this broken window?"

Maggie burst into laughter. "Broken window?" she gasped through the laughter that came, she knew, more from her relief at being free of the basement than it did from Petersen's idiotic question. "The place is practically falling down around him and he's worried about that one little basement window being broken? He is obviously the sort of man who sweats the small details."

No one answered Petersen's question.

The stitching of her arm hurt. "You lied," Maggie told the nurse through clenched teeth. "You said that needle you stuck me with would numb my arm.

My arm is not numb. Having my teeth drilled isn't this bad. It pinches."

"That," the nurse said matter-of-factly, "is because you're watching, Maggie. You feel every stitch because you see Dr. Nelson put that needle into your skin. Quit watching. No one else ever watches. How'd you do this, anyway?"

Helen, hovering anxiously beside the table, answered before Maggie could open her mouth. "She broke a window in the courthouse basement with her arm."

The nurse's eyebrows arched. "The old courthouse, or the new one?"

"The old one, of course," Maggie said testily. "What would we be doing in the new courthouse?"

Nurse Winslow aimed a level gaze at her. "I might ask the same of the old courthouse. Especially the basement."

"We were just exploring. We didn't know a beam was going to give out on us," Maggie explained.

On their way out of the hospital, as the arm began to throb mercilessly, Maggie told Helen, "I know what's been bothering me. Remember what people were saying about the ceiling collapsing? When we were all lying in the parking lot?" Lane, Whit, Scout, and Alex were waiting on the hospital steps. "I heard someone say there wasn't anyone on the first floor when the ceiling collapsed. But that's not true. There *was*. I heard footsteps above me when I was in the coal bin."

Before anyone could answer her, the sheriff and a deputy approached from the parking lot. When they reached the group, Sheriff Donovan first asked Maggie how her arm was. When she shrugged, he said, "I need to talk to you folks. But you look to me," addressing Maggie, "like you could use a nice place to lie down. So I won't ask you to come to my office. Only got one question, anyway, so maybe you could answer it right here, save us all some time."

"What question?" Alex's tone of voice was hostile. The sheriff's office was in the old courthouse, so Alex automatically saw him as part of the establishment that had fired his father.

"A simple one. Anyone else in that basement with you? Besides the lot of you, I mean?"

"Not as far as we know," Whit answered. "We didn't see anyone else, but then, we couldn't see much of anything. We couldn't even see one another. Too dark."

Maggie took a step forward. "But there might have been," she offered. "Because someone locked me in the coal bin room, and my friends all said it wasn't them."

That brought forth a skeptical look from the sheriff. "And you believe them?"

"Of course! They wouldn't lie. I thought one of them was just fooling around, but if it was someone else, it wasn't a joke at all. So . . . I guess there *had* to be someone else down there. Why?"

Sheriff Donovan drew his words out slowly and carefully. "Well, see, the thing is, the city engineer took a look at that beam. A quick look, granted, but still . . . and he says it looks to him like that beam didn't just collapse. It was weak and old, he admits that, but he still insists it would have taken a heavy blow or a sharp kick, maybe someone pushing against it hard, to make it give way like that. So I was just wondering . . . you boys are pretty hefty, any of you lean against that beam, put your full weight on it?"

Alex, Scout, and Whit all said at the same time, "No," and Alex added, "the only thing we leaned against was the wall."

The sheriff thought for a minute, exchanged a look with his deputy, and then asked, "But you did say you couldn't see down there, right? Couldn't see anything? So someone else *could* have been down there?"

"Right."

He nodded. "Okay, then." Waving a hand toward Maggie, he said, "Well, you get that girl on home now where she belongs. We'll talk again when you've all had a chance to pull yourselves together." He and his deputy turned to leave.

"Sheriff?" Whit hesitated, then forged on. "Are you telling us that someone *pushed* that beam out of place? Deliberately?"

"Didn't say that." The sheriff didn't stop walking, didn't turn around. "But looks like, maybe. We'll let you know."

They were still standing on the hospital steps, as slack-jawed and stunned-looking as if he'd told them they were all under arrest, when the tan car with the official emblem on the side pulled out of the parking lot.

# Chapter 12

The awful thing was, once I had done the deed, I couldn't take it back. No matter how much I wanted to, I couldn't change it. It was done, and I was stuck with it. Forever.

I hit her hard. I watched her fall, without a sound, to the frozen ground and lie there, lifeless. Her hair puddled around her. In one of his more poetic moments, Dante had called that hair "like cornsilk." Trite, but in Christy's case it was true. Besides, Dante lived on a farm. He saw a lot of corn.

Christy had landed on her stomach, so I couldn't see her eyes. I was glad of that, because I was sure they had to be wide open, staring at the ground in shock and disbelief. Something had been done to her that she didn't *want* done. I was pretty sure that had never happened to her before.

Had Dante actually been the one to deliver the fatal blow, I think the eyes wouldn't have looked so shocked. Christy knew better than anyone how often she had taunted Dante to the point of striking her. He never had, but I suspected she wouldn't have been surprised if he'd finally done so. But he hadn't. *I* had, and that was something that Christy would never have been able to comprehend.

There was a moment then that is as real to me today as if it had only happened this morning instead of four years ago. I remember everything about it . . . the sound of my own breathing, harsh and ragged from a combination of fury, the exertion of lifting the heavy tire iron and striking the blow, and the shock of seeing her fall and knowing what I had done. I remember the way the frigid air turned my breath visible as it left my body, creating little clouds in front of my face, as if I were The Little Engine That Could, chugging up a steep hill. I remember that my breathing was the *only* sound I heard and I remember thinking that the violence of my act must have frightened even the trees around me. There were no cars roaring along up on the highway. There wasn't a sound from any animal on the nearest farm, which happened to be the Guardinos. The cold, dark winter evening was as deathly still as Christy herself as I stood there in the woods alone with the knowledge of what I had just done.

I remember standing motionless in the underbrush beside the truck. The heavy tire iron, now smeared with Christy's blood and a few long strands of hair (cornsilk), was hanging loosely in my right hand. I remember thinking, *My right hand? But I am left-handed. What is this doing in my right hand?*

I knew the answer to that, of course. The tool lying in the truck bed had been nearest to my right hand and I had been so furious, I had snatched it up without thinking. (Later, this would work against Dante, because unlike me, he *was* right-handed.)

I remember suddenly becoming ill and having to turn away from the truck, as the supper I had eaten earlier in the Guardino kitchen abandoned me, probably in revulsion for what I had just done.

I had called Christy from that very kitchen, after Dante and his parents left. (Another strike against Dante, because the call to Christy's house that night was on the Guardinos' phone bill. The police looked it up. They assumed then that he had called her to set up a meeting in the woods when, in fact, it was I who had called her, and for that very reason.)

I remember leaning against the bed of the truck for what seemed like a long time, looking down at her. I had no idea what to do next. But then, it wasn't as if I'd planned the whole thing. Still, there she was, dead as grass in winter (or so I believed then) and I had no clue what to do with her.

I also remember what had happened right before that awful moment took place. I remember the very last thing that Christy Miller ever said to me. *"Why don't you mind your own business? Dante can take care of himself. Get a life!"* And then she turned away, tossing her head in that maddening way she had.

It would have made anyone crazy. I know it made *me* crazy. Crazy enough to pick up the tire iron.

And what I remember most is, at the very instant that it was happening, as the back of her head turned scarlet and her knees crumpled, something swept over me that was so sickening, so heavy and dark and thick, that it was like being suffocated. Even in my wild state of mind, I recognized the feeling for what it was: gut-deep regret. It was an agonizing need, even as it was happening, for it *not* to be happening. Even as she was falling, even as I knew beyond any doubt that I had killed her, the black blanket of wet wool sweeping down upon me was my fervent wish that I hadn't done it. Everything inside of me was screaming, *No, no, no, don't let it be this way, don't let this happen, I want to take it back, I don't want this to be what it is!*

But it was already too late. And the black, suffocating cloak was engulfing me because I *knew* that. The thing about wanting to change something when it's already too late is, it's just not possible. No matter how much you might want to.

There was another moment then, a moment of utter darkness, when it occurred to me that I wanted to die, too. How could I go on with my own life when I'd taken hers?

I snapped out of that very quickly. First of all, I realized that Dante was safe now, which was what I'd wanted all along. And second, I couldn't very well hit myself over the head with the tire iron. So the moment passed.

If the truck had had a trunk, I'd have hidden her in there. She was smaller than me. I could lift her easily. But there was no trunk, so I had to settle for rolling her limp body underneath the truck and leaving her there. Couldn't very well toss her into the pond. It was one solid, shiny sheet of ice. I kicked a few dead leaves in on top of her, hoping they'd hide the bright red coat she was wearing.

I wondered as I left the woods and loped back along the road toward my house if she'd told anyone she was meeting me. When I'd called her, I'd told her that Dante had a surprise for her, that she was to meet him at his place, on the road by the woods. She had answered the phone when I called, so if she hadn't told anyone else who she was talking to, I was safe enough.

I didn't go straight home. Too upset. I was afraid my mother would see something in my face. I hid out in the Swansons' barn for a couple of hours. They were in Kentucky, antique shopping, I'd heard, and were staying overnight. If anyone asked where I'd been all evening, I could always say I'd hitchhiked to the library in Felicity, so much better than our tiny branch library, and I'd gone down to the computer room. The computer cubicles are private, so I'd have a good excuse for not having been seen.

But I wasn't really worried. There wasn't any reason for me to be a suspect.

And I have to say, it really didn't occur to me that Dante would be. It should have, I know. But it really didn't. Like I said, it wasn't as if I'd thought things through. If I'd ever for one minute thought that Dante would be accused, I wouldn't have done it.

Well . . . yeah, I guess I would have, because she still would have made me furious and I still would have lost my cool. But I would have hidden her somewhere else, at least, and got rid of the tire iron. I just wasn't thinking. *It wasn't as if I'd ever done this kind of thing before.*

What did I feel as I lay huddled in the sweet-smelling hay in the Swansons' barn? Nothing. I felt nothing at all. I kept hearing the sound the tire iron made against Christy's skull. It wasn't the sharp crack of a home run when the bat hits the ball and you know that one's long gone, out of the park. It wasn't like that at all. More like a heavy, booted foot stomping down on a melon. That kind of sound. Disgusting. Sickening. And so . . . final.

There in the Swansons' hayloft, I heard again the shocked whoosh of air that came from her mouth when the tire iron hit, though she didn't cry out. And I saw her fall again, face forward onto the ground. But still I felt nothing. It was as if, after that one black moment when I wanted fiercely, passionately, to take it all back and realized that I couldn't, I had made up my mind that I wasn't going to make myself crazy feeling things. Things like regret. It was too late for that. Regretting is nothing but wasted energy anyway, since it can't change a thing. Better not to have done the deed in the first place.

She deserved it, that's what I had to tell myself. She was ruining everything and then, even when I begged her, she refused to stop. Refused! What choice did I have?

When Dante was arrested the following morning, I wasn't worried. Because he hadn't done anything. Who knew that better than me? He was innocent, so how could anything bad happen to him?

It couldn't.

That's what I told myself.

But I was wrong.

# Chapter 13

When the sheriff's words had sunk in, they tried to make sense of them.

Alex thought the whole idea of someone knocking the beam out of place was crazy. "We were right *there*!" he said in disbelief. "We'd just let Maggie out of the coal bin room. If someone was sneaking around in that passageway, we'd have seen or heard them."

"No, we wouldn't," Helen disagreed. "For one thing, we couldn't *see* anything. That's how Maggie got separated from us in the first place. And for another, we were all talking at the same time."

"Helen's got a point," Lane said calmly. "None of us was paying any attention at all to what was going on behind us. Because we didn't think anything *could* be. We didn't know there was anyone else down there."

"Maybe there wasn't." Scout tightened his protective grip around Maggie's shoulders. "Just because the sheriff is jumping to conclusions, doesn't mean we have to. That building is on its last legs and everyone knows it. If *I* were over one hundred and thirty years old, *my* beams would be collapsing, that's for sure."

"I need to go home," Maggie said suddenly, reaching out with one hand and grasping Helen's arm to steady herself. "I'm dizzy."

Scout lowered her to one of the steps. "Sit down," he ordered. "I'll go get the Jeep. It's in the parking lot. Wait here."

Maggie smiled wanly. As if she were in any shape to do anything *but* wait. "Are you guys in a big hurry to get home?" she asked while they waited. "You could come to my house. I'll feed you." Being alone would almost certainly mean a mental replay of that black, terrifying moment in the dark, airless passageway beneath the courthouse when the ceiling had collapsed. She wasn't ready to deal with those thoughts yet. And now she had the sheriff's weird suspicions to worry about, too. Although Scout was probably right. The building was *so* old. "We'll sit out on the back porch. I can rest there. That should get me into shape for the fund-raiser tonight."

Whit looked interested. "What fund-raiser?"

Maggie let Lane answer. "The Women's Heritage Society is holding a bazaar on the grounds of the old courthouse to raise money for the refurbishing. That's this week. Next week, it's a party at the new courthouse, when they put the statue of Lady Justice up on the roof. That sounds like a lot more fun to me than some dumb bazaar where old women will be selling fattening cakes and cookies, ratty old wicker furniture, and horrible little ceramic figurines."

Alex nodded. "They'll be selling red lampshades with fringe, too, I bet. My grandmother has one."

Scout pulled up in his Jeep. Everyone piled in. Maggie hopped into the front seat, then suddenly cried, "The van! I forgot all about it. It's still in the school parking lot. I can't leave it there."

"We'll get it!" Lane was in the backseat, crammed in with Alex, Whit, and Helen. "Give me the keys. Whit and I will go collect it and bring it to your house. Scout can take us back to Whit's car later."

In the front seat, Maggie's teeth clenched. *"Whit and I"?* Fast work, even for Lane.

"Sure," Whit agreed heartily. "Be glad to. I'll drive. Lane can navigate, since I don't know where you live, Maggie."

Scout was only too happy to stop the Jeep and let Whit and Lane out.

Maggie watched as they ran up Fourth Street. That yachting cap on Lane's head, she thought darkly, is just about the stupidest thing I've ever seen. And what about poor "Scoop," away at college? Stupid nickname. He worked on the college newspaper, so Lane called him Scoop. His real name, Maggie thought, was Paul.

When the rest of the group was settled on her back porch, the sun just beginning to set, the breeze cooling slightly, Helen told Maggie she should call her parents and tell them what had happened. "Your mother probably heard the sirens. Maybe she's worried."

"I don't know where she is. She and Trudy Newhouse were supposed to collect last-minute items for the bazaar tonight, and I know they were going out to Muleshoe and Arcadia for some antique furniture. Anyway, she's probably back at the courthouse by now, getting things ready for tonight. She'll know all about the collapse, but she won't have a clue that I was there, so why would she worry? I'll bet she's upset, though. This could set her renovating campaign back a *lot*."

"Maybe they won't have the bazaar now," Helen said. She was sitting on the top porch step, her back against the railing, her eyes narrowed against the last rays of the setting sun. "I mean, after what happened." Her head turned, and her eyes focused on Maggie, lying on the white wooden swing, her head resting on a huge green-and-white-striped pillow, her feet propped on the swing's other arm. Her injured arm was lying against her chest. "What if the sheriff was right?" Helen asked quietly. "I mean," she added hastily, "not that I think he was. But what if? Who do we know that would want to do that to us?"

"Well, first of all," Maggie said, "I think the sheriff is as bored with Felicity as the rest of us, and he's just trying to create a little excitement. Second, even if there *was* someone down there kicking beams and making ceilings collapse, he or she might not have known that was us down there. He couldn't have seen us, because we certainly couldn't see *him*. Maybe . . . maybe it was an inspector or something, checking out the soundness of the building."

"He would have had a flashlight, Maggie. And he would have hung around afterward," said Helen.

True. And with that inescapable fact came another: Maggie remembered almost running into James Keith, Chantilly Beckwith, and two of their friends, right before they descended into that basement. That meant the nasty little quartet knew for a fact that six members of the peer jury, which the quartet had reason to loathe, were down there. Chantilly might look like a twig, but James and his friends were stocky and sturdy, built like bulldogs. Any one of them alone could have knocked that beam silly.

Could four other people have entered that corridor without Maggie and her friends hearing footsteps or breathing or the rustling of clothing . . . something, anything that would clue them in to the presence of others?

Yes, absolutely, Maggie decided, because I was kicking up such a racket, ranting and raving about being locked in that awful little room. And the quick shove or kick to the beam would only have taken a second or two. One quick shove from bulky shoulders, and down goes the beam.

But . . .

"No," she said suddenly, as if she'd been thinking aloud, "it didn't happen the way the sheriff said, because where would the person or persons have gone after they knocked the beam down? *We* couldn't get out. So how could they?"

"Oh, that's easy," Scout answered. "All they would have had to do was dart around a corner and hide in one of the other passageways until dark. Couple of hours, that's all. Then leave either by the coal chute, or if the mess was cleaned up by then, go back up the stairs and out of the building. I mean, we could have done that, too, but we weren't willing to wait. *You* weren't," he reminded Maggie.

They fell silent again, then Helen said, "I think saving that building would be a big mistake. I think the Bransoms would rather we tore it down. That's what they'd want. That's what they wanted the first time, when Felicity turned their home into a jail. Remember the newspaper articles at the WOH offices, telling how Otis and his wife, Amelia, were so furious when the city took their home for unpaid back taxes and then turned it into a jail? They were both in their nineties then, and in the same nursing home, but they were so angry that criminals were going to be housed in the home they'd lived in forever and raised their kids in." Her voice lowered. "Some people in town say the two of them still wander the halls of the old courthouse. Maybe the renovations would make them even madder."

"We can't make them mad, Helen." Alex's voice was as quiet as Helen's, but firm. "They're dead. You can't make dead people mad."

Maggie wondered if he was thinking about his father. Maybe thinking that because his father was dead, Alex himself had to be mad *for* him, at the city officials who had treated Mr. Goodman so shabbily.

The van pulled up the steep driveway, stopped, and Lane and Whit jumped out. They were laughing.

Oh, goodie, they had a nice time, Maggie thought, slinking lower on the swing. I do so love it when my friends get along well. When they ran up onto the porch, she flashed a brilliant smile at them and said sweetly, "Thank you both so much. It was so nice of you to go to all that trouble."

"No trouble," Whit said easily, taking a seat on the steps. "You feeling okay? How's the arm?"

Lane was beside him in seconds.

"The arm is fine. But you must have had *some* trouble," Maggie continued in that same innocent voice. "It usually only takes four minutes to drive here from school. Did you run into a detour or something? An accident?"

Lane shot her a suspicious glance. "Actually, we ran into your mom. She was at the van, looking for you. Someone at the courthouse told her you were involved in the collapse, and she freaked. Went to the hospital, you weren't there, so she was on her way here when she spotted the van. I think we convinced her that you weren't at death's door. She wanted to know what we were doing down there, and she said it was a good thing you'd already delivered those plans in the morning, because if she thought it was her fault you were in there, she'd never have forgiven herself."

Maggie flushed guiltily.

"I didn't tell her," Lane continued, "that you *were* there delivering the plans. I didn't dare. I was afraid she'd feel too guilty. Either that or she'd have been really mad that you didn't deliver them when she told you to. So I kept my mouth zipped."

"Thanks, Lane. I'll explain it all later."

Whit said, "You'd better have that explanation ready any second now, because I'm not that sure we convinced her you were okay. I'm surprised she hasn't called here already."

The phone rang.

When Maggie had persuaded her mother that not only was she okay, but she had every intention of working at the bazaar as promised, she returned to the porch. "I think I need to sack out for a little while before I go over there," she said reluctantly, not that eager to be in the house alone. Her brother was working and wouldn't be home until late, her mother was staying at the courthouse to put the finishing touches on the bazaar, and her father was going straight there after work to help. But if she didn't lie down, just for a little while, she wasn't going to be in any shape to help in the courthouse kitchen later. God, she was going to have to go back inside that building again!

"Did she say anything about canceling the bazaar?" Helen asked, standing up and dusting off her khaki shorts.

"No. She said it's too late. All the stuff is already on display tables and tagged with prices. And the kitchen, where we'll be working, is in a separate wing from the collapse. Besides, like she said, the bazaar itself is being held outside, and the grounds should be perfectly safe." Maggie laughed abruptly. "No beams out there, holding things up. Or *not*."

Whit stood up, too, and moved toward Maggie to say quietly, "So, I'll see you over there, right?"

She nodded, aware of both Scout and Lane, who must have heard. Then she led everyone down the back steps to the driveway and waved as they all climbed into the Jeep.

A feeling of desolation swept over her as the car disappeared from sight. Twilight had arrived, bathing the backyard in a rosy, purplish glow, but darkness would follow soon after. She'd be left alone in the dark with only questions about the disaster at the courthouse to keep her company.

Maggie was about to climb the steps when the toe of her boot struck something solid. Something that shouldn't have been there. There was just supposed to be the thick, green lawn, and then the wide, wooden steps. Nothing else.

Dog-face had probably dropped something on his way in or out and been too lazy to pick it up.

Maggie looked down. The object lying just below the bottom step didn't belong to her brother, Darren.

The object belonged to her. And before that, it had belonged to Scout's grandfather, and possibly his father before him. Now it belonged to her, because Scout had generously given it to her. Lying at her feet, half-hidden beneath the open bottom step, was the gavel Scout had given her when she was appointed foreperson of the peer jury.

Except . . . except, Maggie realized as she bent to pick it up, thinking it must have dropped out of her backpack, there was something very wrong with it.

The gavel Scout had gifted her with had been one solid piece of smooth, shiny wood. But the gavel she was looking at now in dismay was in pieces. The gavel itself had been neatly sliced—sawed?—into three fat chunks, the handle into two narrower slices.

Picking up the larger chunks and holding them in the palm of one hand, Maggie stood at the foot of the steps, staring down at what was left of the antique gavel Scout had given her.

# Chapter 14

It didn't seem to matter to anyone that Dante was innocent.

I mean, of course no one actually knew that he was, not the way I did. But it seemed to me that they weren't even trying to find out the truth. They presumed right from the beginning that he was guilty. I'd been taught that our criminal justice system was supposed to consider an accused person innocent until proven guilty. But that wasn't what I was seeing. They were all acting just the opposite: the police, the state cops, the sheriff and his deputies, the district attorney . . . like they were all so sure of Dante's guilt.

I'll be the first to admit there was a ton of evidence against him. But it was all circumstantial. He had been in love with Christy, and had dated only her. She, on the other hand, had not been quite so true blue. They had fought in public, many times. The truck under which she was found was on his property. The tire iron belonged to him, and had his fingerprints on it. And there was the phone call, that same evening, from his house to hers.

But no one ever investigated to see if there was evidence against anyone else.

They put him in jail. I couldn't believe it. They actually took him, in handcuffs, and put him in a cell, which was really just an extra room in Sheriff Donovan's house, with bars on the windows. Then, as if that weren't bad enough, because of what the sheriff said was "outrage" over Christy's death in Dante's little farming community, they moved Dante into Felicity. They took him to that disgusting old wreck of a building with the six jail cells in the basement. They said he'd be safer there. And of course, the trial would be held there, in the county seat.

But I was mad. It would be hard for me to go all the way to Felicity to visit Dante.

That courthouse was disgusting! Musty and mildewy and withered, a corpse the town refused to bury. Even the ivy on the outside walls was dead, dry as brown tissue paper, the edges curled like arthritic fingers.

But that's where they took him. And that's where he stayed until they convicted him. Wouldn't even let him out on bail. Not for murder, they said. No bail for murder suspects, not in Greene County.

All the time, while he was in jail, and all during the trial, I was convinced he couldn't possibly be convicted. How could he be? He was innocent. I wasn't worried.

But I should have been.

Because justice is blind. Blind to the truth, and that's a fact.

No wonder that statue up on the courthouse roof is wearing a blindfold. It was explained to me a long time ago that the blindfold means Justice is blind to things like race, creed, wealth, religion, power, and position . . . so that everyone, no matter what their circumstances, is treated the same way under the law. Treated fairly.

But I know now that it means something very different. What that blindfold really means is, Justice is blind to the *truth*.

I could not believe it when they actually convicted him. I was in shock for days. How could they do that? Dante hadn't done anything wrong. He'd just fallen in love with the wrong person, that was all. As far as I know, you don't go to prison for life for that. If you did, the prisons would be overflowing even more than they already are.

Dante hadn't killed anyone. Who knew that better than I?

Of course Dante's fingerprints were on the tire iron. He'd worked on that truck. My fingerprints would have been on it, too, if I hadn't been wearing gloves. Even if I hadn't been wearing them, I don't think my fingerprints would have meant much. Everyone knew I hung around the Guardino farm sometimes, and I was only thirteen . . . much too young to be guilty of such a heinous crime. That's what they'd have said, anyway. Besides, no one had seen me with Christy in a while. But Dante was still very much involved with her. Everyone in town had seen and heard them fighting.

And everyone in town was willing, even eager, to testify to those arguments in open court.

I think the clincher was, Dante had no alibi. His story about sitting down by the pond, alone, sounded weak even to me, and I *knew* he was telling the truth.

And then there was his 4-H pin. He never wore it. But I'd stolen it off his dresser a couple of weeks before that awful night. When Dante wasn't around, which was most of the time, I'd been wearing it on my denim jacket. I just wanted something of his. So I took it.

I never wore the jacket when Dante was around, even though I knew he wouldn't care about the pin. But he might have cared that I'd gone into his room without his permission, since he had jillions of notebooks scattered all over the place with stupid, moony things about Christy written inside, and he'd be afraid that I had read them. Like I'd want to. Anyway, I never told him I'd taken the pin.

What must have happened was, when I swung the tire iron, the clasp on the pin pulled loose and the pin fell off. Landed on the frozen ground without making a sound. And there it stayed. Until one of the sheriff's deputies found it.

It's really not my fault that Dante scratched his initials on the back of that pin.

I did go to the courthouse for most of the trial, until my parents got so disgusted with the whole process, they refused to take me into Felicity. I had to hitchhike in for the reading of the verdict. I had been expressly forbidden to ever hitchhike, but after you've murdered someone, you don't sweat the small stuff.

That was a terrible day, the day they pronounced Dante guilty. It was February by then, still too cold outside to open the courthouse windows. It smelled of stale sweat and cigar smoke inside. There wasn't an ounce of fresh air anywhere in that small, crowded room as the jury foreperson announced calmly and matter-of-factly, as if she were casually mentioning that it just might snow that afternoon, *"Guilty."*

The sound of it rang in my head like bells . . . ding . . . Guilty . . . dong . . . Guilty. Ding dong, the boy is dead.

Not that I thought he'd get the death penalty; he never would, not in Greene County. But he'd be sent to prison for life and was there really a difference? Either way, Dante's life was over.

I was screaming inside. *Nonononononono!* This could not be happening!

But hadn't I thought the same thing as Christy fell to the ground, her skull in two pieces? Hadn't I told myself *that* couldn't be happening? But it happened anyway, didn't it? And she'd died, hadn't she? So . . .

Dante was going to prison and it didn't really matter how I felt about it.

When the verdict was read, Dante's mother screamed. His father clutched at his chest. (Two days later, while he was just sitting in his recliner watching the news but not really seeing it because all he was thinking about was that his only son was going to grow old in prison, Mr. Guardino had a heart attack and died right there in his chair.)

I don't know how Dante's mother survived that ghastly year.

And that wasn't the end of it. That wasn't even the worst of it, although no one but me knows what the worst of it really was.

And I don't want them to know *now*.

# Chapter 15

The bazaar was held, as planned, on the grounds of the old courthouse that evening.

Maggie took the gavel's remnants with her. She arrived at the already crowded site at six o'clock, but she wasn't scheduled to work in the kitchen until eight. A determined look on her face, she found Scout, Helen, Lane, Alex, and Whit and led them to a quiet, solitary spot under an aging elm tree. Then she withdrew from the pockets of her windbreaker the wooden chunks and held them in her outstretched palms.

"What *is* that?" Helen was the first to ask.

Before Maggie could answer, Scout drew in a sharp breath and said, "That better not be what I think it is."

"It is. I'm sorry, Scout. I found it under the back steps right after you guys left. And just enough of it was sticking out that I know someone *wanted* me to find it."

Scout was aghast. He reached out and picked up one chunk, held it in his hands. "You let someone *demolish* my grandfather's gavel?"

"I didn't *let* them, Scout. I don't even know how someone got it. It was in my backpack. I used it this morning at the hearing, and then I put it in my backpack. I know I did."

"I don't *think* so." Scout's tone was harsh. "If you had, it wouldn't look like scrap lumber now." He sent Maggie an accusatory look. "Jeez, I thought you'd take better care of it than this. It was an antique, Maggie!"

Maggie stared at him. "Scout! I *did* take care of it!" She fingered the smooth-sawn edges of the chunks in her hands. "This isn't just *broken*, can't you tell that? It's not like I carelessly threw it on the floor or dropped it, and it broke. Someone *sawed* it into all these pieces. Someone stole it out of my backpack and did this to it."

The understanding that someone had invaded her belongings, invaded her privacy, had taken something that belonged to her and destroyed it, then brought it to her house, to her home, had earlier sent a wave of dizziness washing over Maggie. She had thought, standing at the foot of the steps in the twilight, the wood pieces in her hands, that she couldn't deal with that at all. But she had dealt with it. She had collected all of the chunks, and she had gone inside, and she had rested for an hour. Then she got up, took a shower, changed into jeans and a sweater, combed her hair, stuffed the wood pieces in the pockets of her blue-and-white Bransom High windbreaker, and left the house, just as she would have if someone hadn't violated her privacy.

Because what else could she do?

Now, as her friends tried to comprehend what she was presenting to them and what she had said about it, she lifted her head to ask, "Why would someone *do* this? *Who* would do this?"

Alex answered, "Almost anyone we've sentenced on the peer jury. That gavel was probably a symbol of our power over them, and they'd think they had reason to destroy it. They'd want to make sure you saw what they'd done, hoping it would teach you a lesson."

"James Keith takes shop," Helen volunteered. "He's in my class. He could have used a saw in there. Wouldn't have taken him more than a minute or two. Mr. Norman probably wouldn't even have noticed. No one would have."

Maggie considered that. "But the gavel was *in* my backpack. Unless . . ."

Scout eyed her suspiciously. "Unless what?"

"Well, the way you dragged me out of there this morning," Maggie accused, "maybe it slipped out when I was skidding across the gym floor."

"Oh, right. Blame me. Why can't you just admit that you were careless?"

He really *is* mad that I was picked as foreperson instead of him, Maggie thought with surprise. That's why he's being so mean now. "I wasn't careless, Scout. I'm not a careless person, and you know it." She looked down at the wood in her hands, then looked up at Scout. "I guess it can't be fixed?"

"No. It can't be fixed."

"You know," Lane said, "it could have been that Alice Ann from this morning. The girl who calls herself Chantilly. She was really ticked this morning. And she takes shop, too. I've seen her going in and out of there."

"Well," Alex commented, "it's definitely a message. I guess it was meant for you, Maggie, since it was your gavel. And they brought it to your house, in broad daylight, yet." He thrust his hands in the pockets of his Bransom High athletic jacket and added, "So they know where you live."

"Shouldn't we take this to the sheriff?" Whit asked Maggie. "If the gavel really was an antique, it must have been worth something."

"Only sentimentally," Scout answered, his voice gruff. "I don't think the cops would be that interested. But if Maggie's scared because whoever did this knows where she lives and is mad at her, maybe we should talk to the sheriff." He shrugged. "I mean, whoever it was could come back, right? And then there's that business with the beam today. Maybe the two things are connected."

Maggie shuddered. "It probably *was* James. He was so mad this morning. And I must have dropped the gavel on my way out of the gym. He saw it, picked it up, and decided to get even, just a little bit. Maybe he got it all out of his system."

Helen shook her head. "Maggie, James left the gym *before* we did. He was already gone when Scout hustled you out."

Scout glared at her.

Maggie looked doubtful. "He must have come back. Maybe to yell at me or something. He found the gavel, took it to shop and turned it into alphabet blocks, then brought it to my house. Like he was saying, Nyah, nyah, nyah. That's James's style. I'm not worried."

That was almost true. It was horrible that James had come to her house. The place where she was always supposed to be safe. That, she didn't like at all. But she really did believe it was a one-shot deal. James had been furious, he'd vented that fury, and now he'd leave her alone. He wouldn't dare go beyond this one act of vandalism. He was already on shaky ground both at school and in the community. He wouldn't risk spending time in those dank, dark jail cells in the basement. The new jail cells weren't completed yet.

"I'm really sorry about the gavel," she told Scout sincerely.

He waved a hand. "I guess it wasn't your fault." He took the gavel's remnants from her and tossed them into a nearby trash can. "But we'd better keep an eye on James. Just in case . . ."

"Look," Maggie said, moving out from beneath the tree, "there's a bazaar going on here, and I'm supposed to be helping. Can we just forget about James and try to have some fun before I have to go on kitchen duty at eight? I'm starving, and the smell from that barbecue cart is driving me nuts. Let's get something to eat."

And although Helen muttered, "I just don't see why your mother didn't cancel this thing after what happened today," everyone else followed Maggie into the heart of the teeming crowd. After a moment of hesitation, Helen followed, too.

The damaged wing, Maggie noticed with relief, had been roped off. There were security guards posted at intervals along the roping, to keep children and curiosity-seekers from slipping inside. Her mother wasn't taking any chances on another disaster ruining the bazaar.

With nightfall came a cooling of temperatures accompanied by a brisk breeze. Maggie was grateful for her heavy turtleneck sweater, its color palest blue, and wondered briefly if Lane had noticed that Whit's sweater was blue, too, although a darker shade. Lane wouldn't like that.

The rapidly swelling throng filled the parking lot, examining the merchandise laid out on the dozen or so long, narrow tables lined up side by side, ordering food at one of several wooden food booths and the steaming, aromatic barbecue cart. They all seemed to be in high spirits, apparently not the least bit worried about disaster overtaking them from the building looming over them.

Word had spread that members of the peer jury had been inside at the time of the collapse. Walking alongside the tables piled high with labeled merchandise, they were besieged by questions. People wanted to know, "Are there bats down there?" and "What'd it feel like, Maggie, to be trapped in there?" No one seemed suspicious that the incident hadn't been accidental, so Maggie assumed the sheriff was keeping his opinions to himself, for now.

The questions were annoying. As if she could describe in words the terrible feeling of dread when the ceiling gave way, the fear of suffocation, that one brief moment when she'd forgotten about the coal chute and thought they might be trapped in that basement for hours. She didn't even try. Just shook her head and pressed on through the crowd. The others did the same.

Maggie found her attention drawn to Whit in spite of herself. Although he was wearing the same kind of clothes every other guy there was wearing — jeans and a denim jacket over the blue sweater — his easy air of self-confidence made him seem older than most of Bransom High's male population. Maggie wondered if private school had done that. She also wondered why he had left. He'd said it was partly because of what was going on with the courthouses. That seemed like a silly reason to switch schools at the beginning of junior year.

Because Lane had already pressed in as close to Whit as she could get without climbing up his heels, Maggie said, a bit too sharply, "I go on kitchen duty in twenty minutes. If I'm going to get any dinner, I'd better do it now. I'm going to have to wait in line at the barbecue cart."

It seemed to Maggie that, in spite of the disaster that afternoon, everyone in town who could walk was at the bazaar. The parking lot was one shoulder-to-shoulder, noisy mass of people. Maybe because it was a Friday night, and fun was in short supply in Felicity on a weekend.

Alex was disappointed. "I was kind of hoping," he said glumly, "that what happened this afternoon might lower the turnout tonight. Then the Women of Heritage wouldn't raise enough money, and they'd have to cancel the restoration plans. Especially now that everyone knows how dangerous that building really is."

Scout added darkly, "They're taking a big chance, if you ask me." He surveyed the noisy crowd gathering around the tables, exclaiming over the merchandise on display. "Anything bad happens here tonight, we could lose half of Felicity."

Maggie frowned. "If anything happens? Like what? We're outside, Scout, what could happen? It's not like the ground could collapse under our feet. Felicity doesn't have earthquakes."

He shrugged. "I dunno. I just have this bad feeling. . . ."

"Stop it, will you? You're giving me the creeps!" That business with the gavel must have really upset Scout. He wasn't usually morbid. Maggie's eyes moved involuntarily to the huge, old courthouse. There were lights on inside, in the kitchen wing next to the parking lot where her mother was working. But even that yellow glow shining like cats'-eyes didn't erase the bleak, forlorn look. Though everyone else seemed to be ignoring the building, Maggie was constantly aware of its presence, feeling its yellow-eyed stare between her shoulder blades even when she deliberately kept her back to it.

My friends are right, she thought, suppressing a

shudder. It should be torn down. No amount of restoration is going to bring that rotting old pile of boards back to life. It should be put to rest.

"When are they taking the statue down?" Alex asked of no one in particular. His gaze was focused on the very top of the three-story structure. He was speaking of the giant metal statue of Justice, affixed to the top of the courthouse. Blindfolded and balancing in her hands a set of scales, she had stood proudly atop the building for over sixty years, overseeing Felicity and the surrounding county. Because she was sturdy enough to withstand even the worst of storms, getting her down would be no small task.

"Next Saturday, around noon," Lane answered. She was wearing a pale green sweater and matching slacks, and looked especially pretty, her dark hair spilling over her shoulders like satin. "They have to use a crane, I heard. And the mayor is having some kind of ceremony, because the thing has been up there forever. The peer jury is invited. In fact, we're supposed to be here. Ms. Gross thought it would be 'appropriate.' Said we should be in on what she called a 'history-making event.'"

Whit looked interested. "That might be fun to watch. Am I included?"

"Of course," Maggie answered. "We're supposed to meet here at eleven-thirty. That's *next* Saturday, not tomorrow. Ms. Gross said there'd be chairs set up for us, so we can sit while we watch the removal of the statue, and listen to the mayor's speech. My dad thinks the whole thing is going to take a lot longer than anyone's planning, to get the old girl down off that roof." Maggie began moving toward the barbecue cart. "Personally, if I know the mayor, the *speech* will take a lot longer than anyone's planning."

Whit's eyes met Maggie's, as if to say, *This is just between you and me,* as he asked, "But you're going to be there anyway?"

Her own eyes glinted. "Well, let me think about this." She tapped an index finger against her lips. "A Saturday in Felicity gives me two choices: I can go to the library and check out a couple of books, or I can catch one of four old movies at the mall, none of which were that good to begin with. Tough choices there." She nodded. "Yeah, I guess I could squeeze in a little history-making."

He nodded, smiling at her.

"We'll *all* be there," Lane said. "It's our civic duty, right?" The brittle tone of her voice told Maggie she was offended because Whit had made a point of checking only Maggie's Saturday plans.

"So," Maggie asked lightly, "how's Scoop?"

Lane glared at her. "He's fine, Maggie. Just fine."

Maggie had to eat hurriedly. Used paper plates smeared with rust-colored barbecue sauce piled steadily higher on the kitchen's wide stone windowsills. All trash was supposed to be passed through the two open windows to the kitchen for disposal, but her mother was having a hard time keeping pace. "Be there in a sec, Mom!" Maggie called as she left the barbecue cart with a full plate of her own.

Lane, Whit, Helen, and Alex were still waiting in line. "Man," Scout said, taking a deep breath as he and Maggie took seats on a stone bench, "they should bottle that smell and sell it!"

"They do bottle it, Scout. It's called barbecue sauce." Maggie took a bite of her hot dog and just then spotted James Keith, leaning sullenly against the courthouse wall, his eyes on her. She was tempted to walk over and tell him to stay away from her house or she'd call the police, but decided against it. For one thing, he wasn't alone, and the two boys flanking him looked every bit as nasty as James. His girlfriend was there, too, and beside her stood Alice Ann "Chantilly" Beckwith. Birds of a feather, all of them glaring at her as if she alone were responsible for every bad thing that had ever happened to them.

The other thing that stopped Maggie from confronting James was that she couldn't be certain it really was James who'd dissected the gavel and left it on her porch as some kind of message. She couldn't prove it. Innocent until proven guilty, she told herself, and turned away from his hostile gaze.

She was grateful that Scout hadn't noticed James. He might have felt compelled to start something, in a misguided move to "protect" her. Scout was tall and strong, but the odds were overwhelming.

He wanted to go with her when she went on duty. "Nothing doing," Maggie had to say. "No one's allowed inside the courthouse but volunteers. That doesn't include you. Relax, have fun, okay? I'm only working for an hour. I'll find you when I'm done."

Reluctantly, he went off to join the others.

Maggie's mother was glad to see her. "I've got a splitting headache," she said, wiping a hand across her brow. "I should have asked for more volunteers. Most of the other committee members are already delivering the things we sold, so we don't have to do it tomorrow." Because Maggie was wearing long sleeves, there was no sign of the bandage, so when her mother gave her the once-over to make sure she was as okay as she'd said over the phone, relief shone in her eyes. She passed Maggie a tower of soggy paper plates and motioned toward two huge trash cans lined with black plastic bags sitting in the middle of the kitchen. "I have to leave you on your own here. I want to do some deliveries, too. Less to pack up tonight. Can you manage here by yourself?"

"No problem." Maggie glanced around quickly. The room was small, with dingy yellow walls and peeling black-and-white floor tile. It contained an old, white gas range and a small refrigerator, a tall, wooden cupboard, and a table piled high with new paper plates, cups, and napkins. "With the trash cans taking up so much room, you couldn't get two people in here, anyway. Whew, it stinks, though! The smell of barbecue doesn't mix very well with the odor in this building, does it? It's pretty sickening."

Maggie had thought she would be nervous, being inside the same building that had collapsed on her that afternoon. But the kitchen was so far away from the damaged wing, she told herself there was no danger. And then she got so busy, she really had no time to think about anything except keeping the windowsills clear of dirty paper plates and cups. Lane and Helen helped from the outside, collecting plates from other places on the grounds and bringing them to a window to hand in to Maggie.

The odor grew stronger. In less than fifteen minutes, she had a headache, and after another five, her stomach began churning. Closing the trash bags would have helped, but since she was making steady trips from the windowsill to the cans, repeated opening and closing of the bags would have taken up too much time.

Five more minutes, and the barbecued hot dog she had eaten half an hour earlier revolted.

Maggie had no choice. Hand over her mouth, she dashed out of the kitchen and ran in search of the nearest rest room.

She had just located a door down the hall marked LADIES when there was a thunderous boom from somewhere behind her.

A brilliant flash of light illuminated the hallway.

The hardwood floor beneath her feet rocked violently.

The white plaster wall in front of her, already zigzagged with hairline age cracks, shook, spreading the tiny cracks until, in no more than a second or two, the entire wall looked like a giant road map.

There was a second, louder boom behind her, and

even as her head turned to see what was happening, she was picked up bodily and flung into the road-mapped wall headfirst.

"What?" Maggie cried just before the world disappeared.

# Chapter 16

Maggie was vaguely aware of someone calling her name. At least it sounded like her name. She couldn't be sure. The sound was distant, like someone calling from the other end of a long tunnel.

She shouldn't have eaten that hot dog. Maybe if she'd had a baked potato instead, her stomach wouldn't be grinding like a cement mixer.

Her nose hurt. In fact, her nose was on *fire*.

"Maggie? Maggie, say something!"

Helen's voice. Shaking. Scared. What was scaring Helen?

"Nose hurts." Even to Maggie's own ears, her voice sounded muffled, as if she were gagged.

"What? Say that again, Maggie."

"Nose hurts."

"You're lying on your face. There's a sharp piece of wood in your cheek, from the door frame, I think. But we don't dare move you until the paramedics get here."

Maggie opened her eyes. Helen's face was right next to hers. The hazel eyes were brimming with tears. No, that couldn't be. Helen never cried. She hadn't shed a tear when her parents had gone flying off to Egypt or wherever, leaving her to board with Ms. Gross. Must be an optical illusion. Maybe it was just moonlight shining in Helen's eyes. Except . . . they weren't outside, were they? Weren't they inside? Hadn't she been in the kitchen . . . ? She couldn't remember.

Maggie managed, "Why am I lying on my face?"

"There was an explosion." Lane's voice this time, not Helen's. From somewhere above Maggie. "In the kitchen. We all thought you were dead, because you were working in there. Helen was practically hysterical. We didn't know you'd left. You're very, very lucky, Maggie." Lane's voice moved closer. "Does it feel like you have any broken bones?"

Maggie didn't know what a broken bone felt like. Probably really painful. Like the way her nose felt? Was her nose broken? "An explosion?" She was speaking directly into a pile of debris. Wood and plaster, all in chunks and pieces. Like in the basement. Had another ceiling collapsed? "Is anyone else hurt?"

"A bunch of people who were waiting in line at the barbecue cart." Helen's voice again. Still shaking. "There are ambulances on the way."

"Fire? Is there a fire?"

"No. There was, but some men put it out already. Whit and Alex and Scout helped. Don't talk, Maggie," Helen whispered, as if she didn't want anyone else to hear. "They think there was a gas leak in the kitchen."

"Where's my mom? Was my mom hurt? I would like to see my mother right *now*, please."

"Oh, god, Maggie, she's not here." Helen certainly sounded like she was crying. "She and your dad are already delivering the stuff that people bought. They didn't want to have to pack it up tonight. Your mom had just left when the kitchen blew up."

Maggie tried, very gingerly, to turn her face to the other side, but the piece of wood stabbed her viciously. She lay still. She was very cold, although someone had covered her with a jacket or heavy sweater. She could feel it lying across her shoulders. "The kitchen blew up?"

"Someone said the stove in there was really old." Helen sighed heavily. "I don't know, Maggie, maybe your mom will give up now. This place was bad enough before, but now . . ."

But Maggie was still trying to grasp the information Helen had given her. A gas leak? The smell . . . that sweetish, sickening smell . . . that had been gas fumes, the telltale odor overpowered by the smell of barbecue. The fumes must have caused her mother's headache, her own headache, her churning stomach. If the barbecue cart hadn't been right outside the open window, maybe she or her mother would have recognized the fumes for what they were before it was too late.

But if her stomach hadn't been upset, she wouldn't have left the kitchen. In a bizarre way, the same gas fumes that had caused the explosion had saved her life by making her ill. That struck Maggie as funny, and she laughed softly to herself. The pain was excruciating, so she stopped laughing.

A siren screamed that help had arrived. Maggie's eyes closed in relief.

She learned at the hospital that she had no concussion. "A miracle," the doctor who examined her said when she told him she'd been tossed into the wall headfirst. "You must have a thick skull, you lucky girl."

Maggie wasn't feeling very lucky. The only thing she was feeling was pain. The wood shard on which she had landed had gouged a shallow gash in her left cheek, alongside her nose. No stitches required, but the nurse's careful cleaning of the wound brought tears to Maggie's eyes. Both forearms had been badly bruised when she hit the wall, and the impact had pulled loose the stitches on her earlier wound. Having it sewn up a second time was worse than having the wood splinter pulled from her cheek.

Because her parents still hadn't arrived, her friends were allowed in the small white cubicle when her treatment was completed.

"I heard a fireman tell someone it was probably a leaking gas pipe," Helen said. "I can't believe the whole building didn't go up in flames, like Lane's mother was always saying it would."

"Whit, Scout, and Alex were so brave. They jumped right in to help." Lane gave Whit a brilliant smile, neglecting to include Scout. Both faces were gray with grime, their eyes red-rimmed.

"Wasn't that big a fire," Whit said modestly, smiling at Maggie. "And the firemen were there right away." He shook his head in disbelief. "You just happened to leave the kitchen right before that stove blew?" His eyes on hers were warm with concern and relief. "Man, you got any idea how lucky you are?"

Maggie was beginning to, and the knowledge made her weak and watery inside. If she hadn't eaten the hot dog, would she still have felt sick enough to leave the room? Gingerly fingering the thick gauze bandage on her cheek, she asked if there were other, more serious injuries.

"Don't know," Alex answered. "Lots of people in the barbecue line were knocked silly. I don't think anyone was killed, though."

Maggie gasped.

"It was an explosion, Maggie. Someone *could* have died."

"Well, I'm glad no one did!" She touched the bandage again. "Everything hurts. Even my eyebrows."

"You landed on your face when you hit the floor," Helen said. "But it doesn't look that bad, Maggie, honestly it doesn't. Anyway," her voice shook again, "you're just so lucky to be alive. We were all so sure . . ." Unable to finish the thought, Helen fell silent.

Feeling a pang of sympathy, Maggie reached out to touch Helen's hand. With Helen's parents gone, she relied heavily on her friends. "I'm sorry you were scared." Maggie managed a small, shaky laugh. "If I'd known the stove was going to blow, I'd have hollered out the window that I was running to safety, so you'd have known."

Her parents came rushing in then, her mother's face pale and set, her father's brows drawn together in a worried frown. Whit signaled to the others, and they eased out of the room, leaving Maggie to be comforted by her parents.

When all of her X rays came back negative, she was allowed to go home.

She slept an exhausted sleep and woke up late, to an argument at breakfast about the restoration project.

"After what happened yesterday and last night, you can't possibly be thinking about continuing," her father told her mother. "The old courthouse has served its purpose, Sheila. Let it rest in peace."

Maggie, aching in every part of her body, her cheek and nose throbbing, sat quietly at the table as they argued. Her father had never been all that enthusiastic about the restoration project. But as always, he had eventually supported her mother's efforts to improve the community. Now he sounded adamant. "Maggie was lucky yesterday and she was lucky again last night. Next time," he pressed, "her luck might run out."

Maggie was glad she hadn't told them about the gavel. Not that it had anything to do with the explosion last night, but her dad was already so upset, he'd go ballistic if he heard that someone had brought a nasty message right here to this very house.

"Give it up, Sheila. You've got the damage from the explosion to deal with now, as well as all the other problems. Who knows what might happen next?"

"That explosion was a fluke," Maggie's mother argued. She was standing beside the kitchen sink, sipping orange juice. "A defective gas line. Just *one*, Martin. We'll have all of the old lines replaced. We had planned to do that anyway. And we always intended to get rid of that horrible little kitchen." A frown appeared. "But you could be right. Not about the damage . . . we could fix all of that. But about not knowing what might happen next. It does seem odd, though," she mused aloud, her eyes unfocused, "that disaster struck twice in one day. Seems awfully coincidental to me, and just when public sentiment was swinging in our direction." She sighed heavily. "Maybe the committee needs to sit down and rethink things." Her eyes swung to the bandage on Maggie's face. "I don't want you going anywhere *near* that place in the meantime," she said. "Just stay away from there."

"Can't." Maggie poured cereal into a bowl. "I have to go over there next Saturday. They're taking the statue of Lady Justice down, and Ms. Gross wants the peer jury there."

"After what happened to you last night, she couldn't possibly expect you to show up."

"Sure, she could. And she *will*. I'm foreperson,

Mom." Her mother had finally seen the wound on her arm last night in the ER, but Maggie didn't want to remind her, so she was careful to keep the bandage covered by the sleeve of her robe as she poured milk on her cereal. "I *want* to be there. It's an event." She smiled at her mother. "Felicity doesn't have a lot of those, Mom. I don't want to miss it."

Uncertain, her mother turned to Maggie's father. "Martin? What do you think?"

"Well, it's being held outside. I suppose the grounds are safe enough. If she's supposed to be there, she should go."

"But you said . . ."

"I said you should forget about restoring that dump and use the money you've raised for a recreation center. God knows the kids in Felicity could use one. I *didn't* say Maggie should retreat to her room. Anyway, it's a week away, Sheila. Let's not worry about it now, okay? Besides," smiling at Maggie from around the corner of his newspaper, "she's had her quota of accidents for this year, right, Megs?"

"Right." She hoped. This was probably not a good time to inform them that Sheriff Donovan had his doubts about just how "accidental" the collapsing beam had been.

Their attention turned then to Maggie and how she was feeling, and the discussion ended.

But as she left the table and made her way gingerly up the stairs to her room to get dressed, she thought about what her mother had said. About how coincidental it seemed that two disasters had taken place in the old courthouse in one day.

That it did. Weird. Creepy, especially when Sheriff Donovan had hinted that *one* of those disasters might have had a little help. If that was true, maybe someone was deliberately sabotaging the committee's plans. And if *that* was true, someone must hate the old courthouse a *lot*.

Why would they? It was just a building.

It was a good thing the ceremony honoring the removal of Lady Justice from the top of the building was taking place outside. If it were inside, Maggie honestly didn't think she could attend. She wasn't ready to walk back into that building. And thinking that gave her the same annoyed feeling she'd had in the basement, that she wasn't as brave as she'd been when she was little.

Maybe that *wasn't* bravery, she told herself as she reached the top of the stairs. Maybe it was stupidity. I just hadn't learned enough yet to be afraid.

But now I have. I've learned that ceilings collapse, with or without help, and kitchens explode, and people sneak up on your own private property in broad daylight. I'd be stupid *not* to be afraid. No wonder people say that ignorance is bliss. It *is*.

# Chapter 17

I wanted to tell the truth. I *did*. Dante had already been sentenced to life with no possibility of parole. Because he'd been tried as an adult, he wouldn't be going to juvie. It was straight to the penitentiary for him. With hardened criminals. He hadn't been taken away yet, because his father's funeral was the next day. He was going to be allowed to attend, although I knew he'd be in chains the whole time he was standing at the gravesite.

I went to visit him at the jail. Hitchhiked into Felicity. When I asked him what would happen if someone came forward and admitted to the killing, he said everyone in the county would be really mad at that person. That wasn't what I'd expected him to say.

The jail guard, old Rudy Passamenter, who couldn't have stopped a flea from escaping, was asleep in a chair out in the hallway, around the corner from the cells. I'd passed him on my way in, his belly puffing in and out under his tan shirt, disgusting little snoring noises escaping from his open mouth. Even if he woke up, he was half deaf and couldn't possibly have heard what Dante and I were saying. And the other cells were all empty.

*"The whole county would be mad at anyone who came forward now,"* Dante told me. He was sitting on the faded gray-and-white-striped mattress on his bunk. It hung from chains fastened into the wall. He sat with his hands folded in his lap, his head down, his feet in sneakers kicking at the earthen floor. *"And not just because that person killed Christy. Because they'd obstructed justice all this time, making everyone go through this whole stupid, useless trial."*

He lifted his head. His blue eyes were empty, almost as if the Dante I'd known had already disappeared, even though he hadn't actually been taken away yet. *"It's very expensive, you know, putting on a trial. If someone came forward now and said they knew that I hadn't done it because they'd done it themselves, the first thing everyone in Greene County would think is how much money they'd wasted on my trial. Next, they'd be mad because this new person claiming to be guilty would be saying they'd all been wrong. The sheriff, the deputies who searched our farm, the police here in town, the DA, the judge, the jury, they'd all feel like fools. It'd make them look stupid. No one else in the county would believe it, either, because they'd look like fools, too. There wasn't one person around here who ever believed I was innocent."*

"*I did,*" I said. He was saying that no one would believe the truth even if they heard it? That was pretty dumb. Not that I was planning on coming forward and admitting the truth. Of course I couldn't do that. How could I? That would ruin everything. I still had high school ahead of me, and I was really looking forward to it, especially, frankly, now that Christy wasn't going to be around to spoil everything. No, whatever I did for Dante wasn't going to include giving a full confession. But I couldn't let him go to prison for something he hadn't done. "*I always knew you didn't do it.*"

"*How?*"

"*How what?*"

"*How did you know I didn't do it?*"

"*I just did. I do.*" I was standing, leaning against the white stone wall outside of his cell. "*I know you could never do something so awful.*"

"*And I want to know how you know that.*" His head was still down, his voice very quiet. But then he looked up at me, and there was something in his eyes, after all. Something searching, questioning. He seemed to be studying my face very carefully, almost as if he'd never seen it before.

"*You knew Christy was making me crazy,*" he said. "*Knew it better than anyone. And you know how mad I can get because you've seen it happen. Like the time January got out. Remember? That old cow got out of the barn and trampled all over the pumpkins I was growing for 4-H. I'd sweated over those damn things, and finally got them to almost the right size for the county fair, and then*

January came along and made pumpkin pie out of them. Remember how I yelled and hollered? I think I even kicked the poor old thing."

His eyes came back to life again, just a little, as he talked. "And then there was the time Christy told me she was going into Felicity to the movies with Amy Dunne. But I went into town that night and ran into Amy at the Dairy Queen and she finally admitted that Christy was out with Aaron Clements. Remember? You were with me when I found Aaron's car parked up on Shelter Hill, and there wasn't anybody in it because the two of them were in the woods somewhere, probably laughing at me for being so stupid. So I let all the air out of every single one of Aaron's tires, and smeared mud all over the windshield." Dante laughed bitterly. "Aaron loved telling that story at the trial. He puffed up like a pigeon, relishing every word."

"You had a right to be mad that night."

"That's not the point. The point is, you know I have a temper. So I repeat my question. How do you know I didn't kill her?"

Of course he'd known all along that since *he* hadn't killed Christy, someone else had. But I'm convinced that it wasn't until then that it first occurred to him the someone else just might have been *me.* I could tell by the way his eyes narrowed. He didn't want to believe it. I could see him fighting the idea.

I don't mean that it was impossible for him to believe that I could have done it. He knew I couldn't stand Christy. No, what was really impossible for him to believe was that I was apparently willing to let *him* go to prison for it. That was what he was having a hard time accepting.

I don't remember how I got out of there. I think I mumbled something about knowing he hadn't done it because I knew he didn't have it in him to kill anyone, said I'd see him later, and got the hell out of there.

But he'd be thinking about it, I knew that much. And what would he do when he had finally accepted the truth?

I went home and tried to figure out what *I* was going to do.

# Chapter 18

Maggie's friends called to say they'd be over later. Expecting the third call to be Scout or Alex, Maggie was surprised to hear Whit's voice. "You're answering the phone, so I guess that means you're still in one piece, am I right?"

"One *painful* piece," she answered dryly, cradling the phone against her shoulder as she pulled on a pair of socks. "Have you heard any more about what happened last night? Was it really a defective gas line like my parents said?"

Whit didn't know, but said the damage to the old courthouse wasn't as bad as it might have been.

"I don't think it matters. My mom's on the edge of throwing in the towel. I think she's going to cancel the whole renovation project."

"No kidding?"

She didn't like the way his voice lifted. "I thought you cared about history. You're not disappointed that the building might come down? Disappear, as if it had never existed?"

"Well, sure. I mean, I'm all for preserving history. But," he added, "considering the fact that *we* almost disappeared yesterday, and you came close to being obliterated last night, can you blame me for thinking your mom is right?"

Maggie shuddered. How close they had all come. Especially *her*.

Scout called next, complaining that he'd tried before, only to find the line busy. He sounded indignant because she'd been talking to someone else. She didn't tell him who it was. When he said he'd be over later, something Whit, too, had promised, Maggie didn't argue. If she was going to spend the day at home, might as well have company.

When she went back down the stairs and into the kitchen, her father was gone. Her mother was on the telephone. She hung up just as Maggie walked in and slid into a white wooden chair at the table.

Mrs. Keene turned around, her brows knit together. Her face was very pale. "I don't like this," she said slowly. "I don't like it at all."

Maggie looked up inquiringly. "What don't you like?"

Her mother's words came slowly. "That was Trudy Newhouse. Her husband, Sam, is a volunteer fireman. She said they couldn't find anything wrong with that old stove."

Maggie's heart plummeted. First the sheriff and his questions about the beam, now this . . . "Then what was it?"

Thoughtfully fingering a blue plaid dish towel she was holding, Maggie's mother said, "Well . . . Trudy's husband has the weirdest idea." Her eyes on Maggie's were very wide, and perplexed, as if Trudy had handed her one of those maddening, multicolored cube puzzles. "Sam thinks someone deliberately turned the gas on, but didn't light the burner—to let gas seep out into the room, knowing no one would identify the smell because Billy Scully's barbecue cart was right outside the open windows. He thinks that's why you and I had headaches. From the fumes."

Maggie nodded. "And my stomach was upset, too."

Sheila Keene's mouth was set grimly. "I just can't believe Sam's right. The stove could have been turned on accidentally. Maybe I brushed up against one of the knobs when I was rushing back and forth. As for the explosion, Sam thinks someone tossed a lit match through the window. But I think that's reaching, too. The gas fumes would have been drifting outside, through that open window. Anything could have set off that explosion. Maybe Walter Meadows lit one of those foul cigars of his. Or a spark from the barbecue pit could have done it."

Maggie's knees felt soupy. She wanted to accept her mother's theory. Because what Trudy's husband was suggesting was just too . . . too *ugly*. Too scary. The idea that someone might have deliberately planned to blow up the kitchen in the old courthouse was terrifying. Especially since *she* was the person who had been inside that kitchen at the time.

But the sheriff had said maybe the beam hadn't collapsed all by itself. Clearly, he hadn't shared that theory with Maggie's parents, or her mother wouldn't have that skeptical look on her face.

Trudy's husband had to be wrong. The sheriff had to be wrong, too.

But what if they weren't?

"Of course," Maggie's mother continued, "if Sam *is* right, and that gas was turned on deliberately, it was turned on by someone who is against us."

Maggie heard again the blast, saw again the flash of light, felt the floor rock beneath her feet. "Against *us*?"

"Well, not you and me, dear. I meant the Women of Heritage. And our move to save the old courthouse, that's what I meant."

"But *I* was the one who almost became landfill." If someone had done it on purpose, had they known she'd left the kitchen? Or hadn't they cared?

"I'm sure that part *was* accidental, Maggie." Sheila Keene tossed the dish towel aside, as if it were getting in the way of her thought processes, and indeed, her eyes cleared when she was no longer burdened by the checkered cloth. "Even if the gas was turned on deliberately, and I'm not saying it was, I'm sure it was by someone who expected the kitchen to be empty. After all, the bazaar was being held outside."

Maggie wanted her mother's words to calm her fears, as they were meant to. But after what the sheriff had said . . . "But if the person who turned on the gas was watching from outside, waiting to toss a lighted match in through the window, he'd have seen me in there."

Her mother's lips pursed. "How could someone standing outside the window toss in a lighted match without being seen?"

"Oh, Mom, it was so crowded at the food lines, he could have tossed a bomb in that window and no one would have noticed."

"Well, then," her mother said, "look at it this way. If he *was* watching and waiting for just the right moment, he waited until you were *out* of the kitchen, right? That means he never intended to hurt anyone. All he was trying to do—and that's if there even was such a person—was screw up our plans to renovate. That's all."

"That's *all*?" Maggie cried. "Isn't that enough? People could have died!"

Walking over to the table to slide into a chair opposite Maggie, her mother said slowly, as if she were just now making up her mind about something, "Maggie, since we're discussing this, I have to ask you something. Did you show those plans I gave you to anyone yesterday?"

"Plans?" Maggie thought for a minute. "No. Why?"

"Oh, nothing. Never mind. I just wondered. But if you didn't . . ."

"Don't *do* that! I hate that! Tell me why you asked me about the plans."

It was her mother's turn to sigh. "Oh, all right, I

guess I might as well." She slid a paper napkin out of the chicken-shaped red-and-white plastic holder on the table and began folding its edges as she talked. "The beam that gave way in the basement yesterday was clearly marked on the first page of those plans."

"Marked?"

"There was a note on it stating that the beam was weak and needed to be replaced. That beam and two others. They were clearly visible in the drawing, and it would have been obvious to anyone looking at the plans that the beam in question was the one nearest to the coal bin door. Which would make it easy to locate. Anyone who saw that first page would have known that it would take very little to make that beam collapse. A well-placed kick, a hefty shove . . ."

Maggie stared at her mother. "You've been talking to the sheriff."

"Donovan? No, I haven't." Alarm flared in Sheila Keene's eyes. "Why?"

"Nothing. Listen, that beam just caved, that's all. Why is everyone so surprised? The building is ancient."

Her mother sighed heavily. "I know. And I've decided to talk the committee into canceling the courthouse renovation. I've been thinking a lot about it. And it's just too risky." The regret in her eyes slowly gave way to the glimmer of a new idea. "What about that old warehouse down on Second Street? It's big, and looks solid enough. It might just make a great children's museum." She got up, went to a drawer for pencil and paper, and left the room, murmuring under her breath, the old courthouse apparently forgotten, at least for the moment.

Well, my friends will be thrilled, Maggie thought. Looks like they're going to get their rec center, after all.

She knew she should have told her mother that she'd had the plans with her all day at school. Because it *could* mean that someone had seen those plans. But who? The backpack had been with her all day.

Well, *almost* all day. She'd left the backpack, with the plans inside, on the bench outside the jury room when they went in to deliberate. And again, during PE, she'd left the pack on a bench in the locker room. Should have put it in her locker, but she'd been late, as usual, and had just dropped it and changed and run to the gym.

But the broken gavel couldn't have anything to do with any of the courthouse stuff. That had to do with the peer jury. Which was *not* her mother's problem.

Her friends weren't coming over until later, and her parents went to deliver the last of the bazaar merchandise. Dog-face was working, so Maggie had the house to herself. She soaked in a hot tub to ease her aches and pains, then lay on her bed reading. Reading kept her from thinking about Trudy's husband's theory and the sheriff's suspicions.

She was almost asleep when the doorbell rang. Scout.

Conscious of a dull, throbbing headache, Maggie called in the direction of the open window, "Come on in! I'm upstairs!" She sat up, picked at her hair with her fingers in a halfhearted attempt to smooth it, and waited for Scout to pound up the stairs and burst into her room.

When she didn't hear the front door open, she called out again, waited again. It wasn't like Scout to hesitate on the front porch. She got up reluctantly and went to the window, intending to call to Scout from there.

But the Jeep wasn't in the driveway, parked on the incline the way it should have been. And something else caught Maggie's eye immediately. A sedan. Old. Blue. Parked across the street. There was only one distinctive thing about the car. It didn't belong there. It wasn't Mrs. Garber's brand-new Cadillac with the custom turquoise paint job that was always parked at the curb because Mrs. Garber was afraid of her very steep driveway. When she was home, the Cadillac was always parked right there in that very spot. If she wasn't home, she couldn't very well have company, so what was the old blue sedan doing there?

Maggie pulled the curtain aside to get a better look. Hadn't she seen that car somewhere recently? It looked familiar. But then, there were probably hundreds of cars just like that in Greene County. Still, it wasn't the kind of car normally parked at Mrs. Garber's house when she entertained.

The doorbell rang again, more insistently this time.

Feeling foolish, as if she'd been caught spying, Maggie drew back from the window.

She was too stiff and sore to hurry down the stairs, but it didn't matter, because when she finally pulled the front door open, Scout wasn't standing on the porch. No one was. And the blue car was gone.

But there *was* something on the front porch. It was lying just across the threshhold, at Maggie's feet. She had already begun to swing the door shut when the object caught her eye, drawing her gaze down, down. . . .

She stopped the door in midswing. Stared at the object. Looked up again, glanced around for some clue as to how it had arrived on her porch. Nothing. The street below their slope was silent and empty.

Maggie backed away a step, took another look. What sat in front of her, perched on the threshold like a gift, was an old-fashioned scale, very old, probably antique. She'd seen one like it in an old western. It was a miniature version of the scales Justice was balancing on the old courthouse roof, and in the movie it had been used to weigh gold dust. But this wasn't an old western, and no one weighed gold dust at her house.

Extending over the gold base was a lightweight brass arm. From each end of the arm hung a slender chain. Each chain supported a round brass scoop. The twin scoops were loosely covered with squares of aluminum foil.

Maggie realized what must have happened. The scale, which looked to be an antique, perhaps even valuable, must have been left behind in all the excitement at the bazaar last night. Someone had spotted it and been kind enough to bring it here, so her mother could deliver it to the person who had bought it. The scoops were probably covered to keep them free of damaging dust and grime.

Why hadn't the person who'd delivered it waited to be thanked?

Because you took forever getting down here, she told herself, and bent to pick up the scale. She'd just take it inside and park it in the kitchen for her mother.

As she bent, a brisk spring breeze blew across the porch. First it increased the swaying motion of the scale's twin scoops, then it reached in underneath one square of aluminum foil and tugged on it until it had lifted an edge. Slipping in beneath the edge to set the foil free, it yanked it all the way off and dropped it to the porch floor before wafting along on its merry way.

As the foil uncurled from the scoop, and slid off, Maggie's body froze in midbend. She stared, her eyes filled with confusion.

The uncovered scoop was brimming over with a thick, bright red liquid that, no longer kept in check by the foil, rolled to the edge of the swaying scoop and spilled over onto the gray porch floor, where it began to puddle at Maggie's feet.

She stood up straight, still staring at the scale. The confusion in her eyes turned to revulsion as she realized what she was looking at. Slowly, very slowly, as the sun continued to shine and the breeze set the porch rocker to rocking, it sank in, though she fought it as long as she could. The thin red stream spilling out of the scoop and pooling at her feet was blood.

# Chapter 19

I had to get Dante out of that jail before it was too late.

His father's funeral was scheduled for the next day. When that was over, Dante would be carted away in chains, straight to the penitentiary. I couldn't let that happen.

When my parents had finally fallen asleep, I biked into Felicity. It was cold, with an icy rain falling. Took me over an hour. When I got there, I went straight to the old courthouse and sneaked around to the side of the building that held the coal chute. Hid my bike in some bushes, unlocked the outside lock, and pushed open the inside latch with the knife I'd brought with me because I knew I'd need it.

The bin was still nearly full of round, black nuggets delivered before the new gas furnace had been installed. Getting out of the room was easy. I used my knife to remove the small hinges on the door. Wasn't the first time. Christy and I thought it was stupid to keep that door barred, since no one but kids ever went near the coal bin. Besides, it was barred on the corridor side, so any prisoner who wanted to use it as an escape route could just lift the bar and open the door. Most of them weren't there long enough to think about escaping. But that was exactly the way I planned to get Dante out of there.

He was asleep on the cot in his cell, one arm hanging down over the edge of the bunk as if he hadn't known where else to put it. He was lying on his stomach in his repulsive orange jail clothes, his eyes closed, his face turned in profile toward me. His hair could have stood a good combing, not to mention a shampoo, and he looked about eight years old.

I hurt then, real bad, deep down inside somewhere, in a place I hadn't felt before. No matter how much I blamed Christy (and I did) for what had happened, the fact was, Dante wouldn't be lying on that musty cot in that damp, dark cell if it weren't for me. That really hurt.

But I was going to fix that.

There were no guards in sight, but I hadn't expected any. If there was a guard on duty in the dead of night, he'd be sound asleep around the corner. Or over at Shorty's, having a cup of coffee and a piece of Shorty's coconut cream pie. Felicity wasn't used to having murderers in its jail. And Dante was a local boy, so the guards weren't watching him as carefully as they might have a stranger. Lucky for me.

He was the only prisoner in the six basement cells. That was lucky, too. For *us*.

He woke up when I called his name for the third time. Rubbed his eyes with a fist. Sat up. Looked at me as if he thought he was still dreaming.

I told him I'd come to set him free. *"You're sixteen,"* I said, *"old enough to run away and make a life for yourself someplace where no one knows you."* I'd stolen fifty dollars from my mother's purse, and as I talked quietly, urgently, I held out a fistful of bills.

Dante didn't take the money. He didn't even get off his cot, just sat there listening to me with a sleepy-eyed look. I had to repeat myself twice before he finally got what I was saying.

Even when he nodded to show me he understood why I was there, standing just outside the barred door of his cell, he didn't say anything. Just sat there, nodding his head and swiping at his messy hair and studying the dirt floor. Not even looking at me.

When he finally did speak, still not looking at me, what he said stopped my heart cold. *"It was you, wasn't it?"* His voice was flat and emotionless. *"You did it. You killed Christy. I knew it wasn't me, but I figured it was maybe one of her other boyfriends. I never thought of you. Not once."* He lifted his head then, his eyes red-rimmed with sleep and just plain old weariness and probably tears over the death of his father. *"Why? Why did you do it?"*

There was so much anguish in his voice that I knew then he still loved her. And that made me so mad. So really, really furious. Did he still not know how bad she was for him? For his family? For our friendship? What was the matter with him?

I talked faster then than I ever had in my life. I didn't tell him exactly the whole truth. I couldn't do that. I told him we'd fought, Christy and I, and that I was only defending myself when I hit her. I told myself that might make him feel better than the truth would, but of course it was really *me* I was protecting. Whatever. When I'd finished, I added that he had to understand, he really *had* to. Because I couldn't deal with him not understanding.

He listened, although his eyes were focusing on the floor again, which made me mad. I was there to rescue him. He could at least look at me. When I'd finished, he did look at me, but what he said was, *"You have to tell. You know you do. You have to confess, and you have to do it yesterday."*

I couldn't believe it. What was he *talking* about? Was he nuts? I had no intention of telling anyone but him the truth. Ever. I hadn't even planned to tell *him*. He'd *guessed* the truth.

*"Dante, don't be ridiculous! No one would believe I did it! I'm not even fourteen yet! Besides, there isn't one shred of proof that I had anything to do with Christy's death. Anyway, you've already been convicted. Like you said, no one wants another trial. It's all over. I'm sorry she's dead,"* (a lie, but after so many, what's one more?) *"but I'm here to make it up to you."*

*"The only way you can make it up to me,"* he said firmly, *"is by telling the truth. I want people to*

know I'm not a murderer. You owe me that."

"What do you care what people think? Anyway, even if I confessed and enough people believed me to get you off the hook and send me off to juvenile detention, there would be just as many people in Greene County who would never believe you were really innocent. Never. They'd think I made a false confession to save a friend from prison. Because I'm younger and would only get juvie. I'll bet even your own mother would never be sure it wasn't you."

It took a while, but in the end I convinced him. He was pretty bitter about the people in Greene County by then anyway. I could tell by the look in his eyes that it finally had sunk in . . . that even if he were somehow freed, he wouldn't be able to stay around Felicity. People would never really trust him again. They wouldn't let it rest.

But I could also see that he didn't think it was right for me to get away with murder.

I asked him, "Are you going to tell?"

After a couple of long minutes, he shook his head. "You're right. No one would believe me," he said in a hopeless voice. "They'd think I was just trying to get myself off the hook, that I'd somehow talked you into taking the rap for me because you're younger and wouldn't be sent to prison like me. They might even think you'd volunteered, just like you said, because we're friends."

That was heartening. He'd been so preoccupied for so long with Christy, I wasn't even sure he still thought of me as a friend.

But the way he looked worried me. So drained and lifeless, as if his sentence *had* been death, and it had already been carried out. I wasn't sure he had the energy to climb up the coal chute and run to the railroad tracks to grab a freight train on its way out of town, which was how I'd planned his escape. I also wasn't sure he'd be willing to split before his father's funeral. But he couldn't afford to wait. No way could I get him out of town if he insisted on attending the service. There'd be too many people around tomorrow. Tonight was perfect. He *had* to agree. For both our sakes.

He did, although it took a while. But he knew it was his only chance. I made him see that.

Getting him out of there was a cinch. Those cells were a joke. The wooden frame around his cell door was rotting. I used my knife again, and in minutes Dante, looking surprised, was standing beside me outside the cell. Using my flashlight to guide us, I led the way to the coal bin. I left the door off its hinges. It wasn't like they weren't going to *know* Dante had escaped. What difference did it make if they knew *how*? Even if they figured out that he hadn't done it alone, they'd never in a trillion years think it was me who had helped him. I was perfectly safe.

We scuttled up the coal chute and outside.

I wriggled through that window on my stomach and heaved an enormous sigh of relief. Dante, close on my heels, gulping in fresh air as if he couldn't get enough of it, was out of jail and would soon be on his way out of Felicity and Greene County. I had made amends. I couldn't bring Christy back even if I wanted to (which I *didn't*), but Dante wasn't going to spend the rest of his life in prison for my crime, after all. That was such a relief, my whole body suddenly felt as light as air.

I had set Dante free.

# Chapter 20

Maggie slammed the front door shut, flipping the lock, and leaned against the cool wood, her arms and legs trembling uncontrollably.

Blood? *Blood?*

She was still there, frightened and too bewildered to think what to do next, when footsteps bounded up onto the porch. There was a startled moment of silence, then Scout's voice crying, "What the hell . . . ?" He had spotted the scale. After a stunned moment or two, the doorbell rang and he shouted Maggie's name.

Maggie opened the door.

Helen, Alex, and Lane were just coming up the steps, and down on the street, Whit had just jumped out of a shiny black Lexus.

Standing in the doorway, Maggie watched silently as each of them exclaimed over the repulsive object on the porch.

When she had let them all in and shut the object

out again, Whit led her to a chair and pushed her gently into it. Helen ran into the kitchen to get her a glass of water, and Scout went to the telephone to call the sheriff, saying bluntly to Maggie, "That's *blood* on there, Maggie. He has to see this."

While they waited, Maggie told them about the blue car.

"I know who it belongs to," Alex said when she had described it. "Alice Ann Beckwith. Better known as Chantilly."

"From the peer jury hearing?" Maggie set her glass of water on the end table. "How do you know that?"

"I've seen her in it. Somebody said her grand-mother died and left it to her. Beckwith supposedly hates it, but it's better than nothing, so she drives it."

"I think she's been following me. I've seen that car before. Never got a look at the driver, though."

Scout shrugged. "Well, she's mad at you. We already knew that. I guess that thing out there on the porch is her idea of revenge. Maybe she wrecked the gavel, too. She was there in the gym Friday, like James."

"She might have left her fingerprints on that scale," Helen suggested. "Or on the gavel."

"The gavel's gone," Maggie said. "But we have the scale. Is she dumb enough to leave finger-prints?"

"She was smart in grade school," Helen said.

Lane shot back, "But she's dumb enough to keep getting herself in all kinds of trouble. Anyway, the sheriff can check for prints." Of Maggie, she asked, "Does your mom know about this?"

"Not yet. She's not home. She'll freak." Maggie shared with them the information her mother had gleaned from Trudy Newhouse. They weren't as surprised as she'd thought they would be, probably because the sheriff had already planted a seed of suspicion about the basement beam.

Whit was sitting on the fireplace hearth. "You can't seriously think that Beckwith girl is responsible for kicking that beam out from under us, can you? She doesn't look like she'd have the strength to lift an eyebrow."

Maggie bristled. "I didn't say Chantilly did anything all by herself. James and his cronies probably helped her. I'll bet they're all in this together, to get back at the peer jury." She thought about that for a minute. Then, brightening visibly, she added, "Which could mean that none of this had anything to do with the renovations, after all. Maybe my mom shouldn't cancel the plans."

"Your mom is giving up?" Scout asked.

Maggie nodded. "She says she is. But maybe when I tell her what *we* think, how it's the peer jury that's the target here, she'll change her mind."

Helen shifted uncomfortably in her chair. "Maggie, I never said I agreed with your theory. The girl I knew in grade school, that shy, quiet little thing, wouldn't blow up a kitchen just to get back at the peer jury."

"She's not *in* grade school now," Maggie said testily. "And she's probably especially mad at me because I'm foreperson. She could have overheard me telling someone I was going to help in the kitchen last night."

Whit was watching her, and the look on his face was one of amusement, which Maggie didn't understand. Until he said, "Do you do track and field, too?"

"What?"

"Well, if you're this good at jumping to conclusions, you'd probably ace the hurdles, the broad jump, and the high jump."

"Very funny. You can apologize to me when the sheriff tells you I'm probably right."

The sheriff didn't tell her that. Not even close. "Hold on there, Maggie," he said, shaking his head when Maggie had explained her theory. Her parents had arrived just ahead of the sheriff and were still tense and shaken by the "greeting" they'd found awaiting them on the front porch. Because the sheriff had arrived only a moment later, Maggie hadn't had to explain twice what she'd been thinking. Once had been bad enough. "Let's just back up here a minute," the sheriff added, sinking into Martin Keene's black leather chair. "No point in jumping to conclusions."

Maggie didn't look at Whit.

"First off, there's no law against parking at the curb out there. It's perfectly legal. Second, you didn't see anyone walking up on your porch, and I happen to know Lena Garber, your neighbor across the street, is in Hawaii, so she couldn't have seen anything. The nearest house up the street is too far away for anyone to see anything, so you've got no witnesses. Third, even if that car *was* the Beckwith girl's, you can't prove she was driving it. Maybe she let someone else drive it. Maybe it was stolen." He leaned forward, propping his elbows on his knees. "You gotta give me more than that, kid. I can't do diddly with what you're telling me. 'Course, we'll check out that thing on your porch, see if there's any prints, see if anyone saw someone pick it up at that to-do last night. And I'll talk to the Beckwith girl, see what she's been up to lately." He stood up, slapping his hat back on his head. "But that girl's got no love for uniforms or badges, probably won't even give me the time of day."

As he left, he said to Maggie's parents, "The girl Maggie's talking about hasn't been afraid of anything since she hit puberty. She sure as hell isn't scared of *me*. She's been in and out of that courthouse so many times, we were thinkin' of puttin' up a plaque in her name, right out there in the lobby. Would, too, if the building wasn't bein' torn down."

"Well, it *is*," Sheila Keene said firmly, and Maggie saw her friends exchange looks. The looks weren't ones of disappointment. But then, she hadn't expected that they would be.

"Just as well." Sheriff Donovan pulled the door open. "A plaque would fire that girl up, and makin' Alice Ann Beckwith mad is not a smart thing to do, believe me. If we had coyotes in these parts, the farmers out around where she lives would be more afraid of her than they are of the coyotes." To Maggie, he warned, "Don't go messin' around with that girl. You let us handle her, you hear? Like I said, I'll talk to her. Just don't expect her to be happy about it."

Maggie didn't answer.

When the sheriff had gone, taking the disgusting scale with him, Maggie's parents considered canceling a planned engagement that night. "Your brother won't be here, either," her mother said worriedly. "He's staying over at Clark's house."

Maggie insisted they not cancel their plans, saying she wasn't going to be alone. Her friends would stay. "Anyway," she told her parents, "the word will spread around town that the renovations are being canceled, so if you're right and I'm wrong, we can quit worrying. If everything that's happened was aimed at stopping your plans instead of getting back at the peer jury, all this awful stuff should stop, right? So relax, go to your party, and I promise I'll relax, too. And I *will* now that the sheriff has taken that repulsive thing away."

"Mrs. Bannister bought that scale," her mother said absentmindedly. "Paid a fortune for it. I suppose she'll have to wait a while for it now." Shaking her head, she went upstairs to change into party clothes.

When they had gone, Maggie and her friends watched a video, a comedy that eased the tension and made them all laugh.

But when it was over, in that sudden moment of quiet as the tape began rewinding, she could feel uneasiness in the air again.

"Hey, relax, everybody!" she surprised herself

by saying. "No more renovations, no more problems, and we'll probably get our rec center, right? As for Chantilly Beckwith, I still think the sheriff will take care of her. Justice will triumph, right? Doesn't it always?"

It was Alex who said solemnly, "Not always. It didn't for Dante Guardino."

"Oh, jeez, Alex," Scout groaned, "don't get started on that! It's old news."

They all knew about the case. Everyone in Greene County knew. It had happened three or four years ago. The bludgeoning death of a young girl . . . just thirteen . . . by her sixteen-year-old boyfriend, driven to violence by jealousy, according to newspaper reports. The boy, who lived on one of the area farms, had been tried as an adult, convicted, and sentenced to life in prison. He'd escaped from the old courthouse jail the night before he was to be moved to the penitentiary, and had never been caught.

Maggie and her friends had discussed the case occasionally. Their opinions were divided. Helen and Scout, who had known the older boy slightly through 4-H, had believed him innocent at first, saying the Dante they knew, however slightly, hadn't seemed the murderous type. But when he escaped, they had changed their minds. Their reasoning was, if he'd been innocent, he would have waited for the "system" to correct the injustice done him. So he must have been guilty all along. Alex and Maggie still believed him innocent, as did Lane, although she said she didn't see what difference it made what they thought. "A jury of his peers found him guilty and he was sentenced. Isn't that the way it's supposed to work?"

"I knew him," Whit said now. "I knew Dante Guardino."

They all turned to stare at him.

"And I followed the case. Read everything that was ever printed. His attorney didn't do squat for him. Guardino would have been better off acting as his own lawyer, even though the theory is that anyone who does that has a fool for a client."

"You knew him?" Scout sounded as surprised as the rest of them felt. "How could you have known him? Dante was from Arcadia, lived there all his life. And I'm from Muleshoe, right next door. Helen's from Updown, and Lane lived in Sugar Hill for a while, and Alex still lives in Thompson. The only townie here is Maggie. How come none of us ever ran into you?"

"I've lived in Muleshoe, at Picadilly, just a stone's throw from you, Scout, since I was twelve," Whit said.

Scout's jaw came unhinged, and Lane gasped. "Picadilly? That's *your* place?" Lane asked, clearly awestricken.

Whit laughed. "Well, it's not *mine*. We lived in Shaker Heights until I was eleven, and then my dad decided I'd be better off in the country, so he had Picadilly built. Took a year. But we spend almost as much time back in Cleveland as we do here. My mom is a city girl. She doesn't really dig fresh air and roosters crowing at sunup."

Scout said, "I watched that place go up. I couldn't believe how big it was. Bigger than my house, even." There was unabashed envy in his voice. Until Picadilly was established, Scout's family had owned the nicest country home in all of Greene County.

The house at Picadilly was impressive, an enormous structure made of stone and white frame, set back far from the road, surrounded by rolling green lawns, all of it encompassed by a pristine white wooden fence that stretched for miles. It was truly gorgeous, all of it, and Maggie had often wondered what it looked like inside. She was convinced there had to be a sparkling pool, probably a tennis court, too, somewhere on the grounds. That explained Whit's October tan.

His statement that his parents spent a lot of time in Cleveland explained a lot, too. No one in Felicity knew the Whittiers well. Maggie hadn't even known they had a son. Her mother had tried, more than once, to get Mrs. Whittier to join the Women of Heritage group, with no luck. "They keep to themselves," she had told her family, "and maybe that's just as well. Most of us would be uncomfortable around people with so much money."

"L.F. Whittier may be a famous judge," her father had said matter-of-factly, "but he puts his pants on one leg at a time, just like me."

"I can't believe," Lane said now, "that you've lived out there that long and none of us ever ran into you." Her tone was heavy with regret.

Maggie hid a smile. Lane was thinking of how

much time she'd wasted. If she'd known Whit was at Picadilly that whole time, she could practically be engaged to him by now, and her college boyfriend would be history.

Whit shrugged. "I already told you, I went to Cutler Day. Not to the local schools. My parents drove me, so I never rode on a school bus. It looked like fun to me . . . rowdy fun . . . the kind you don't find at Cutler Day. And I never joined 4-H because except for my dad's horses, animals are not a part of life at Picadilly." He smiled ruefully. "My mother. Dog hair, you know, gets on everything, and chickens and pigs are dirty, and cows terrify her. I couldn't see my dad letting me take one of his valuable thoroughbreds to a 4-H meeting." The smile widened into a grin. "It always amazed the hell out of me that he'd even let me *ride* them."

"If you didn't go to grade school here, and you weren't in 4-H, how did you know Dante?" Alex asked.

"We bought hay from his dad. Dante came with him on deliveries. He was older than me, but he didn't seem to care about that. Neither did I. I liked him. He was smart, and had a sense of humor . . . except when it came to that girlfriend of his. Sometimes, when he brought the hay himself, without his dad, she tagged along with him. I never saw in her what Dante did. She seemed kind of sly to me, like a fox. When she didn't come along, he talked about her all the time. I was only thirteen and thought girls were stupid, but Dante was so far gone, he couldn't see straight. I still don't think he did it."

"You're crazy." There was derision in Scout's voice. "There was a ton of evidence against the guy."

"All of it circumstantial." Whit wasn't giving an inch.

Neither was Scout. "Yeah, well, Dante was good with animals, but he had a temper. I saw him lose it once, when a dog at the county fair went after the calf Dante was showing. Man, he was furious! And I never met that girl, that Christy, but everyone in the county knew she ran rings around him."

"Do we have to talk about this now?" Maggie cried impatiently. "Don't we have enough going on here *now*? Why do we have to rehash an *old* crime?"

The boys subsided guiltily. But the conversation about violence had unnerved Maggie again, and she decided to send them all home.

Only Whit stayed behind.

# Chapter 21

I did it, I did it, it worked! They're giving up. *She's* giving up! It's going to be torn down, that dangerous old relic of a building. Dangerous in more ways than one. I can't believe it. This is so great!

Well, yeah, I can believe it. After all I went through, after everything I did, how could the committee keep going? Sheila Keene isn't that stupid. Anyway, I don't think the good citizens of this community would have kept supporting her, not after that deal at the bazaar. Which was almost *too* easy.

I know what really stopped her. What really stopped her was her own daughter coming so close to being erased permanently from the blackboard of life, so to speak. And that lunkhead Newhouse was a big help to me, too, although he doesn't know it. It was very kind of him to spread his suspicions around town that the explosion wasn't an accident. I'll bet *that* gave Maggie Keene's mother something to think about.

Just the same, I don't trust her . . . not quite. She's feeling scared right now, but that might not last. She could change her mind again.

That can't happen. Just to be on the safe side, maybe I'd better think about insurance. Something to keep her focused on tearing that place down.

Then I can relax. At last. They'll raze the building, pour a ton of cement over what's left, and bury a page of the past forever. And all of my bad memories with it.

Now, how do I put the final nail in the coffin of that building?

# Chapter 22

There was a moment as Scout was leaving, with Helen and Lane and Alex already on their way down the steps, when he realized that Whit, still sitting on the hearth, had made no move to leave with the others. The look in Scout's eyes as he turned back to Maggie was a mixture of hurt and confusion, and maybe a little anger. He knew she wasn't going to ask Whit to leave, and he didn't understand that. Or didn't want to.

She was tempted, then, to say, "You stay, too, Scout." But the truth was, she didn't want to do that. She wanted a few minutes alone with Whit. Was that so terrible?

"See you tomorrow, Scout," she said, and closed the door.

Whit helped her carry the empty glasses into the kitchen. "You don't seem all that relieved that your mom has halted the renovation plans," he commented, depositing his load on the kitchen counter. "Everyone else is glad. But not you?"

"I just don't think it's right to give in to bullying," she said firmly. She stashed a half-empty bottle in the refrigerator, and turned to face him, leaning against the refrigerator door. "And isn't that what this is? The broken gavel, the bloody scale, the beam collapsing . . . if the sheriff's right that it wasn't accidental, and then the explosion. If they really were done on purpose, and if it really was because someone doesn't want the old courthouse to stand, then it's just the worst kind of extortion. I thought extortion was illegal."

There was obvious admiration in Whit's brown eyes as he returned her gaze. "You don't scare easily, do you?"

"I'm not sure," Maggie answered honestly. "I haven't had any reason to be scared since I was four and a huge, black spider crawled across my pillow when I was getting ready to go to sleep. I screamed the house down. My poor parents probably thought I was being ripped limb from limb by a serial killer who'd crawled in my bedroom window." She sipped the drink in her hand and then said, "I guess I don't need to be scared now, do I? I mean, if it's all over. I still think Beckwith was behind the gavel and the scales, because of the peer jury, but maybe Donovan will take care of her."

"I don't know if you should be scared or not. But I hope not." Whit smiled at her, then surprised her by pulling her to him so that her head rested against his chest. He smelled of autumn air and mint, and when he put his arms around her, Maggie closed her eyes and let herself relax for the first time that day. "I don't especially want to think of you afraid," he said quietly into her hair. "I couldn't say why. Just don't like the idea."

She didn't, either. The image of herself cowering in a quiet corner somewhere stiffened her spine. "I'm not. I'm not afraid," she murmured into his chest. And she wasn't, not at that moment. But she couldn't stay in his arms forever, could she? Too bad.

Pulling slightly away, she looked up at him to ask, "Are you still going to the ceremony next Saturday?"

"Sure. Why not? I haven't had any nasty messages on my porches."

Maggie smiled. "Do you *have* porches?"

"Several." He grinned. "And I'd like you to see them. My folks are giving a party at Picadilly next Friday night. We'd be the only two people there under the age of forty, but we could keep each other company. Interested?"

Maggie wasn't in the mood for a party. But . . . she *might* be by next Friday night. And she'd get to see what Picadilly looked like inside.

Scout would not be happy. Neither would Lane. But was she going to live her entire life worrying about how Scout and Lane felt? I don't *think* so, she told herself emphatically.

"Interested," she answered, smiling. "Definitely interested. I'd love to go."

Whit hesitated, then added, "You and Scout . . . you're friends, right? Like you're friends with Lane and Helen and Goodman?"

Maggie decided on honesty. "More than that," she admitted, then added quickly, "but not a *lot* more than that." Although Scout might not feel the same way.

He nodded. "Great!" Then he bent his head and kissed her thoroughly, as if they were sealing some kind of bargain.

Maybe they were, she thought later as she got ready for bed.

Sunday was a quiet day. Although the news had indeed spread that renovation plans for the old courthouse had been canceled, Maggie's friends were too drained physically and emotionally to celebrate the probability of a recreation center. They talked on the phone off and on all day, but made no plans. That was fine with Maggie, whose injured arm was hurting. And she wasn't eager to appear in public with a bandage on her cheek.

She had only one brief conversation with her mother about the cancellation. "You never gave up before," Maggie said as she was setting the table for dinner. She had tried to keep her tone from sounding accusatory, but she was pretty sure she'd failed.

"I never came so close to losing my daughter before." Her mother paused, then added, "I'll make a deal with you, Maggie. If the sheriff comes up with proof of your theory, that all of this has to do with someone angry at the peer jury, and the courthouse isn't involved, I'll think about the renovation plans again. But keep that to yourself, okay? Just in case ..."

Maggie was satisfied with that. But she was impatient for Sheriff Donovan to come up with something. When she called his office, she got an answering machine and his pager number, but decided the call could wait. If he'd found out anything, he'd have come to the house to tell her mother.

By the end of that week, Maggie had to admit that the atmosphere in Felicity had lightened considerably. Talk at school was excited and anticipatory, centered around the new rec center, which gossip claimed might be available to all as early as next spring. There were no more ugly incidents. Even the students "sentenced" by the peer jury that week seemed to take their punishments in stride, without ugly threats or dire looks.

And Maggie saw Whit every single night that week.

Monday, he arrived at her house unexpectedly, with a book on architecture, saying he thought she might like to read it. Unlike Alex, Maggie had not the slightest interest in architecture, and in fact, the very mention of the word "building" still tightened her jaw.

But there he was, standing on her porch in his suede jacket, his light brown hair a little windblown, smiling down at her as if he hoped she might think of the book as a dozen, long-stemmed red roses.

"Thanks," she said, "this is great," and invited him in.

Before he left, he pressed his advantage by asking her to take in a movie with him the following night. "If we're going to spend a whole evening at Picadilly on Friday, with only each other to talk to, we should get to know each other better, right?"

"Um, I don't know," she teased. "Maybe I don't have that much to say. If I say it all tomorrow night, I might bore you to death Friday night."

He laughed. "Oh, I think you probably have a *lot* to say. And you, boring? I don't think so."

Wednesday morning, Scout was waiting for Maggie when she pulled into the school parking lot. "So," he began awkwardly as she jumped out of the van to join him, "I guess you're busy this weekend, right?" There was pain in his face and in his voice, and Maggie felt it as if the knife were in her own heart. Although Scout had money, like Whit, he hadn't had it as easy as Whit . . . as far as she knew. Still didn't.

"Yeah, I am. But I'll see you at the ceremony on Saturday. When they take the statue down."

He nodded, and fell silent, although they walked into school together.

Her parents had heard nothing from the sheriff. Maggie saw James Keith in the halls several times at school, but there was no sign of Chantilly Beckwith. Maggie hoped fiercely that she'd dropped out of high school and run away to join the circus.

Wednesday night, Whit and Maggie took a long walk in the woods behind her house, and made plans to attend the Thursday night pep rally at

Bransom High for the upcoming Friday night game.

"Helen's going to freak," Maggie told Whit as they sat on the cool ground beneath a huge old oak tree, surrounded by underbrush and the skittering nighttime noises of small animals. A nearly full moon lit their faces, and a mild autumn breeze toyed with Maggie's hair. An owl somewhere above them hooted in its husky voice. "When she finds out I'm not going to the game, she'll freak. We always go together."

"Well," Whit said, putting an arm around her shoulders and gently turning her head so that she faced him, "tell Helen we'll go to the game next week. But not this week. You tell Helen that on *this* Friday night, I'm taking you out to Picadilly to show my parents why I haven't been home one night this week. When they meet you, they'll get it. Now quit worrying about Helen, because I'm about to kiss you and I don't want you distracted."

"Helen who?" she murmured during the brief interval between the first and second kiss.

At lunch on Thursday, Helen shrieked, "You're not going? Maggie, you traitor!"

Lane, who had seen the way Whit and Maggie looked at each other and had accepted the truth in her usual cool, okay-I-get-it-and-so-what attitude, said, "Helen, you don't really expect Maggie to turn down an invitation to Picadilly for a dumb high school football game, do you?" If there was envy in her voice, it was well-disguised. "Do you think she's insane?"

"But . . ."

Maggie interrupted Helen. "We'll all go next week, Helen, and watch Scout play. Whit's decided not to go out for the team, but he wants to go to all the games, so we'll all go together, okay? But *this* Friday night," she added firmly, "I am going to Picadilly. Now forget the game and help me figure out what I'm going to do with this hair. I'm up for anything that doesn't involve purple dye or shaving my head."

Thursday afternoon after classes, Lane and Helen helped Maggie find exactly the right dress at the mall, a deceptively simple black sleeveless sheath with a matching cropped jacket.

"Only a size six could wear that dress and get away with it," Helen said wistfully.

Lane commented on the price tag, but admitted that the dress looked fantastic on Maggie.

They all attended the pep rally Thursday night together. Maggie almost opted out, thinking of how much she had to do to get ready for the party at Picadilly, but she felt guilty about spending so little time with her friends all week, especially Helen. And she was glad, later, that she'd gone. Everyone seemed to like Whit. He had fit in right from the start. And Lane was being such a good sport about things.

She had good friends. And maybe, just maybe, more than that in Whit.

Thursday night when she got home, the sheriff's car was parked in front of her house.

He had more questions for her about the renovation plans. Her parents sat by silently while Maggie answered as honestly as she could. "I don't think anyone saw them," she said, "but I can't be sure." And she explained that she hadn't delivered the plans first thing in the morning as her mother had asked, and that she hadn't had the backpack with her every single second.

Her mother was annoyed, Maggie could see that. She should have told her the truth sooner. "This is about the beam, isn't it?" Maggie asked the sheriff. "You still don't think it just collapsed, do you?"

"Doesn't look that way," was all he would say. "We're workin' on it. Let you know what we come up with."

Her mother was too distracted to lecture Maggie about not delivering the plans as she'd been asked.

Friday afternoon after PE, Maggie dashed through her shower, dressing hurriedly because she still had so much to do . . . her hair . . . finding the missing black heel . . . her nails . . . she would never be ready by eight when Whit came to pick her up.

Shouting a good-bye to Lane and Helen, she snatched up her backpack and ran from the locker room and up the stairs, thinking, Shoes . . . hair . . . nails . . . what am I forgetting?

She reached the top of the stairs in record time, only to be stopped in her tracks by a voice saying coldly, "Going somewhere, are we? I don't *think* so."

Maggie's head shot up. She was staring directly into a pale, bony face topped by very black, spiked hair standing straight up in the air as if something had frightened it half to death. The eyes she was looking into were cold, black, and expressionless, the scarlet mouth opened slightly to reveal unevenly spaced lower teeth. The voice that came out of the mouth was low and harsh. "You sicced the sheriff on me, you little creep!"

Maggie was staring into the face of Alice Ann "Chantilly" Beckwith. True to the sheriff's prediction, she clearly was *not* happy.

And the person she was not happy with was Maggie Keene.

# Chapter 23

Maggie, her backpack in her arms, found herself balanced precariously on the top step of a steep, enclosed staircase. As if that weren't bad enough, when Chantilly began talking, she also began jabbing at Maggie's chest with an index finger for emphasis.

"The sheriff came here to school," *jab*, "yanked me out of class," *jab*, "made me stand out there in the hall where everyone could see me," *jab*, each jab gathering strength, pushing against Maggie with added force, "asking me all kinds of stupid questions about my car and some stupid scale!" *Jab, jab.*

Maggie wobbled on the step. If I fall backward, she thought, I will fall hard, and I will fall far. There'd be no Picadilly for me tonight. She thought about dumping the backpack so she could grasp at something for balance, and quickly realized despairingly that there was nothing to hold onto, nothing but flat, smooth walls on both sides of her. She kept the backpack. It was heavy. If she had to, she could slug Chantilly with it. Knock her silly.

Chantilly's voice rose. "James is right. You all let that dumb peer jury go to your heads. You see yourselves as caped crusaders, sitting in that gym dispensing justice! You're crazy, you know that, Keene? Just like that mother of yours. They should lock up both of you and throw away the key, instead of locking me up." Her bone-white face was ugly in its anger. And what struck Maggie as odd was that as angry as the girl was, there was still no life at all in her eyes. They were black, empty orbs, like lumps of coal in a snowman's face.

"Maggie?" Helen's voice, from the foot of the stairs. "Maggie, what's happening up there? Something wrong?" And Lane called, "Who *is* that? Is that Alice Ann Beckwith?"

Reinforcements. Better yet, witnesses. When Maggie went to the sheriff this time, she would take witnesses with her. Then he'd *have* to listen.

Feeling braver now that she was no longer alone, Maggie said heatedly, "That was your car in front of my house that day. If you weren't in it, you don't have anything to worry about. But I have a right to tell the sheriff what I saw."

Chantilly's index finger hung in the air between them, as if it were uncertain about its next move. "You can't prove that was my car." Her eyes narrowed. "Just stay out of my way and out of my business, you got that?" *Jab.* Maggie came close to losing her balance, regaining it at the last moment.

"You go to the sheriff about me again, and that peer jury of yours could be minus a foreperson."

Maggie fumed. This unpleasant girl was ruining what was supposed to be a really good day in her life, spoiling her excitement about the party at Picadilly. "I am just *so* scared," she said defiantly. She held up a hand, steady as a rock. "See? Look how I'm trembling. Go find your grungy little friends, and tell them to stay away from my house. The sheriff is going to be watching all of you."

"You'll be sorry," Chantilly hissed. Then she turned and ran down the corridor, disappearing around a corner in a blur of black.

Helen and Lane ran to the top of the stairs. "Gotta hand it to you, Maggie. You made it sound as if the sheriff intends to spend his every waking moment following that girl and her cohorts in crime all over town. You don't really think that, do you?"

Maggie leaned against the wall, her knees weak. That girl had been so angry. "Maybe he will when we tell him what she just did. How she threatened me. You heard her. Three people saying the same thing is better than one person saying it, right? But," Maggie added hastily, "I can't do it right now. I have *got* to get home and pull myself together. Tomorrow morning, okay? It's Saturday. Donovan should be in his office. We'll go then. Meet me in front of the old courthouse. Does either of you need a ride?"

They said they'd let her know, told her to have a great time that night, and Maggie rushed off to get ready for the party.

It was a strange evening. Not what she'd imagined at all.

Picadilly was as gorgeous on the inside as the outside. Maggie wasn't disappointed about that. Everyone was nice to her, including Whit's very good-looking parents. Whit looked movie-actor handsome in a black blazer over a white turtleneck, and once, when they were dancing, Maggie overheard two women sitting along a wall comment, "Don't they make a striking couple?" and knew exactly who they meant.

But she found it impossible to relax. She had been in Scout's home many times. It was a lavish, sprawling, brick ranch big enough to lose a herd of cattle in. Though that home, too, was filled with expensive furnishings, paintings, and carpet, she had never felt uncomfortable there, not even during the divorce when Scout's mother had stormed through the house angrily slamming every door she could get her hands on. The house had always felt warm and lived-in and welcoming.

Picadilly wasn't like that. Maggie wasn't sure why. It was as beautiful inside as anything she had ever seen in any magazine or movie. Everything matched perfectly, down to the tiniest figurine on the mantel in the ballroom. Too perfectly, maybe. There was so much gloss on the hardwood floors, she was nearly blinded when she walked into the dining room. Every doorknob shone like pure gold. As far as she could tell, there wasn't a single sofa cushion that needed adjusting, not a picture hanging crooked anywhere, no sign of dog hair or newspapers or magazines, and she was reluctant to use any of the hand towels in the guest bathroom because they were folded so precisely in thirds on the brass racks. The monograms were perfectly centered. Might ruin the whole look if I use one, she thought glumly, and wiped her hands on tissue instead.

The very instant that someone set a glass down on any flat surface it was immediately whisked away by a waiter before defacing beads of moisture could even think of marring the highly polished mahogany or glass.

It was all just a tiny bit too perfect.

Maggie thought of her own chaotic household, her parents rushing in and out, Dog-face drinking out of the milk carton, the floor of her own room carpeted with discarded clothing and books and shoes and purses. And she wondered what it would be like to grow up in a place as perfect as Picadilly.

Wouldn't you be expected to be perfect, too?

Whit's parents were really nice, but how did Mrs. Whittier keep every single strand of her upswept platinum blonde hair so perfectly in place while she made the rounds in all of the first floor's nine rooms? If that were Sheila Keene, there'd be naughty little tendrils of coppery hair trailing along the back of her neck, over her ears, and down her forehead.

What am I doing here? Maggie asked herself. And then Whit led her back out onto the dance floor in the ballroom, and she remembered what she was doing there.

"I know what you're thinking," he said when they took their buffet plates out onto one of several stone terraces abutting the house. "It's too perfect, right? I can see it in your eyes, which, by the way, look as terrific as the rest of you. The dress is great."

"I'm glad you approve," she said lightly, moving to the heavy stone railing to set her plate down. "And yeah, you're right. I feel kind of like we're on a movie set. Like it's not real. I mean, where did you put your muddy shoes after you and that friend of yours . . . Dante Guardino . . . unloaded the hay?" She smiled at Whit. "Or were muddy shoes just not allowed?"

He returned the smile. "There's a mud room. Back near the kitchen."

Of course. With eighteen rooms, there almost certainly would be a mud room.

"It's my mother's doing," he said, forking a baby carrot on his plate. "She's got a great eye for perfection. And just as good an eye for what she calls 'disharmony.'"

"The trouble is, I don't have her eye. Neither does my dad. And I can tell you right now, when I build my own house someday, I'm building it for fun and comfort. Maybe a log cabin. You can do some really great things with logs these days."

As they ate, she insisted that he describe his ideal house to her, and he did. It sounded wonderful, and she was happy to hear that he didn't intend to stay in Felicity. "I was thinking California, maybe Marin County. Work in San Francisco, law or architecture, I haven't decided yet, and live in the country, in a nice, big, sloppy old log cabin."

He was still talking when other voices emerged from the French doors open to the ballroom. Maggie didn't turn around, and wouldn't have listened at all if she hadn't heard the name, "Christy Miller." She knew who that was. The girl who had been killed, allegedly by Dante Guardino, Whit's friend.

The name caught Whit's attention, too. He had stopped talking, stopped eating, and was listening as intently as she was, though they both kept their backs to the ongoing conversation behind them.

" . . . a brutal crime," one woman was saying. "Such a young girl, no more than a child, really."

Another woman's voice, which Maggie recognized as belonging to Whit's mother, commented, "That may be, but she certainly didn't *act* like a child. She was a terrible flirt, you know. Nearly drove the boyfriend mad." Her voice lowered slightly, but Maggie could still hear her clearly, and knew that Whit could, too. "You know, I worried about Thomas when that girl was around. He was only thirteen then, and so impressionable. And I admit it, she was a pretty little thing. In a common sort of way. Tons of blonde hair, far too much makeup, that sort of thing."

Thomas? Maggie glanced up at Whit. If she'd been uncertain that he was the Thomas in question, she knew it was a fact when she saw the way his mouth had tightened. He wasn't looking at her, but out over the enormous, well-lighted, smooth green lawn and flower beds.

The terrace was huge, and there were other people sitting on benches and standing at the railing. Whit's mother hadn't noticed that her son was one of those people.

"I tried to warn him about her," her voice went on. "He seemed to be listening, but later I suspected that he was running off somewhere to meet the two of them, the girl and her boyfriend, away from the house. At least, I hoped it was the two of them. I'd have been sick if I'd suspected he was meeting just the girl. I wasn't happy about his association with the boy, either, mind you. His father was a *farmer*. He delivered our hay! But Thomas had made no other friends out here. . . ." Her voice trailed off, as if she'd been suddenly distracted.

"Your boy must have been very upset when the girl was killed."

Maggie couldn't look at Whit. Half of her wanted the discussion to end, while the other half wanted to hear the rest. Whit had said he knew Dante Guardino and the girl. But he had never said he knew them as well as his mother was implying.

"Oh, he was very upset. But that's understandable, don't you think? Thomas had never encountered violence of any sort before, not even in the city, and he's always been very sensitive. But," Mrs. Whittier added hastily, "he got over it, of course. He's made of strong stuff, my son, and it would take more than the death of a girl he hardly knew to throw him off course."

Well, which *is* it? Maggie thought irritably. He knew Christy well enough to worry you, or he

*179*

hardly knew her at all? Make up your mind!

Whit remained motionless and silent.

His mother's companion sighed. "Well, George said he could have got that Guardino boy off. Insanity plea, or diminished capacity, something like that, because of the girl's reputation and the boy's age. Of course," she added with a small laugh, "my George always thinks he can get someone else's client off. Humility is not one of George's problems. But," she sighed, "once the boy escaped, there was no hope of clearing him. One can't very well defend a client in absentia, can one?"

"I've often wondered," Whit's mother mused aloud, "if that boy might not someday make his way back here. His mother still lives here, you know. And you do read about criminals returning to the scene of the crime." She paused for a moment, then added, "I've wondered, too, if someone like that might ever kill again?"

"Well, as long as he doesn't do it around here," her companion said in a bored voice. "Let's go see what our husbands are up to. I wouldn't mind another dance. It's so hard to get George to bring me to these things. I don't want to waste a moment of it."

When the voices had ceased, Maggie looked up at Whit again. She sensed that he had completely withdrawn from her, and sensed, too, that it might be a really terrific idea not to pursue the matter.

But that just wasn't possible. It wasn't as if the two women had been talking about the merit badges Whit had earned in scouting when he was thirteen, or the number of times he'd fallen off his bicycle, or what he liked to eat at Sunday brunch. They had just told her, unwittingly, that Whit had lied about his relationship with a dead girl and her murderer. Or, at the very least, not told the whole truth.

Maggie took a deep breath, let it out. When she spoke, her voice was quiet, but determined. "Whit? Why didn't you tell us you knew Christy Miller and Dante Guardino so well?"

# Chapter 24

Laying his fork on his plate, Whit turned then to face her. "I told you I knew them." His voice was flat, emotionless.

"Not that well. I got the feeling, and I know everyone else did, too, that you knew Dante a little bit and Christy hardly at all. But that's not how your mother made it sound."

"My mother doesn't have a clue," he said harshly. "Remember what I said about how she can sense disharmony? Well, that doesn't just apply to which color coordinates with which other color, or how you should place the furniture in a room. It applies to people, too." He turned away from Maggie again, to stare out into the night. "Her son associating with any farm kids is her idea of a 'disharmonious' relationship. I knew that. So I let her think there *was* no relationship. I thought she bought that story. I never knew until now that she was worried about me sneaking out to see Dante."

"*Did* you sneak out?"

"Yeah, I did. But not for the reasons she thinks. I did it to cover for Dante. His folks didn't want him seeing Christy at all. They couldn't stand her. So I'd bike over, meet him at his house, put my bike in the back of his father's truck, and we'd drive off together. As soon as we were out of the sight of the house, I'd hop out, grab my bike, and go on home by myself. And Dante would go meet Christy. If I wasn't available to cover for him, one of his other friends would."

Maggie said nothing. She didn't know what to think.

"So I didn't have to do it that often," Whit continued. "If it seemed more often than that to my mother, it's because she didn't want me having anything to do, ever, with either one of them." Whit laughed harshly. "Like I said, it was 'disharmonious.'"

Instead of feeling that he had explained, Maggie felt that there was more he wasn't telling her. "You could have told us that," she said quietly. "My friends wouldn't have thought it was so awful. We would have thought you were just doing a favor for a friend."

"The girl was *murdered*, Maggie. And a friend of mine was convicted of committing that murder. That's not exactly a great subject for conversation."

Ordinarily, Maggie would have agreed. "But that *was* the subject. That's what we were talking about. And *you* brought it up. You said you knew them. It just seems weird that you didn't say how well." Then she got it. It hit her as if someone had just written it on an invisible blackboard in front of her. It was the only reason for Whit's lack of honesty that made any sense. "Oh, god, you had a crush on her, didn't you? On that girl?" Of course. What had his mother said? That he'd been "upset" when the girl was killed. "That's why you lied. Or . . . didn't tell the whole truth."

He turned his head even farther away from her, to the left. She couldn't even see his profile, couldn't read any part of his expression. "I don't think I did lie. I just didn't elaborate. As for having a crush on her, I told you I didn't like her. And, god, Maggie, I was only thirteen."

"When I was thirteen, I thought I would die if Scout didn't ask me to go to the county fair with him." She hadn't known Scout that well. But all she'd required then was that a boy be gorgeous, and Scout was that. Now, she asked for more from a relationship. Like total honesty.

But she wasn't about to get it from Thomas Aquinas Whittier, not tonight. He let out a sound that spelled impatience, even annoyance. Maybe anger?

Maggie knew she had a choice. She could drop the subject and enjoy the rest of the evening . . . or not, and ruin everything. Like he said, he hadn't really lied to them. Not exactly. He'd just left out a lot. And what did it matter? It had all happened a long time ago. Silly to make an issue of it now.

Still . . . something just didn't feel right. If

his mother hadn't come out on the terrace, if they hadn't overheard the conversation, she still wouldn't know that Whit had been friends with two principals in a murder case. "Would you ever have told me?" she asked.

He was silent for a very long moment. Then he finally turned toward her and, his face expressionless, said, "Frankly, I didn't think it was any of your business."

So. She had ruined the evening, after all. Or he had. Or his mother had, without knowing it. Whatever. It was ruined.

"I think I'd like to go home now," she said carefully.

He nodded and said, "I think that's a good idea."

She was very gracious in her thank-you to the Whittiers. As they left, Whit's mother said warmly, "Do come again, Maggie," completely unaware that she had been instrumental in the ruination of Maggie's first, and no doubt last, evening at Picadilly.

Come again? Not likely. But, Maggie thought, blinking back tears of disappointment and anger as she climbed into Whit's black Lexus, I guess that means she thinks we make a "harmonious" couple. If she only knew . . .

The drive back into Felicity was painfully long and silent. Maggie sat as close to the passenger's door as possible. Whit insisted on walking her to the door, though she didn't want him to. But once there, standing at the door, he didn't attempt to kiss her good night. She wasn't sure what she would have done if he had. After that long drive home, she felt as if they were occupying separate planets. Kissing him now would feel like kissing a stranger.

"Well," he said, standing at least a foot away from her on the porch, "I guess I'll see you at the courthouse tomorrow. When they take the statue down. You're still going, right?"

Her lips seemed unwilling to move. She forced them to say, "Right."

Nodding, he turned to leave. He was at the edge of the porch when he turned around to say, "I was only thirteen, Maggie. Didn't you do anything at thirteen that you'd like to forget? That you don't want to talk about now because that brings it all back, and you don't want it back?"

She didn't even have to think about it. "Yes," she said without hesitation. "But I would have told *you*." And she turned around, yanked the door open, and went inside.

It was still early enough that her parents weren't home. Her mother had had a WOH meeting, and as he always did when her mother had meetings, her father was playing poker at a friend's house. There was no hard rock music coming from upstairs. Maggie's brother was out, too.

This was supposed to be *my* big night, she told herself bitterly, peeling off the black jacket and tossing it on the sofa, and now here I am, home at ten, and everybody else is out having fun. How did that happen?

She knew perfectly well how it had happened. He was stubborn, she was stubborn, neither of them had given an inch, and here she was, all alone in an empty house.

I don't care, she thought, still stubborn, he should have told me the truth. I would have told *him*.

*Oh, you would not*, an inner voice argued. If Scout, the boy you had a mad crush on when you were thirteen, had been violently, viciously murdered, would you, at seventeen, have confided that gruesome fact to some person you'd only met a week earlier?

The thought of Scout's skull being bashed in by a blunt object made Maggie physically ill. She went immediately to the telephone by the door to call him, as if she needed to be reassured that he was still alive and breathing.

He wasn't home. At first his mother said he was home, but a few minutes later she returned to the telephone to tell Maggie he wasn't in his room. "I guess he went out," she said, sounding uncaring.

She'd been drinking, Maggie could tell. She did that once in a while now, since the divorce, and Scout wasn't very happy about it. But he didn't know what to do about it.

Wondering who he was out with ... the guys? ... a girl? ... *what* girl? Maggie hung up the phone and went into the downstairs bathroom to take something for her upset stomach.

She dreaded calling Lane and Helen. They'd be horrified that she was home this early, and they'd need to know all the gory details of her evening at Picadilly. What was she going to tell them? The truth? But it was really Whit's truth, wasn't it? If she told, she'd feel like she was reading from his diary or something.

But she had to call them to see if they needed a ride in the morning. She hadn't forgotten she intended to visit the sheriff, and she hoped they hadn't, either.

She'd just tell them she'd had a little disagreement with Whit. That wouldn't surprise either of them. They both knew she occasionally opened her mouth first and regretted later.

*Only occasionally?* the nasty little inner voice questioned sarcastically.

Deciding to call from her bedroom after she'd changed into her robe, Maggie climbed the stairs, wishing the house weren't so dark and empty, and went into her room.

She didn't see the package on her bed until she'd changed her clothes and dutifully hung the black dress in her closet. Then she flopped down on her bed. And there it was, sitting on the blue-and-white comforter.

It was wrapped in plain brown paper, addressed to her in black print, and had no return address. But there was a blue Post-It note on the front in her brother's hieroglyphical handwriting.

*"This came for you. Secret admirer? Lucky you."* It was signed, simply, *"D."*

Maggie held the package in her hands, turning it over, then shaking it gently. Who would be sending her a present? Her grandmother would have put a return address on it.

I haven't had such great luck with people bringing me things lately, she thought, setting the package aside. Maybe I'll just wait until Mom and Dad get home to open this one.

But by the time she had called Lane and Helen, answering their questions about Picadilly in the most cryptic fashion and making arrangements to pick them both up in the morning, her curiosity about the package sent her fingers fumbling at the string. If it were a bomb, it would be ticking, and she didn't hear a sound in her room but the faint sigh of the night breeze outside her open window.

Off came the string.

Off came the paper.

Off came the lid of the box.

Tissue paper, slightly wrinkled and clearly not new, covered the contents. There was no card.

There should have been a card.

Maybe it was inside, beneath the wrinkled tissue paper. Probably was.

Her grandmother would have put the card on top, so that she would see it first thing.

Her hands were not shaking as she unfolded the tissue paper, because there was absolutely no reason in the world to be afraid. None at all. Someone had sent her something in a box, and she was going to open it just as anyone would open a package they'd received. Anything else would be sheer cowardice, and she was not, was *not*, a coward.

When she had uncovered the object lying deep within the tissue paper, she sat perfectly still, her eyes not veering away for a second, her breathing deep and even. "I'm okay," she murmured, staring at the contents of the box, "I am perfectly okay, there is nothing the least bit scary about this, nothing at all. It can't hurt me."

Which was true enough. Inside the tissue paper lay nothing but a doll. A rag doll, its features embroidered on the round face, its hair orange. A soft, stuffed doll in a red dress and red-and-white-striped stockings, lying in the box on its back, its boneless arms folded limply over its chest.

Harmless. Dolls were perfectly, absolutely harmless. Couldn't hurt anyone, ever.

But they could send messages. Nasty messages. Messages meant to frighten, to intimidate. Meant to make the hands start shaking, after all, though they didn't want to, and the stomach roil and the little pulse at the temple start throbbing with alarm, no matter how concentrated the effort to keep it from doing that.

A doll could do all that if it was wearing a blindfold over its blank, black eyes. The blindfold, too, was black, amateurishly cut out of construction paper and taped to the round, soft little head. And a doll could send a nasty message if it had a thick, rough rope tied in a hangman's knot around its little neck.

# Chapter 25

Unaware of passing time, Maggie sat unmoving on the bed, the open box still on her lap, until the sound of the front door opening and closing, then voices below, roused her.

A few minutes later, Maggie's mother poked her head in the open doorway. "Hi, sweetie. I stole your father away from the poker game. He smells like a box of cigars. Did you have a good time among the very rich?"

Maggie didn't answer, but she lifted her head. When her mother saw the expression on her face, she hurried over to the bed. "What's wrong?" Seeing the box, she reached for it, asking grimly, "*Now* what?" Then, "What on earth . . . ? This is disgusting!" Sheila Keene lifted her head and called, "Martin! Come up here!"

By the time her parents and then Darren, who arrived ten minutes later, had thoroughly examined and exclaimed over the contents of the package,

Maggie was wishing she'd hidden it. What good was all this fuss doing? It didn't change anything, and it was giving her a headache.

"It's okay Mom, Dad," she said wearily. "It's just a joke, really. Someone the peer jury sentenced probably thought it was a terrific way to send a message. I mean, if you think about it, it's kind of funny. When my hair is wet, I do look a little like that." She managed a weak laugh.

No one echoed it.

"Some joke," her brother muttered. "Even my sense of humor isn't that gross."

"This blindfold . . . " her mother murmured, "and that noose! It's horrid." She shuddered visibly and almost tossed the box at her husband, who caught it and said, "I think Donovan should see this."

"I'll take it to him." Maggie lay down on her bed and pulled up the comforter, hoping they'd take the hint. "I'm going to see him tomorrow." She didn't want to scare her parents further by telling them about Chantilly's threat, so she added, "To talk to him about that scale. But take the package downstairs, okay? I don't want it in my room overnight. Just put it by the front door. I'll get it in the morning."

Her mother stood beside the bed, looking down at Maggie. "Are you sure you're okay? It must have been horrible, opening that box, thinking it was a present, and then finding . . . that. Where did it come from?"

Maggie looked at her brother. "You left it on my bed. Who gave it to you?"

"No one. The doorbell rang while I was fixing a sandwich. By the time I got there, the package was just sitting on the porch. I didn't see anyone."

"You didn't see a plain old blue car pull away?" Maggie asked him.

"It was dark. Maybe I saw taillights. I don't remember."

"Mom, it was just a joke," Maggie repeated, wanting desperately to be alone.

Her mother nodded, looking unconvinced. "Did you have a good time at Picadilly?" she asked then.

"Yeah, it was great." To avoid any further questions on *that* subject, Maggie asked, "How was your meeting? So is it absolutely settled about the courthouse?"

Defeat showed in her mother's face. "We're definitely razing it. Tearing it down, building a rec center on the site." She smiled at Maggie. "I'm sure your friends will be happy. I should have let you break the news to them. You'd be their hero. Heroine. But there was a reporter at the meeting, so I'm assuming the story was on the eleven o'clock news." Glancing at her watch, she said, "We missed it. A lot of Felicity residents, especially those under eighteen, must be rejoicing right about now." She asked again, "You're sure you're okay? You'll be able to sleep?"

If you people ever leave, I will, Maggie thought darkly. But she felt bad for her mother. All that planning, all that energy, all those meetings, and now the historical building she'd tried so hard to save was actually going to be history. Depressing.

And then to come home and find *this* ... "Yes, Mom, I'll sleep. Don't worry, okay? I'm fine."

But when the room was empty, the door closed, the nasty little box and its contents on their way downstairs, sleep didn't come easily. If bad things really did come in threes, the way people said, this particular Friday was a terrific example. First the unnerving encounter with Chantilly Beckwith, then the disappointing evening at Picadilly, and last, but certainly far from least, that creepy little doll. Ugh. Someone had gone to a lot of trouble. You'd think people would have better things to do with their time.

Maybe tomorrow morning the sheriff would tell her they now had proof that both incidents at the courthouse had been absolutely accidental. "Nothing sinister about either one of them," he would say. "Just plain old bad luck, bad karma, bad timing." Which would mean that the broken gavel and the bloody scale and the ugly little doll had nothing to do with the other incidents. If the courthouse was no longer an issue, the sheriff could concentrate solely on who was torturing Maggie Keene.

Comforted by those thoughts, Maggie fell asleep.

But on Saturday, she never got the chance to ask the sheriff what he'd found out about the cave-in and the explosion, because when she, Lane, and Helen arrived at the courthouse, the sheriff wasn't in his office.

"He's already up on the roof," a deputy told them. "Seeing to it that the work crew takin' that statue down doesn't drop it straight down off the roof and crush seventeen people standin' on the ground watchin'."

Disappointed, Maggie asked him if he knew anything about the investigation into the two disasters, but just then his phone rang. When he turned his back on the trio to answer, they knew they'd been dismissed.

They still had an hour before they had to meet the rest of the peer jury for the ceremony on the courthouse grounds, so they went to the food court at the mall. They ate and talked, Maggie trying as hard as she could to avoid the subject of her evening at Picadilly.

Impossible.

It was easy enough at first. She had showed them the doll and they discussed that for a while, both suggesting that James Keith or Chantilly Beckwith or both had sent it. Then, because they already knew about the cancellation of the courthouse renovation project and were delighted, Maggie kept them on that subject. They were already enthusiastically planning dances and parties and concerts at the new recreation center.

"It hasn't even been built yet," Maggie pointed out dourly. "And nothing's on the drawing board yet." It wasn't that she didn't want a rec center. She did. But she didn't think they should plan anything new until someone knew what had happened at the courthouse. Wasn't that more important than anything else? People had almost died.

The moment she'd been dreading came when, exhausting the subject of the rec center, Helen and

Lane insisted on hearing the details of her evening at Picadilly.

"Maggie," Helen cried in exasperation, "if you don't tell us this very second what happened last night, you're going to be *wearing* this taco!"

Even then, Maggie was cautious about how much she shared. Whit had made it painfully clear that his relationship with Dante Guardino and the Miller girl was his business. If he wasn't willing to share it with *her*, he certainly wouldn't want Helen and Lane to hear about it.

"We had a little argument, that's all. Nothing major. You know me," she added with what she hoped was a nonchalant shrug. "I'm hard to get along with."

"No, you're not," Helen said loyally. "But," she added, "sometimes you take things the wrong way. Then you get defensive, and that mouth of yours goes into overdrive." She stared intently at Maggie. "Is that how you got last night? With Whit?"

"No!" Maggie said defensively, and then, hearing the tone in her voice, laughed ruefully. "Well, maybe. Anyway," sweeping her trash onto her tray to carry it to the can, "it's history, okay?"

Lane laughed, in better spirits now than she'd been in days. And Maggie knew why. "Please don't mention history. That's what almost lost us our rec center. Thank goodness your mother came to her senses."

When Helen said, "Come on, we'd better get going," Maggie found herself involuntarily recoiling at the thought of going back to the site of the explosion. Going to the sheriff's office hadn't been difficult. It was in one of the "newer" wings, on the opposite side of the kitchen wing.

But the ceremony was taking place in the same area as the bazaar, which made it hard for her to leave the safety of the van when she reached her destination. She parked, but then she sat there, for what seemed like the longest time, battling the need to start the engine again and go back home. She could sit on the couch with her father and watch football, eat popcorn and chips, yell at the set when their team fumbled. She could forget all about the ancient old building with the hole in its basement ceiling and its first floor corridor, and no kitchen left to speak of. She could just go home. *She* was the one who had been tossed like a Frisbee by that explosion. No one would blame her if she didn't show up for the ceremony today.

No, no, no. Wrong, all wrong. She couldn't do that. Because if she did, she'd be a coward. The thought made her cringe. In the old western movies her dad was so fond of, which she occasionally watched with him, she'd be the character known as a "yellow-bellied, lily-livered coward." But thinking of the westerns reminded her of the antique scale, and her spine tingled.

She was *not* yellow-bellied. She was *not* lily-livered. She was *not*, would not be, could not be, a coward.

She took three deep breaths and let them out. Then she jumped down from the van to follow Helen and Lane.

# Chapter 26

Most of the refuse from the blast had been cleared away, although a good-sized pile of stone rubble still lay inside the roped-off area. Every window on that side had been stripped of its glass.

Still, the damage wasn't as bad as Maggie had expected. Averting her eyes from the building, she focused instead on the rapidly swelling crowd.

The rows of folding chairs next to the building sat like soldiers waiting for inspection. Although the other members of the peer jury were already seated, there was no sign of Whit. She felt a twinge of disappointment. Had he changed his mind? Scout hadn't arrived yet, either, and she wondered again who he'd gone out with last night. She waved to the other members as she, Helen, and Lane took seats beside Bennie and Tanya, in the front row.

The two cheerleaders looked as perky as ever, in jeans and matching blue-and-white Bransom High windbreakers. Tanya's cupid's-bow mouth rounded into an "O" of surprise when Maggie joined them. "Oh, you poor thing," she breathed in the whispery voice that Scout called "sexy." "Look at your face!" Maggie had removed the bandage, but the laceration beside her nose was still an angry red. "Does it hurt a lot? We didn't think you'd be here today, after what happened last week." Waving a hand toward Bennie, she added, "We were sure you wouldn't ever come near this place again."

"Are you staying for the ceremony?" Bennie asked. A small, blonde girl with wide blue eyes and a friendly smile, she had no enemies, and Maggie felt a twinge of envy. No one would ever blow up a kitchen with Bennie in it.

"Yep. I hope the mayor doesn't talk forever." Maggie glanced toward the speakers' platform, a hastily constructed wooden structure. Her mother wouldn't be giving a speech, now that her project had been canceled. Maggie's eyes moved to the left and up. "How are they doing with Lady Justice?"

Bennie pointed to the very top of the old courthouse. "See those guys way up there at the top? They've already unfastened the metal bolts on the bottom of the statue. They were up there first thing this morning, and they've been working ever since. Someone said the statue is just about ready to be taken down. The crane's right over there." She pointed again, this time to the bright yellow machine sitting some distance from the rows of chairs, on the only stretch of green lawn that hadn't been uprooted and replaced by cement.

Maggie's eyes followed Bennie's finger. "Well, it's

big enough, but I still don't see how they're going to get Justice down from there."

Before either girl could answer, Scout appeared at Maggie's side, slid into the chair beside her, said hi, and answered her question. "See that big metal jaw on the end of the crane? Looks like a scoop?" He, too, pointed.

Maggie saw it. A giant scoop, dangling like a child's sandbox toy from the end of the crane's long, uptilted arm. "That bucket? Is it big enough? The statue is huge."

"It better be. If that thing tumbles out of the bucket, guess who it's going to land on. They put these chairs too close to the building."

"It's not going to tumble out of the bucket," Tanya said confidently. "You shouldn't think bad things, Scout. Sometimes thinking them can make them happen. I honestly believe that."

Scout grinned at Maggie. It was the same slightly crooked grin she had first fallen madly in love with. At thirteen. It seemed a thousand years ago now. "That's our Tanya," he whispered, "the poster child for positive thinking."

"I called you last night around ten-thirty. Your mom said you were out."

The grin vanished. "How would *she* know? She was pretty out of it when I got home." Then, in a different tone of voice, "I thought you were busy last night. Must have been a short evening if you were home making phone calls at ten-thirty."

Before she could answer him, Whit arrived and took a seat on the end of the front row. He looked tired, and Maggie wondered if he'd been lying awake all night . . . thinking about her? Nice thought, but probably not true. He didn't look in her direction, and she realized it must appear to him that she and Scout had come here together.

"I got home early," was all she said to Scout. Then, lightly, "So where were you?"

His eyebrow arched. "I can't ask you where you're going, but you can ask me where I've been? Doesn't sound like equality to *me*."

Maggie laughed. "You could have asked me where I was going."

"Would you have told me?"

"Sure." Liar. She wouldn't have said, "I'm going to Picadilly," because the look of pain on his face would have been too much for her. She really *was* a coward!

But she was here, wasn't she? In the place that she least wanted to be. She could have stayed home, and she hadn't. So maybe she was getting braver.

Maggie looked in Whit's direction twice, but his eyes remained steadily on the rooftop, as if he thought the crew of workers struggling with the heavy statue couldn't function properly without his scrutiny.

"I don't know why we all care so much about that rec center," Scout said. "I mean, we're all out of here in two years. We won't have much time to use it."

"It'll be for adults, too. When you're living here and working for your dad, you and your family can use the center."

Scout's head whipped around and he stared at Maggie. "I'm not staying in Felicity! I'm out of this town the minute I graduate, putting it as far behind me as I can."

"You're not going to work for your dad?" Hadn't he said, a long time ago, that he probably would? When had he changed his mind? And why hadn't he told her?

"You're kidding, right? After what he did?" Scout's father had divorced Scout's mother so he could marry another woman. They were living in Nestegg, in a house even larger and more impressive than Scout's. "I wouldn't go to work for him if he paid me in gold bullion. He cheated on my mom, Maggie! And dumped her. And he can apologize until he's purple, but that doesn't change anything." His blue eyes bleak, he shook his head. "Man, if there's one thing I can't stand, it's a cheat!"

Chagrined, Maggie realized how long it had been since she'd spent time alone with Scout. She'd known the divorce had upset him, shocked him, as it had everyone in Felicity. But she'd had no clue that he was still so bitter. She knew that he saw his father occasionally. To Maggie's surprise, Scout's mother insisted on it. But clearly, Scout hadn't forgiven him.

To change the subject, she asked, "Why are they even giving speeches today? Wouldn't it make more sense to have a ceremony when the statue is placed on the *new* building?"

Scout, his anger gone as suddenly as it had appeared, laughed. "Oh, they're doing it then, too.

There's another ceremony scheduled for next week, when they raise the statue to the roof of the new courthouse. You know our mayor. Carter P. Rockwell wouldn't miss an opportunity to sound off. The old windbag does love an audience."

Maggie groaned silently. Another ceremony? Another opportunity for disaster, if you asked her. Unless Sheriff Donovan had solved, by then, the mystery of who was doing what and why it was being done, gathering so many people together in one place again was just inviting trouble. Even now, she could feel a sense of dread gathering inside her like the dark clouds beginning to block out the sun overhead.

They all sat and talked quietly among themselves. People were arriving in spite of the threatening skies. There wasn't that much to do in Felicity on a Saturday afternoon. But even if there had been, Maggie thought few residents would be willing to miss this. The statue had been in place on the old courthouse for more than sixty years. If the workmen were successful and Lady Justice made her way to the roof of the new courthouse, she would probably be up there even longer than sixty years. So what was taking place today wouldn't happen again for a very long time. No one wanted to miss it.

"I've never understood why that statue is blindfolded," Tanya said. "I mean, how is she supposed to know if someone is guilty if she can't even see them?"

"She doesn't do the judging," Whit pointed out.

"People on juries do that. Like our peer jury. What that statue represents is how fair and impartial Justice is supposed to be."

Maggie, not interested in the discussion, had already tuned out. She was more interested in watching the workmen at the top of the old courthouse, struggling with the huge, heavy statue. As she watched, the crew on the top of the building, using ropes and chains in some sort of pulley arrangement that Maggie couldn't see clearly, suddenly tipped the statue forward, letting it fall slowly, heavily, until it landed in the uplifted scoop of the crane.

To Maggie's surprise, the statue settled in firmly, though its head extended beyond one edge of the scoop. Still, it looked secure enough that it seemed certain to stay in place during the long, slow descent.

Maggie breathed a little easier. The statue was *not* going to fall on them. Like Tanya said, why anticipate disaster? You just might get it.

Because the burgeoning crowd had begun to collect in front of the peer jury's chairs, Whit suggested they stand up and move to one side to get a better view. "Over there," he said, pointing, "below the speakers' platform. We can see the whole thing from there."

The chain suspending the scoop whined a protest as the loaded bucket began its descent.

The statue came down without incident. But as it slowly lumbered closer to the lower floors, it became harder to see over the heads of the crowd.

"I want to see how they get that big old thing out of the scoop," Maggie said to Lane, and signaled to her to push her way through the crowd.

Lane shook her head. "Impossible. It'd be easier to break through a stone wall. We'll have to go around."

Realizing that she was right, Maggie leaned forward to tug on Scout's sleeve. "We can't see. We're moving. You guys coming?"

He nodded and alerted Whit, Alex, and Helen. Lane had already rounded the speakers' platform, keeping one arm in the air as a directional signal. Maggie tried to keep her eyes on the red sweatsuit as she fought to find an opening in the solid mass of shoulders and arms and legs and chests.

"The statue's almost down," someone behind her said.

"Oh, I want to see it land!" Maggie declared irritably, and darted out into the open.

She emerged in a clearing on the edge of the crowd, behind the speakers' platform, and glanced around for Lane. There she was, up ahead, one arm still in the air signaling as she hurried forward, intent on seeing the statue land.

Maggie turned to make sure her friends were still following. She saw Whit advancing straight toward her, and satisfied, turned back toward Lane.

"It's down!" someone shouted, and the ground did indeed shake, just a little, beneath Maggie's feet as the scoop containing the giant statue landed.

"Oh, darn!" she muttered. But she still had time to watch them remove the statue from the scoop, though she couldn't imagine how they would do that or how many strong backs it would take. She would have broken into a run then, across the only patch of thick green grass left on Otis Bransom's property, if someone hadn't screamed.

The scream came from just ahead of Maggie. It was loud and shrill, and startled the crowd into a shocked, questioning silence.

But the oddest thing about it was that while it began as a shriek of terror so thin and high it assaulted every ear, it instantly dwindled to a fainter, hollow wail, as if the person making the sound was being swiftly carried away.

Maggie was frozen in place by the paralyzing sound ahead of her. She saw the statue, still in its yellow scoop, lying on the ground, the blindfolded face uptilted toward the sky. She saw the crane, motionless now. And she saw, on her left, the crowd, stricken motionless, like her. She saw, looming above all of it, the old courthouse, its dingy, uncurtained windows staring blankly back at her.

What she *didn't* see was Lane Bridgewater.

"Lane?" Maggie questioned as the crowd waited in silence for someone to tell them it was okay . . . the scream wasn't anything . . . just some kid playing around . . . nothing to worry about, folks.

No one said that. And Lane didn't answer Maggie's call.

Whit arrived at Maggie's side. Alex, Scout, and Helen were right behind him. "Where's Lane?" Alex asked. "I thought she was with you."

"Well, she was," Maggie said slowly, her eyes

searching for some sign of Lane. "She was right *there*, just ahead of me." She pointed. "But ... but I don't see her now."

The four began moving forward slowly. People closest to them in the crowd sensed a puzzle and turned their heads to watch.

They almost didn't see the hole. Maggie would have walked right into it if Whit hadn't suddenly grabbed her elbow and shouted, "Watch out!" He waved a hand toward the ground.

They were looking then at a round, black hole. A hole large enough for someone as thin as Lane to tumble into. Dipping into the hole from around the edges was a thin carpet of grass, beneath that an inch or so of dirt, like carpet padding, and beneath that, a layer of boards, like flooring.

Maggie caught her breath. "Lane?" she asked quietly. Then, because there had been that thin, high scream, and because Lane had disappeared as if she'd been vaporized, and because she had this very bad feeling in the pit of her stomach, Maggie got down on her knees at the edge of the black hole and called in a louder voice, "*Lane?*"

Her only answer was a groan floating up from below. It was distant and very faint. But it was enough.

Maggie sank back on her knees and lifted her head to look up at Whit. "That's where she is," she said. "She's down there."

# Chapter 27

There was no need to call for help. Enough people had been watching to know that something was very wrong. Before Maggie could really take in what had happened, they were surrounded by town officials, the sheriff, Maggie's mother, and members of her committee. They had to step over a jumbled pile of rubble collected from last week's explosion to reach the edge and look in. Soon there were far too many people gathering at the same time in the same place to see what new disaster had taken place on the grounds of the old courthouse.

"I *knew* it!" Helen declared in a shrill voice. "Every time we come near this place, something awful happens. Poor Lane!"

The sheriff peeled Maggie away from the edge of the hole and ordered his deputies to move everyone else back as well, so that he could assess the situation.

Gathered in a group a short distance away, Lane's friends waited with fearful eyes.

Whit appeared at Maggie's elbow, put a hand on it, and pulled her gently backward until they were slightly separate from the others. His face looked strained, his easy air of self-confidence no longer apparent. "I thought it was *you*," he said in a voice so quiet, Maggie had to strain to hear him. He kept his hand on her arm, careful not to touch the fresh bandage covering her injury. "Someone said a girl had fallen into a deep hole, and I'd lost sight of you in the crowd, so I . . . I thought it was you." The lines of tension around his mouth began to ease, and the merest hint of a smile appeared. "I should have known better. You're too sharp to walk right into a hole in the ground."

Maggie felt Scout's eyes on them. But Whit had clearly been scared . . . for *her*. And now he seemed so relieved, she couldn't just walk away. But if he cared that much, why had he told her to mind her own business?

"I'm fine," she said coolly.

"It's Lane?"

"Yes. She was trying to get closer to the building. I don't know what a hole is doing right there where anyone could walk right into it," Maggie added with indignation. "I guess she didn't see it because she was trying to watch the statue coming down. I was behind her, following, and she just sort of . . . disappeared."

"So it *could* have been you," Whit said, and she

knew she wasn't imagining the tension in his voice. "Maggie, look at me."

"No."

"*Look* at me. I can't apologize if you won't look at me."

"You don't owe me an apology." She kept her eyes on the sheriff, lying prone now on the ground at the edge of the hole, aiming a large flashlight into its depths. "And I can't think about this now. I have to find out if Lane is okay." She pulled her arm free and turned away.

"I'm sorry," he called softly after her. "I'm really sorry."

Alex had just returned from the edge of the hole.

"Is she . . ." Helen's voice quavered, "is she dead?"

"No," Alex answered quickly, "she's not dead. We heard her. She made a noise."

Whit asked if anyone knew how far down Lane had fallen. "How deep is the hole?"

"It's plenty deep," an old man volunteered from behind them. "I know what that hole is. That's Otis Bransom's old well, the one he dug when him and his dad built this place." He nodded toward the building. "Otis had the well boarded over when he got indoor plumbing. Boards musta rotted through."

Maggie wondered why Lane hadn't *seen* the hole. It was perfectly visible, and not really small enough to overlook, even if you were in a hurry.

"Girl wouldn't be dead, though," the man continued. "Might not even have any broken bones. That well's partway filled in with dirt. Otis's wife insisted. She was afraid one of their own girls would fall through the boards. George, their handyman, was supposed to fill it in all the way, but he had hisself a heart attack before he finished. All that shoveling, I'd guess. So Otis just covered it up, then added dirt, planted grass. But there'd be plenty of dirt down inside there to cushion your friend's fall. If you're sure she's down there."

As if he'd overheard, the sheriff, still lying prone at the edge of the well, turned his head to call out to Maggie, "She's down here, alright. We can see her plain enough. Not that far down, either. He's right about the fill."

"Just get her *out*," Maggie called back. "Get her out of there!"

It took a while. The speeches forgotten, Lady Justice lying ignored, still in the scoop, all efforts went to rescuing Lane from Otis Bransom's old well. Scout put a comforting arm around Maggie while they waited. What was *not* comforting was Helen repeatedly mumbling, "I *knew* it, I just knew it, bad things always happen here."

Maggie wanted to throttle her. She settled instead for hissing, "Helen, if you don't stop that right this second, you're going to join Lane in that well!"

Helen clamped her lips together.

Instead of dispersing, the crowd swelled as word of the accident spread throughout Felicity. Lane's parents, who had chosen not to attend the ceremony, arrived.

"I *told* her to stay away from here," Lane's mother said, sounding like Helen. She directed a malevolent gaze at Maggie's mother, standing nearby. "If anyone in this town had half a grain of sense, this building would have been torn down long ago. My daughter may have complained about being bored out in the country, but at least she was *safe*!"

Just once during the lengthy process, Maggie moved close enough to peer down into the well. The lantern propped at its edge illuminated the interior as the sheriff and a deputy attempted to rig up some sort of harness. Maggie could see Lane's still, silent form resting on a narrow stone outcropping, as if she had chosen this deep, dark spot to take a nap.

If she had been conscious, they would have lowered a rope to her. But she hadn't stirred. And no one could be sure that a ladder would have a firm enough footing on the mounded dirt.

"How long has she been down there?" Maggie asked Helen.

"Don't know. Can't find my watch. But it feels like hours."

Just about the time that Maggie felt like she had to start screaming at the top of her lungs for somebody to do something, a group of men including Lane's father and two deputies began lowering the sheriff, wearing the harness, into the well.

There wasn't a sound in the watching crowd.

The silence was broken once by the distant rumble of thunder, a second time by a shrill train whistle at the railroad crossing five blocks away. The only other sound was the scraping of the sheriff's boots on the stone walls of the well as he descended.

Maggie's neck began to ache from looking steadily downward. When she lifted her head to ease the ache, the first thing she saw, still in its yellow scoop, its blindfolded stone features blankly facing upward, was Lady Justice . . . the reason they had come to the old courthouse today. Forgotten now.

The sheriff's voice floated up from inside the well. "Got her!" he called. Scout, Whit, Alex, and several Bransom High football players rushed to help the men pull on the rope attached to the harness. They were careful to hold the rope away from the edge of the well to keep the sheriff and Lane from being slammed against the stone wall.

A loud cheer went up from the crowd as the sheriff's head emerged, then his shoulders, chest, and arms . . . with Lane folded up inside them. The way she looked reminded Maggie of the doll in the box. She'd forgotten all about it, but now it came flooding back, and her knees went weak.

Lane's red sweatsuit was chalky with stone dust, and there was a small cut on her left temple, trickling blood. But to everyone's surprise, as they emerged into the fresh air, she began stirring, and by the time her father lay her gently on the ground, she was conscious, her eyes open. She began murmuring to her father, her voice low and husky.

"See?" Scout said, bending his head toward Maggie. "Didn't I tell you? She looks okay, right?"

But Maggie wasn't agreeing until she saw and heard for herself that Lane was okay. She ran to kneel beside Lane, who lay quietly, gingerly moving a leg, then another leg, then an arm, and another arm.

"I didn't break anything," she said, sounding amazed.

Everyone began talking at once then, some people congratulating the sheriff, others wondering aloud if someone was going to do something about the statue now that the girl had been rescued. Others began deploring the state of the well's cover.

Maggie reached out to take Lane's left hand in hers. She couldn't do that. The hand wasn't empty. It was a closed fist, with something inside. Maggie couldn't see what it was.

"Hey, Maggie," Lane murmured, her eyes clearing somewhat. "What happened?"

"You fell. The covering gave way on Otis's old well. The boards were rotted through. But," she added hastily, "you're going to be okay."

The sheriff, kneeling at the edge of the hole and fingering the edges of the broken boards, said to no one in particular, "Oh, this wood wasn't rotted. Not at all. Old Otis always used only the best materials. The cover that was nailed over this well prob'ly would have lasted another fifty years or so. If someone hadn't sawed it in half."

Uncomprehending, the crowd fell silent again at his words.

Lane's father, kneeling beside her, asked,

"Sawed? What are you talking about, Donovan?"

"What I'm talkin' about," the sheriff answered, climbing to his feet, "is, someone came at that cover with a saw and sliced right through its center, grass, dirt, boards, and all. It wouldn't have taken that long with a small power saw. See, it's got a slit all the way across it. Like a slot in a piggy bank, you might say. It wouldn't have looked any different, though. Not unless you checked real close."

No response from the crowd, which he now had in the palm of his hand. He might have been reciting a Shakespearean soliloquy, so rapt was the attention of his audience.

"The minute she stepped into the center of the cover, it gave. Just like it was meant to."

Maggie gasped.

The sheriff took his hat off, wiped his brow with a handkerchief, put the hat back on. "That's what happened. I knew it the minute I saw how smooth the edges of those boards were. Sliced as neatly as cheese. Right through the center."

"It was done on purpose?" There was both anger and disbelief in Mr. Bridgewater's voice. His daughter was popular. Why would someone want to hurt her?

"Couldn't have been meant for her, especially," the sheriff said. "The thing is, with this ceremony business here today, whoever did it knew for certain that someone was bound to fall in. Musta meant for that very thing to happen, you ask me."

Understanding exactly what he was saying, Maggie felt sick. Someone had deliberately created a trap, a trap that Lane had fallen into. Why would someone *do* that?

As if he'd read her mind, the sheriff asked of the crowd, "Anyone here know why someone would do that?"

No one answered him.

# Chapter 28

Whit spoke up. "Sheriff, how would anyone know there was a well on this property?"

"It's outlined on the diagrams of the property at the Women of Heritage offices," Maggie's mother answered. "Anyone could have found it. If they were looking for it, that is. Of course, there wouldn't be any notations about the well being filled in. That came later."

Which meant, Maggie realized, that the maniac armed with a power saw had expected any prey he caught in his trap to fall all the way to the original bottom of the well. Almost certainly to his — or her — death.

As paramedics loaded Lane onto a stretcher, Helen turned to Maggie to say, "Your mom must be having a hard time with this. I mean, bad enough that all that stuff happened inside the building. But now the outside looks jinxed, too." She sighed heavily. "She must be glad, though, that she's already canceled the restoration plans."

Maggie would have retorted angrily if the sheriff hadn't called out just then, "Anybody know what this is?"

Maggie turned to look.

Lane was already inside the ambulance and the paramedics were closing the doors. The sheriff was standing at the rear of the vehicle, holding up in the air a dirty square of cloth. It looked like it might have once been white, though it was hard to tell.

"The girl gave it to me," the sheriff continued. "She was holding it in her hand."

Maggie nodded. The closed fist.

"Looks like a handkerchief, but she says it's not hers. Said it was on that ledge in the well. Could have been there for years, I suppose. Or maybe not." He glanced around the crowd. "Anyone know whose it might be?"

The mayor, a short, heavyset man with a thick crop of graying hair, removed his straw hat, scratched his head, and said, "Maybe it belongs to one of the construction workers," pointing to the roof of the old courthouse. "Coulda dropped it when they were traipsing through here with their equipment on their way to pulling that statue down. In fact," he added, clearly hoping that this unpleasant event could be dismissed as quickly as possible, "maybe they accidentally split the well cover, too."

The sheriff uttered a disgusted sound. "Your construction crew uses linen hankies, do they, Carter? And how do you 'accidentally' saw straight through the middle of a wooden well cover?"

Carter P. Rockwell put his straw hat back on and fell sullenly silent.

"Nope," the sheriff said, shaking his head, "nothin' accidental about this." He let that sink in. Then he waved the scrap of cloth again. "So let me ask again, anyone know who this here hankie belongs to?"

Into the tense silence that followed, Alex's voice said, "That looks like yours, Helen. Isn't Ms. Gross always giving you those? With your initials on them?"

Helen gasped. But she didn't move forward to examine the grimy piece of cloth. She stayed where she was, safely situated between Whit and Maggie. "Of course not!" she declared hotly. "What would one of my hankies be doing in that well? I didn't even know there *was* a well there!"

But in the next second, as the sheriff turned the handkerchief over in his hands, he was saying aloud, "H. E. M." He tapped a finger against the embroidered initials, so dirty they were indecipherable to the onlookers. He lifted his head, repeating, "Anyone here know who H.E.M. might be?"

Helen's middle name was Electra. Her face had gone ghostly white. She shook her head vehemently. "No, no, that's not *mine*! I wasn't anywhere *near* that well."

But all eyes in the crowd were on her, and many of them were full of suspicion.

"He didn't say you did anything," Maggie urged in a low voice. "Don't get all upset. Just go check out the hankie, see if it's one of yours, and then tell him the truth." In a more normal voice, she said, "We all know you didn't have anything to do with this, Helen." She waited for Alex and Scout to echo that sentiment, but they didn't. She wasn't expecting it from Whit, who didn't know Helen that well, but he surprised her by saying, "Considering what's been going on around here lately, Helen, someone could have filched one of your hankies and put it there, just like they took Maggie's gavel. Just go talk to the sheriff. We'll wait for you."

Maggie sent him a grateful smile, and Helen, with obvious reluctance, did as they had suggested.

When Helen had thoroughly examined the handkerchief, she spoke to the sheriff so quietly that no one watching could hear her. But they saw her nod her head.

Maggie, sickened, half expected the sheriff to whip out a pair of handcuffs.

Instead, he simply nodded, and said, "Thank you, miss. We'll talk about this later. Right now, I'm goin' along to the hospital to talk to that girl who fell, see if she can remember anything important."

Helen's steps back to her friends were heavy with relief.

"Sheriff," Maggie called, not caring who heard her, "if you want to talk to someone, talk to Alice Ann Beckwith! She's furious with the peer jury, and she knew we were all going to be here today. She threatened me yesterday. You talk to *her*!"

But the sheriff was already walking away, and the crowd, awash in mutterings and grumblings, began to dissipate, as workmen from the roof brought new boards to nail across the well.

Lady Justice continued to lie in the scoop next to the building, still forgotten.

In the heavy silence that followed Helen rejoining them, Alex was the first to speak in Maggie's group. "Well, that tears it!" he declared, his voice low and angry. "This place always *was* unlucky for the Goodman family. From now on, I'm steering clear of it. You guys will just have to get along without me when you start moving stuff out of here to the new building. I'm not setting one foot inside this one."

"I'm not either," Helen said.

The mayor, to Maggie's surprise, canceled his speech, announcing that he would save it for the following week at the new courthouse. With the statue still lying in the yellow scoop as if it were lolling in a bathtub, the ceremony was canceled and a deputy began to disperse the crowd. "No speeches today, folks. Excitement's over, go on home now."

Shrugging and muttering, the crowd began to disperse. One woman said loudly as she walked away, "This better be the end of it, that's all I've got to say! The sooner we tear this old eyesore down, the better off we'll all be."

Other people mumbled agreement.

But something was nagging at Maggie, and as she led her friends to the van to follow the ambulance to the hospital, she voiced her thoughts. "Someone set a trap, knowing there would be lots of people here today, and that somebody was sure to fall in. And they couldn't have known that well had been filled in."

Thunder rolled above them, the skies opened, and it began raining lightly at first, then harder. They broke into a run. When they were settled in the van, Maggie wiped her face with her sleeve and continued, "What I don't get is, my mother had already announced that the renovation plans had been scrapped. If the cave-in and the explosion were meant to stop the remodeling, the way I thought maybe they were, why did *this* happen today? Isn't that overkill? What's the point?"

Whit, sitting behind her, speculated, "Maybe we were wrong. Maybe none of it was because of the renovation plans. Could be someone who just hates the old courthouse. Someone who was jailed there once, or someone who was fired."

Maggie was glad she couldn't see Alex's face. He had to be thinking of his father.

"I always thought," Whit added, "that Dante would come back here one day, to clear himself. I was always surprised that he didn't."

The sudden reference to Guardino startled all of them.

"Oh, get real," Scout said. "You think Dante did all this stuff? He's long gone. He'd be crazy to come back here. And if he *was* here, someone would have seen him."

"No, they wouldn't. He wouldn't dare appear in daylight. He'd be arrested first thing. He'd have to do things at night."

But Helen said, "The sheriff hasn't even said the cave-in and the explosion were deliberate."

"No, but he's certain about the well cover being deliberately sawed through," Maggie said. "So doesn't it make sense that the other things were, too?" She wondered if Whit was right. What if the violence at the courthouse didn't have anything to do with the proposed renovations? Then canceling them wouldn't do any good, would it? When things had quieted down after the cancelation was announced, it had seemed so clear that this had been the goal all along. But now . . . if it wasn't that, what was it? Why was someone so angry?

Maybe Whit had a point. If Dante Guardino really had been innocent, *he* might be that angry. Angry enough to come back to Felicity and take revenge.

Hard as that was to believe, it was even less likely that a stupid recreation center could mean so much to anyone. Ridiculous.

"At least it wasn't you who fell into that well," Alex said to Maggie. "When you came so close to becoming part of the ozone layer last week, I thought someone was after *you*. Maybe because you're peer jury foreperson. But I guess not. Lane's the one in the hospital now."

If it hadn't been raining, Maggie would never have seen the blue car. It was parked next to a big old station wagon that dwarfed it, hiding it from sight. But the rain had already made the roads slick, and as she braked at the parking lot's exit, the wheels skidded and the van spun sideways in the road. Maggie found herself staring straight at the blue car that had been parked outside her house one night last week. The night of the bloody scale.

"That's Chantilly Beckwith's car," she said, staring at it through the rain. It was empty. "I didn't see her at the ceremony, did you? Or James, either."

"Maybe," Scout said, "they didn't *want* anyone to see them."

# Chapter 29

They were barely out of the parking lot when Scout exclaimed, "Hey, what the hell is this weird thing in the box, Maggie?"

Oh, damn. The doll. She'd forgotten. Forgotten it was back there, forgotten she'd ever received it. It seemed so unimportant now, after what had happened to Lane. "I got it last night," she said, wishing Scout weren't quite so observant. She really didn't want to talk about the doll.

"Who sent it? And what's the blindfold for?"

"How should I know? Somebody's sick joke, I guess."

When Whit, too, had examined the contents of the package, he said calmly, "The blindfold is probably supposed to represent how blind justice is, at least in the opinion of the sender. And the noose looks like a threat to me. Was it left on your front porch like the scale?"

"Yes. Now can we please talk about something else?"

Although Maggie refused to talk about the doll, she couldn't stop the others from proposing theories about what it meant and who had sent it. Helen suspected someone they'd sentenced on the peer jury, though she didn't suggest who it might be, and Scout and Alex said James Keith and/or Chantilly Beckwith were the most likely candidates.

And they don't even know that Chantilly threatened me yesterday, Maggie thought, glad she hadn't told them. She didn't want Scout deciding to rush to her defense and confront Chantilly and her friends. That would not be so terrific.

Helen opened her mouth to begin, "Maggie, did you tell them about yester — ?"

Guessing what was coming, Maggie took her foot off the gas pedal long enough to deliver a gentle but telling kick to Helen's left ankle, and shot her a look that even a no-brainer would have recognized to mean, "Shut up about that." Helen got it, and fell silent.

Scout might have pursued the matter if they hadn't pulled into the hospital parking lot then.

When they went inside the hospital, they saw Lane sitting on a table in an emergency room cubicle. Although there were visible bruises and scratches on her face and hands, nothing was bandaged or in a cast. Her father had gone back to work, but her mother was seated in a chair beside the table.

"You look worse than I do," Lane told Helen.

"You're not mad at me for giving the sheriff that hankie, are you? I didn't know it was yours."

Instead of answering, Helen astonished everyone by crying out, "God, I *hate* that stupid old courthouse! I wish it had burned to the ground last week! I wish it would disintegrate into ten thousand tiny pieces. And I *wish*," glaring at Maggie, "that your mother hadn't taken so long to cancel the stupid renovating."

"Well, *I* wish she hadn't been bullied into changing her mind, that's what I wish!" Maggie replied. "It stinks. And maybe it was all for nothing. We don't know for sure that the project is the real reason any of this stuff has happened. If it is, why is Lane sitting on this table right this very moment, when the plans have already been canceled?"

No one had an answer for her. She hadn't expected one.

Helen let out a little sound of misery. "I just don't understand how anyone could think that I would set a trap for some innocent person to fall into." Her eyes moved to Lane. "Are you really okay?"

"I guess. The doctor who was in here before said that if it was summer and I'd been wearing shorts and a tank top, I'd have been cut up really bad by that stone ledge." She held out the edges of her red sweatsuit top. "He said, and I quote, 'Being swathed in fleece saved you.'" Lane laughed. "Swathed in fleece! Yes, Helen, I'm okay. Just sore, that's all. I feel like I was bounced along a sidewalk like a rubber ball. And," she added kindly, "no one who knows you thinks you're behind this."

"The sheriff had to ask you about the hankie," Maggie added to console Helen, "because of where Lane found it. All you have to do is tell him where you were last night, when he says it must have happened, and he'll know you didn't do it."

Helen looked even more worried. "I was home." She paused, then added, "Alone. Ms. Gross had a library board meeting." Paused again, and then said, "And I went for a run. But I did that alone, too."

Whit didn't think it mattered that Helen had no alibi. His opinion was, a lone hankie wasn't grounds for arrest. Or even further questioning, although he wasn't sure about that.

The doctor came in to tell Mrs. Bridgewater she was free to take Lane home, and made her friends leave. "There are way too many people in here. What do you think this is, your new recreation center?"

Out in the hall, Helen said plaintively, "What I want to know is, *how* did that hankie get into that well? Hasn't anyone besides me wondered about that?"

Yes, they all had, but no one had any useful ideas.

Maggie felt sorry for Helen. She was so pale, and seemed so worried. Being confronted by the sheriff must have scared her half to death. Helen didn't cross in the middle of the street, had never had a traffic ticket, and had never once been called to the principal's office at school. She was probably imagining those grim, dark, jail cells at the old courthouse and wondering how soon one of those doors would slam shut on her.

Impulsively, Maggie said to her, "How about staying overnight at my house? We'll toss around all the stuff that's been happening, see if we can come up with some answers. Two brains are better than one. We'll play Nancy Drew, okay? It'll be fun."

Helen glared at her. "You think I want to talk about any of this? Guess again. That's the last thing I want. I want to forget about it."

"Okay, okay." Maggie pretended to zip her lips shut. Helen really did look terrible. Like she hadn't slept in years. "Mum's the word. We'll watch a couple of videos. Comedies, I promise. We'll laugh ourselves silly. Come on, Helen, we can cheer each other up."

Helen looked reluctant, until she remembered that Ms. Gross wouldn't be home again. "She's driving into Cleveland with friends. Maybe you're right, Maggie. I don't think I want to spend another night alone. Okay, I'll come. But I don't want to even *hear* the word 'courthouse.' "

"I promise."

As Lane, walking more slowly and carefully than usual, left with her mother, Maggie made her promise to call later. Then she, too, left to drop Scout, Whit, and Alex at their respective cars.

"Can I call you tonight, too?" Scout asked teasingly as he left the van.

"Sure," Maggie said heartily, wondering if Whit would take the cue and repeat the question. He'd hardly said two words to her since he'd apologized. An apology which, of course, she'd barely responded to. No wonder he wasn't speaking to her. But then, she'd had Lane on her mind. Not her fault.

All he said was, "See you guys later."

In Maggie's room, Helen, her face still strained with tension, lay on the wooden park bench Maggie had dragged home from a garage sale and covered with blue-checked cushions. Maggie stretched out on her stomach on her unmade bed. Her parents and brother were out, and the house was quiet except for the *smack-smack* of the rain against the windows. The smell of the popcorn she had made hung heavy in the air, and should have been appetizing. But the thought of food made her queasy.

"It was so awful," Helen said quietly. "Ghastly! The sheriff signaling to me, and all those people watching me go tell him that was my handkerchief. I felt like I was walking the plank." She let out a deep sigh. "Everyone's going to be talking about me and pointing at me in school on Monday, like I'm already wearing prison stripes and ankle chains. I'm *not* going, that's all. I can't. I'll tell Ms. Gross I have malaria and stay in bed all day. Maybe all year."

"Oh, yeah, that'll work," Maggie said dryly. Since she had no appetite, she stretched out an arm to hand the popcorn bowl to Helen. "That's the perfect way to get people to stop talking. Hide out in your house as if you really *are* guilty of something. Works every time."

Helen laughed. It wasn't much of a laugh, but it eased some of the tension in her face. "When you're right, you're right."

"Anyway," Maggie joked, glad to see Helen relax just a little, "no one's going to buy malaria. Felicity is about as far from a tropical island as you can get." Helen laughed again. Maggie hated to spoil the moment of relaxation, but she had to ask. "So, how do *you* think your hankie got into that well?"

Helen lay back against the bench, munching and studying the ceiling. "I *told* you, I don't want to discuss any of that." But in the next breath she added, "I don't know. Everyone knows I carry hankies. I'm a running joke at school for being the only teenager in the civilized world to blow my nose on linen. And a lot of people know those hankies are monogrammed, too, because Ms. Gross monograms everything. She tells everyone that no thief will steal anything that's initialed. Who would want something with the initials M.S.G. already on it?"

"Monosodium glutamate," Maggie said, rolling over onto her back.

"What?"

"That's what M.S.G. stands for. Monosodium glutamate. You know, that stuff they put in food. It makes some people sick. Allergic reaction. We read about it in science, remember?"

Helen laughed again. "What you're saying is that Ms. Gross has the same initials as something that gives people a bad rash?"

Maggie laughed, too, and once they got going, they couldn't seem to stop. They were drained and exhausted and tired of controlling their emotions. It felt good to laugh.

They laughed so hard, Helen had to get up and grab a handful of tissues from the box on Maggie's dresser. As she sat back down, swiping at her tearing eyes, she gasped, "Where's a good hankie when you need one?"

"In the well," Maggie answered, and they both shrieked with laughter.

When they finally settled down, Helen asked, "So, what happened between you and Whit? I know you didn't want to go into it with Lane there, since she's been panting after him since the very first second she saw him, but you can tell me." Sternly, she said, "What did you *do*, Maggie? He looked pretty bummed today."

Maggie explained. She had to tell someone, and Helen was her best friend.

If she had expected Helen to say, "No wonder you're mad," she was disappointed. What Helen said, looking perplexed, was, "You're mad at him because he knew Dante Guardino and Christy Miller? He already told us that, Maggie."

"No! I'm mad because he knew them a lot better than he let us think he did. And because I think he had a crush on that girl, but he wouldn't admit it."

Helen shrugged. "It's none of your business."

"That's what *he* said."

"Well, he's right." Helen paused, and then added, "Actually, Maggie, I might as well tell you, *I* knew them, too. Better than you thought I did. Christy, too. Most of the kids who came to Bransom from out in the country knew them. It's just that no one wants to talk about it now, because who wants to admit they were friends with a convicted killer?"

Curious about the girl Whit might have been infatuated with at thirteen, Maggie asked, "What was she like?"

"Christy? A champion manipulator. She could twist people around her little finger so cleverly, you didn't even realize you'd been turned into a pretzel. And her favorite form of exercise was tossing that long, blonde hair of hers. I think one reason I keep mine short is, I don't want to be like her." More seriously, Helen added, "Christy really wasn't very nice. Being pretty went to her head. I never could understand what Dante saw in her. He was so smart. But he fell for her act, and in a big way."

"So Scout and Alex, even Lane, might have known both of them better than I thought they did?"

"Beats me. They might have. We all went to different elementary schools, so I don't know for sure who knew who. Whom. Like I said, no one wants to talk about those two now."

"The thing is," Maggie said slowly, "if he really was innocent, if he didn't kill her, someone *else* did. Someone in Greene County. Maybe someone right here in Felicity. But the police wouldn't have looked for that person because Dante had already been convicted."

"What's your point?"

"My point is, that killer might still be here, Helen. Somewhere. Maybe he didn't leave after the trial. He wouldn't have had to. He got away with murder, and was perfectly safe."

"Are you deliberately trying to scare me more than I'm already scared, or is it accidental? Isn't it bad enough that Whit thinks maybe Guardino's back in town?"

"Sorry. He probably did do it. I mean, a jury convicted him, right? They must have had plenty of evidence."

"I have a super idea. Let's not talk about this anymore, okay? It's too creepy." Helen took a handful of popcorn, chewed, swallowed, then asked, "So, is Picadilly as nice inside as out?"

Maggie laughed. "Calling Picadilly 'nice' is like saying Whit isn't bad-looking. Both are masterpieces of understatement."

"Whatever. I'll bet Scout's relieved that you and Whit didn't hit it off."

Uncomfortable because she suspected Helen was right, Maggie asked, "Helen, doesn't it look like someone put your hankie into that well to make you look guilty? I mean, how obvious is that? Doesn't it make you mad?"

"Well, at first I was just scared." Helen dropped the empty popcorn bowl on the floor. "But now, yeah, I'm mad. And getting madder. Someone did me wrong and I don't know why. If Lane had been killed, the sheriff would never have let me leave. Not with Lane lying in that well dead as a doornail."

Maggie knew she was right.

After a minute or two of quiet, Maggie lifted her head. "Helen?"

"Yeah?"

"What exactly is a doornail? And how did it die? And how can we be sure it was ever really alive in the first place?"

They were off again, laughing until their sides hurt.

But sometime in the middle of the night, Maggie was awakened, shaking and sweating, by a nightmare. She was locked in the coal bin of the old courthouse, completely sealed in on all sides by thick wooden boards fastened with giant-sized nails. Every few minutes, a voice from above, deep and evil, would call down to her, "You can't come out. Your sentence isn't up yet."

Though she screamed until her throat was raw, the voice never relented and never let her out.

When she was fully awake, she wondered if Lane had at any time regained consciousness in that cold, dark well. If she had, she must have felt very much the way Maggie had while she was still deep inside the nightmare.

# Chapter 30

The following morning, even though it was Sunday, the sheriff came for Helen at ten forty-five.

Maggie and Helen, thoroughly exhausted, had just awakened. They were debating whether to get dressed before or after they ate breakfast. The debate ended when Maggie's mother knocked on the door and called out their names.

"Enter!" Maggie reached for her robe.

Her mother's expression was very serious. "Helen, I think you should get dressed. Sheriff Donovan is downstairs. He wants to talk to you."

Helen paled. "The sheriff? Do I have to?"

"Not without a lawyer," Maggie cried, a favorite television show springing to mind.

"Oh, Maggie, she doesn't need a lawyer," her mother said. "He just wants to ask her some questions, that's all. I'm sure Helen can clear things up right away."

But when they got downstairs, haphazardly

dressed in jeans and sweaters, clearing things up became complicated.

"Turns out," the sheriff said in a tone of voice that Maggie instinctively realized was deceptively nonchalant, "that someone saw you leaving the grounds of the old courthouse on Friday evening, Ms. Morgan. Saw you running from there. One of the construction workers, checking on some equipment. He's sure it was you. Said it was 'the girl with the hankie.' Now, what I'm wondering is, why you didn't volunteer that information yesterday afternoon when we found that hankie in the well."

Helen, seated beside Maggie on the plaid couch, sat with her head down, her hands folded in her lap. She said nothing.

Maggie spoke up. "If Helen says she wasn't there Friday night, then she wasn't! And you shouldn't be interrogating her like this without a lawyer."

The sheriff raised graying eyebrows at the word "interrogating." "I just want the truth, Maggie, that's all. We know she was there. It could be she saw or heard something that might help us."

Helen remained silent.

"Well," the sheriff said, holding out one hand, "maybe you could tell us if this belongs to you, too."

Maggie recognized the object in his hand right away. A wristwatch. The band was plain brown leather, the kind Helen wore. And the sheriff wouldn't have that look on his face if he didn't already know who the watch belonged to. Ms. Gross had given Helen that watch, so of course it had to have her initials on it somewhere.

Helen nodded, and reached out for the watch.

The sheriff withdrew his hand. "Nope. Can't let you have this just yet. But I bet you can guess where we found this. And it *does* belong to you, am I right?" He turned the watch over. Helen's initials were clearly visible on the smooth gold backing.

Defeat showed in her face. "Yes. Okay, yes, it's mine. And yes, I can guess where you found it, or you wouldn't be here. And yes, I *was* there Friday night." Her voice became more agitated as she spoke. "And *yes*, I *did* see something!"

"There, now," the sheriff said, leaning back in the chair, "that wasn't so hard, was it?"

"Helen," Maggie warned, "I don't think you should say any more."

Helen waved a hand. "It's okay." Her eyes on the sheriff, she began slowly, "I went out for a run. I decided to swing by the old courthouse because I hadn't found my watch yet. I'd looked everywhere else, so I figured I must have lost it during the explosion last week. It was almost dark out, but the parking lot has lights, so I thought I'd be able to see okay."

Maggie, her parents, and the sheriff were listening intently.

"But when I got there, before I could look for the watch, I heard this sound . . . I didn't know what it was then. But now I know it was a saw. I think a small power saw. My dad has one. He used it to saw broken limbs off the trees in our apple orchard when we lived in the country. It sounded just like what I heard at the courthouse that night."

"Did you see anyone?"

Helen nodded again. "But I don't know who it was," she said quickly. "I couldn't even tell if it was a woman or a man. I was too far away, and the person I saw was wearing a jacket, maybe an athletic jacket, and a baseball cap."

"Helen," Mrs. Keene asked gently, "why on earth didn't you tell the sheriff this yesterday?"

"Because he'd already found my hankie in the well!" Helen cried. "When I saw that person kneeling on the ground Friday night, I didn't know he was doing anything wrong. Or dangerous. I didn't know that until the next day, when Lane fell in the well. When I realized that was just about the spot where I'd seen the person, I knew then what he'd been up to. But that night, I just thought he was one of the workers getting ready for the ceremony."

Maggie nodded. "I would have, too."

But Helen hung her head again. "When Lane fell into that well, I knew I should have told someone what I'd seen. They'd have checked out that spot then, and she never would have fallen in. When she did, I was too ashamed to tell anyone. And then the sheriff found my hankie. I was terrified that if I told him I'd been there the night before, he'd be positive I was the one with the saw, and I was just inventing the other person to get myself off the hook."

The image of Helen armed with a power saw would have made Maggie laugh if the circumstances hadn't been so serious, and Helen weren't so scared.

"I wouldn't have thought that," the sheriff said quietly. "Not without more proof. But," he sat forward, "I'm going to need you to take a little trip down to the office with me, Ms. Morgan. You can call a lawyer first if you want, but what I mainly want from you is a description of the person you saw near the well."

"But I *told* you, I didn't really see him. I didn't want to hang around while someone else was there, and I decided it was too dark to see something as small as my watch anyway. So I left. I can't describe whoever it was."

"Well, let's just give it a try, okay? Anything you can tell us will help."

Helen didn't call a lawyer. But when she had left with the sheriff, Maggie went to the phone to call Whit. His father was a judge. He'd know what to do.

"Baseball cap? Jacket?" he asked when she had explained. "What kind of jacket?"

"I don't know," Maggie answered impatiently. "What difference does it make? So, should she have a lawyer or not?"

"No, I don't think so. Not yet. Sounds to me like the sheriff believed her story. Did she say what the baseball cap looked like? Any emblem? Team name?"

"It was dark, Whit. Why are you asking me all these questions? She *said* she didn't get a good look at the person."

"It just sounds familiar, that's all . . ." Whit's voice trailed off. "So," he asked then, "are you still mad at me?"

"I don't have time for this now," Maggie said curtly, and instantly regretted the words. But they were true, weren't they? She had to get to the courthouse. She had to be there for Helen, who had looked like she was on her way to death row when she left. "But no," she added hastily, "I'm not mad. You were right. Your . . . friendship with Christy Miller *isn't* any of my business."

"No," he said just as quickly, "I wasn't right. There wasn't any reason to hide anything. I was being a jerk. Listen, anything you want to ask me, just ask away. Honesty is the best policy, from now on, I promise."

Maggie saw an opportunity, and took it. "Okay, then. Do you *really* think Dante Guardino is back in town? And taking out his rage on the old courthouse? Since you knew him, what you think might mean something. Is that why you asked me about the jacket and cap? Is that the kind of stuff he wore?"

It took him a minute or two, but when he answered he sounded sincere. "Yeah, he did. He wore a Bransom High jacket and a Cleveland Indians baseball cap almost all the time. But I don't know what I think, Maggie. Why would he come back here?"

"I don't know. But if he was really innocent, who would have more right to hate the courthouse than him? Felicity, too. Listen, I've got to get over there with Helen. I'll call you when I get back."

And if Guardino *was* innocent, she thought, her spine tingling, there is another killer out there somewhere. Someone who got away with murder.

She didn't call Lane before she left, knowing Lane would be resting. But she tried Scout and Alex, thinking they would want to be there for Helen as much as she did. They weren't home.

"Well, you can't see her *now*," the deputy in the outer office said when Maggie asked for Helen. Her tone of voice implied that Maggie should have known better than to ask. "She's in with Sheriff Donovan."

Maggie stood her ground. "I know that. But I think she should have someone with her, and I'm her best friend. If she isn't being arrested, why can't I go in?"

"He said he wasn't to be disturbed."

"I just *told* you, it shouldn't *disturb* him if Helen has someone with her."

The deputy stood up, smoothing her tan slacks. "You got a mouth on you, don't you? No visitors, period. Run along now. Your little friend's just fine."

"My *friend* is five feet, eight inches tall!" Maggie snapped. "At least three inches taller than *you*." Then she whirled on her heel and stomped out of the office.

But she didn't leave the building. She wasn't going anywhere until she knew Helen was okay.

She found a pay phone and tried Scout again. Still no answer. Alex was home, though, and offered to join Maggie at the courthouse. "For moral support," he said.

"Okay, if you're sure you feel up to it. But find Scout first, okay? He's probably playing touch football in the park. Helen needs all the moral support she can get."

"She hasn't been arrested, has she?"

"No." Maggie quickly filled Alex in on what Helen had told the sheriff. "Of course someone stole her watch and planted it near the well, just like they planted the hankie. Hurry up, okay? I hate being here alone. The only people here on Sunday are the sheriff and one deputy."

Before he hung up, Alex asked, "Is Whittier showing up, too?"

"I don't know. I didn't ask him to, if that's what you mean. He doesn't really know Helen that well."

"Right. Okay, I'll be there as soon as I can dig up Redfern." He hung up.

While Maggie was waiting, she decided to go in search of a rest room. She would just be very careful to avoid the kitchen wing and the coal bin wing. Like Tanya said, why borrow trouble?

As she walked the dim, deserted corridors, looking left and right, she thought about Alex's last question. Why *hadn't* she asked Whit to lend moral support, too? He seemed to like Helen, and he would have driven into town if Maggie had asked.

But then, why hadn't he offered?

She was so lost in thought, she didn't hear the footsteps behind her until they were only a few feet away. When the *tap-tap* did sink in, Maggie stopped walking. Alex? Couldn't be. It would take him longer than that to drive into town. Maggie turned around, hoping to see Scout. Or maybe Whit.

But it wasn't one of her friends catching up to her in the hallway. Instead, she found herself staring directly, once again, into the black, empty eyes of Chantilly Beckwith. She was holding a thick, solid board with jagged edges in her left hand. And she wasn't smiling.

# Chapter 31

"What'd I tell you about siccing the sheriff on me?" the girl snarled, advancing toward Maggie, who began backing up along the corridor. "He was at my house again this morning, nine o'clock, yammering at me about threatening you."

"You *did* threaten me."

Chantilly's upper lip curled. "You don't have a clue how much I hate you and your snotty friends, do you? You know what? I was following you, before my hearing, thinking about asking you to take it easy on me, so I wouldn't be suspended. Everyone says you're so fair, so I thought maybe you'd listen. But you never even noticed me. It was like I didn't exist for you, you know?"

The blue car. It had been following her even *before* the bloody scale?

"I should have known you'd never help me. I don't know what I was thinking."

Emboldened by the knowledge that the sheriff

was in the building, although he was a good distance away, Maggie warned, "Stay away from me, or I'll scream this place down."

"I don't think so," a deep, harsh voice said from behind her, and a rough hand clapped itself over Maggie's mouth. It smelled like an ashtray. She knew immediately who it belonged to. James Keith, who never went anywhere without a cigarette. Chantilly had distracted her so she wouldn't hear James's footsteps coming down the hall from the opposite direction.

An arm of steel pinned Maggie's arms against her sides. Chantilly smiled, though her dark eyes held no humor. "Well, hey, Madame Foreperson," she said softly, "how would you like to see justice in action? Witness it with your very own eyes?" She raised the board over one shoulder, as if she were poised to hit a home run.

It had happened so fast, Maggie felt dazed. Almost too dazed to think. But, not quite. And instinct and indignation helped. Who did they think they were, these two barbaric thugs, threatening her? Did they really think she was just going to stand there and play helpless while they pummeled her into pulp with that board?

She was wearing heeled boots. She lifted one swiftly and brought the heel down, as hard as she could, on James Keith's left foot. He yelped in pain, and weakened his grip, just a little. Maggie took advantage of the moment to yank her left arm free and drive that elbow into his midsection with all her might.

He let out a *whoosh* of air. And let go.

Maggie ran. Chantilly, her face a startled mask of fury, was barring the way back to the sheriff's office, so Maggie had no choice. She had to run in the other direction.

She ran wildly, her legs pumping furiously, the heels of her boots pounding out a *rat-a-tat-tat* on the worn floorboards. She had no breath to spare for screaming, and instinct told her it was more important to flee than to summon help. If she didn't run fast enough, Chantilly would catch up, and by the time help arrived, it would be too late.

So she ran, fast and furiously and blindly.

Too blindly. She had no sense of where she was, wasn't aware that she had flown down corridors so fast and far that she had entered the older wing. The same older wing that housed the coal bin. The same older wing where the cave-in had taken place. The same older wing where a bass-drum-sized portion of the corridor floor was missing.

There were no barricades around the hole. Mr. Petersen, the town clerk, had not yet made up his mind that barricades were necessary. He would not decide to do so until the following Tuesday.

The floor disappeared from beneath Maggie's feet suddenly and completely. She had no time to scream. She simply fell, hard and fast, feetfirst, landing in the coal bin. The momentum of her fall drove her downward into the hill of black nuggets like a shovel, until the mountain had made a place for her in its middle.

When she came to a rest, buried in coal up to her

waist, her arms free, it took her several stunned minutes to understand what had happened. When it sank in, she realized where she was, and waited for her eyes to become accustomed to the semi-darkness. The window she had shattered with her elbow had not yet been replaced, and the opening allowed in more light than the old, dirty glass had.

That was unfortunate. Because when her dizziness had passed and her eyes had become accustomed to the dim light, what met her eyes was so shocking, so unbelievable, she stopped breathing entirely.

If her legs hadn't been hurting fiercely from her drive downward into the hill of coal, she might have convinced herself that she had struck her head as she fell and was now unconscious, that she wasn't really seeing anything at all. She was only dreaming it . . . or, rather, nightmaring it.

Because how could she be seeing what she thought she was seeing?

White — the cold, raw white of bare bone — protruding right there in front of her. And in the white bone . . . horrible, horrible . . . two empty, hollow eye sockets staring back at her as if to say, what are you doing here, this is my pile of coal, I was here first. There were cheekbones, high and angled beneath the eye sockets . . . there was a hard, unyielding bony white jaw . . . an open, grinning mouth . . .

Still not breathing, Maggie stared.

White bones and empty eye sockets and grin-

ning mouth . . . no skin . . . no flesh . . . no covering
of any kind to hide the white bone . . .

What she was looking at, what had popped up
right beside her like the feature attraction in a
haunted house at an amusement park, was a skull.

The bony, unseeing, grinning, white skull of a
person long dead.

Maggie opened her mouth then, and began
screaming.

# Chapter 32

Maggie was told later, at the hospital where she was treated for shock, that she couldn't have been in the coal bin more than a minute or two before the sheriff, the deputy, Helen, Scout, and Alex, who had just arrived, heard her screams and followed the sound to the coal bin. There, they found James Keith and Chantilly Beckwith cowering in the hallway above Maggie's head, staring downward into the bin, their mouths open, their eyes blank with horror.

They were arrested the minute Maggie had been taken away in an ambulance.

At the hospital, she was given a very strong sedative and kept overnight. She awoke several times, screaming.

She was allowed to go home the following morning, but was advised not to go to school that day. "Rest and quiet," the doctor ordered, and Maggie was far too shaken and sore to argue with him.

When Alex, Helen, and Lane came to visit her that afternoon, she flatly refused to talk about what had happened. Couldn't. Impossible. She hadn't accepted it, couldn't, and struggled to convince herself that it was all just a terrible nightmare.

Her mother said gently that it would be better if Maggie came to terms with it. "Then you can put it behind you, sweetie."

Maggie thought that was a crock, and said so.

And her mother said, "I suppose you're probably wondering . . . who . . . who it was."

Maggie wasn't wondering any such thing. Because in order to wonder that, she first had to admit that the bony-white, nightmarish thing in the coal bin with her had once been a living person. No way was she ready to do that.

She just wouldn't think about it.

So she slept all day, and when the trio arrived, she said, "We can talk about anything you want except *that*. Don't even think about bringing it up. Where's Scout?"

Helen sighed and sat down on the foot of the bed. "At the bus station. His father has arranged for his mom to go to rehab. In California. Twenty-one days. She refuses to fly, so Scout had to get her a bus ticket."

"He's going to bunk with me while she's gone," Alex said.

Maggie didn't know what to say. That's awful? That's great? Wasn't it both? It was awful that Mrs. Redfern needed to go, but it was great that she'd finally agreed to get help. Maybe when she came back, life in Scout's house would improve.

"Don't say anything to him about it," Alex warned. "He doesn't want anyone to know. He only told me because he needed a place to stay. And I told them," waving toward Lane and Helen, "and you, so no one would ask him why he's staying at my house."

"What I want to know," Helen said to Maggie, "is if you're okay. I feel bad that this happened because you were hanging around the courthouse waiting to lend me moral support. That's what the deputy told me. Are you okay?"

Was she? No, probably not. But she could pretend that she was. She could do that. Maybe she could even fool herself.

The sheriff had visited that morning, asking her only about Chantilly and James. Maggie had given him the details of their threatening visit, and he had taken notes. When he left, he said he would see to it that they gave her no more trouble. She believed that he meant it. But she didn't see how he could promise that unless he was willing to keep the two of them in jail forever. Or at least until Maggie left for college.

When asked, Helen said that the sheriff had been "nice" to her yesterday morning, not treating her like a criminal or anything. But she felt bad that she hadn't been able to give him a description of the person wielding the saw at the old courthouse.

Lane seemed to be okay, although her right cheek was bruised a little, and she moved stiffly, as if she'd overdone a workout.

Scout arrived, looking very tired. Maggie felt sorry for him, but she kept Alex's warning in mind, and didn't ask him where he'd been. He held her hand and asked her if Whit had been to see her.

"No," she said truthfully, and Scout looked relieved.

But ten minutes after they had all left, the doorbell rang again, and a minute or so after that, there was a knock on Maggie's open bedroom door. When she looked up, Whit was standing in the doorway, a fat bouquet of golden autumn flowers filling a glass vase in his hands. "Your mom's vase," he said as he entered the room. "But the flowers are from the garden at Picadilly. They're mums."

"I know what they are," she said. "We wear them for Homecoming."

Her bedside table was too cluttered for the vase, so he set it down on her desk, then moved to stand beside her bed. "I heard what happened. You okay?"

"Sit," she said, pointing to the chair Scout had vacated not ten minutes earlier. "Yep, I'm okay. I guess." Pretending to him didn't seem like such a good idea, after her hissy fit about *his* lack of honesty. "It was pretty grim. Chantilly and James scared ten years off my life. I felt really helpless at first. He came up behind me and there she was in front of me with that board . . ." To her horror, tears sprang to Maggie's eyes. She was mortified, and turned away to hide them.

But Whit reached out and turned her face back toward him, saying, "It's okay. Shedding a couple of tears doesn't make you helpless, Maggie." Keeping his hand on her cheek, he said, "And you can avoid talking about that nasty business in the coal bin all you want, but it happened." He handed her a tissue from the box on her table. "I can't believe how wrong I was."

"Wrong?" She swiped quickly at her eyes. "About what?"

His eyes regarded her carefully. "You don't know? You haven't heard?"

Feeling unsteady, Maggie sank lower in her bed, clutching the edge of the comforter as if it might balance her. "I don't *want* to hear it," she said angrily. "Whatever it is, don't tell me. It won't kill me not to know, will it? So don't tell me. Not now. Next month, maybe, or next year . . . "

He took one of her hands in both of his. "You need to know this. Quit pretending you don't have the guts to hear it. And quit pretending that you don't know what I was wrong about. We both know you do."

Maggie thought about ripping her hand out of his and clapping both her hands over her ears. But she knew he was right. It was silly and childish to keep pretending. It didn't do any good anyway. It wouldn't change anything that was real. "What were you wrong about?" she asked, although she already knew the answer. She hadn't guessed it in the coal bin because she hadn't been thinking then, not thinking at all. But later, in the hospital . . .

"I was wrong about Dante coming back here."

She looked at him then. "He never left, did he?"

Whit shook his head. "No. They think he tried. His cell door had been jimmied. But something went wrong. Maybe the coal chute window was locked from the outside and he couldn't get it open without breaking the glass and rousing a guard. Or maybe he was climbing up the chute and fell backward, into the bin. Hit his head or something. We won't know that until the medical examiner has done his thing."

"How do they know it's him?"

"Dental records. They went to his mother, then to his dentist, right here in town. It's Dante, all right. No question."

"Your friend."

Whit nodded. "My friend." Still holding Maggie's hand, he leaned back in his chair. "It's weird, you know? I hadn't seen him in so long, but as long as I knew he was out there, I figured there was always this little bit of hope that something would happen to clear him, and he could come back to town someday. Now . . ." He shook his head, his brown eyes bleak.

"Well, this is weird, too," Maggie said, "but I was just thinking, if it weren't for James and Chantilly, we might never have known that Dante didn't escape. If they hadn't come at me like that, I wouldn't have run, and I wouldn't have fallen into the coal bin. The courthouse would have been torn down, cemented over, and no one would ever have known." She laughed without humor. "Hard to believe we have something to thank those two for, but isn't it better to know what happened to Dante?"

"That's just it," Whit said, frowning, "we *don't* know what happened to him."

"Well, I meant . . . "

"I know. But it bothers me, not knowing. Dante was athletic, and he was smart. If he'd really wanted to get away, I think he could have. What stopped him?"

"If he was innocent . . . " she began, but he interrupted her.

"If he was innocent, he wouldn't have tried to escape. Looks like I was wrong about that, too. Let's not talk about it anymore, okay?" He hitched his chair closer to the bed. "So," he said, smiling at her, "are we okay now? You've forgiven me?"

"I don't know. I've been kind of busy lately, you know? Preoccupied, you might say. Haven't had much time to think about who I'm mad at and who I've forgiven. Except, of course, for James and Chantilly. I'm pretty sure about that one."

"You're avoiding the subject at hand again. Are you going to look at me or not?"

Maggie turned to him. They talked for a while, carefully avoiding certain subjects. Whit said that although his mother liked Picadilly, she disliked the country, which was why they spent so much time in Cleveland. "They argue about it a lot," he confided. "But I figure, if that's the worst I have to deal with, I'll survive. Everybody has something. I mean, Helen's parents are off in Egypt, Lane's father lost their farm, Scout's parents are splitsville, and Alex's dad died. So," he asked Maggie, "what's your deal?"

She laughed, almost bitterly. "You won't believe this," she said, "but my deal *was* boredom. I mean heavy-duty, no-holds-barred, terminal boredom. Nothing ever happened here, and I couldn't wait to get out of Felicity. Now, I still want to get out of here, but it's not because I'm bored, it's because I'm scared."

"I guess you'd settle for being bored again, am I right?"

"You are so right."

She saw no need to explain then that kissing him was not the way to boredom, as he seemed to think it was. She'd set him straight later. Or not.

# Chapter 33

I hate her, I hate her, I *hate* her! She's ruined everything!

I can't believe this has happened. It was all set, all finished, the plans canceled, the building about to be destroyed, once and for all. I'd done what I set out to do. And I'd never been so relieved in all my life.

And now *this*! Everything I went through destroyed, useless, a waste of time and risk, all because of her. I was almost caught sawing through that well cover . . . some runner, couldn't see who it was. That would have ruined everything. Maybe it *was* overkill. But I needed one last thing, just one, to make sure the WOH didn't change their minds again. And it worked perfectly, thanks to the very detailed plans and charts at their own offices. I knew exactly what I was doing.

This is just the worst. But I should be fair here. It wasn't really *her* fault. It was *theirs*, Alice Ann, better known as "Chantilly" — stupid name — and that Neanderthal, James. If they hadn't attacked her in that hallway, she wouldn't have run. And if she hadn't run, she wouldn't have fallen into the coal bin.

The coal bin . . . god, I can't believe my filthy luck!

It'll all come out now. Bound to. I have to leave now. Long before I was planning to. What choice do I have, if I don't want to spend the rest of my life where Dante almost spent his?

But first, I have one more thing to do. Make that three. Three things. I'm not leaving here without paying all three of them back for ruining everything, when I had worked so hard to protect myself. God, I tried so *hard*! And I almost made it.

I don't have much time. I'll have to hurry.

I feel like killing all three of them.

The last time I felt like killing someone, I picked up a tire iron and did it.

Why did they have to go and ruin it all?

Just . . . like . . . Christy.

# Chapter 34

*The nondescript blue sedan travels along a dark country road, weaving on the blacktop to avoid deep puddles left by recent rain. Inside the car, the girl driving, who has black hair stiffened with gel and sticking out about her head like spokes on a bicycle wheel, is laughing at something the short, burly boy beside her has said. They are so lost in their hilarity that they don't see the headlights of a car approaching from the rear until it is less than two car lengths behind them.*

*Its lights are too bright.*

*"Hey, what the hell . . . ?" the girl cries out, only angry at this point, not frightened, because she believes she has nothing to be afraid of, and because she doesn't frighten easily. She believes that after what she saw sticking up out of that coal bin in the old courthouse, it would take a lot to scare her now.*

*Well, maybe not so much. Like most bullies, she*

*is truly brave only when she's doing the attacking. So maybe it doesn't take more than a few hard thumps to her rear bumper to make her heart pound in her chest and make her hands shake on the steering wheel. The blows send her car skidding dangerously close to the deep, overflowing culvert beside the road.*

*"Cut it out!" she screams, hunching over the wheel and holding on tighter. Then, "James? What's he doing back there?"*

*But before James can figure out what the girl wants from him, the car behind them suddenly pulls out around them, its left wheels riding on the berm because the road is narrow.*

*The girl says with relief, "Oh, good, he's passing!"*

*But he doesn't pass. He travels alongside of them for thirty seconds or so, then, just as the girl has decided that if she slows down he'll pass them, the driver of the other car whips the steering wheel viciously to the left and slams into the side of the blue car with full force.*

*There is nothing the girl can do. The road is slick, the tires of her car old and smooth.*

*The nondescript blue sedan skids to the left, sliding wildly like a sled on hard-packed snow. The two left tires slam into a completely submerged stone barrier, hitting it hard. The car flips over, into the flooded culvert, landing upside down in the water.*

*The other car slows, but doesn't stop. It hesitates,*

*engine running, just long enough to make certain that no one climbs up over the embankment to safety.*

*No one does.*

*With a satisfied shifting of gears, the predatory car speeds away, its taillights glowing a triumphant red on the dark country road.*

# Chapter 35

She stayed home from school again on Tuesday. They had no peer jury hearings scheduled, and she was having serious trouble sleeping. She wondered if she would ever close her eyes again without seeing that grinning, hollow-eyed skull lying beside her on her pillow.

Dante's picture was in the paper on Tuesday. It wasn't a very good picture. He was wearing the Bransom High jacket and baseball cap Whit had told her about, and the cap cast shadows over his face. But she thought he was very good-looking. She also thought he looked familiar, and then realized he looked a little like Whit. Same bone structure. Not quite as gorgeous, of course. But almost.

Wednesday, they were supposed to begin emptying out the few remaining items in the offices of the old courthouse. She had promised Ms. Gross. And she was foreperson. Unless she wanted to resign that position — maybe hand over the reins to Scout — she had to help.

"You're not going over there," Lane said in disbelief when Maggie talked to her on the phone Tuesday night. "I don't believe you! After what happened to you? It had to be ten thousand times worse than what happened to me. How *can* you, Maggie?"

"I have to. If I don't, I'll be running from shadows my whole life. I'll just steer clear of the two damaged wings, that's all. Anyway, they took that ... Dante ... out of there. Mrs. Guardino is arranging for a memorial service. I wonder if anyone will go?"

"Whit will. Probably Scout, too, and maybe Alex. Helen won't. She isn't helping with the moving stuff, either. I just talked to her, and she says no way. Neither is Alex."

"Are you?"

"If you are, I am. My mother will have a fit, though. Maybe I'd better not tell her exactly where we're going to be this afternoon. What she doesn't know can't hurt her, right? If she finds out I went within ten feet of that place, she'll ground me till I'm ninety-six."

"It's going to be a grubby job. I'm wearing the oldest, rattiest clothes I own." Maggie asked Lane if the sheriff had come up with any news about the well cover.

"Nope. Not as far as I know, anyway." Lane paused, then added, "You don't think it was Helen?"

Maggie gasped. "Lane! You told Helen you knew it wasn't her. Were you lying?"

"I wasn't really lying. She was so upset, I was just trying to make her feel better until we knew more, that's all. She could have done it, Maggie. She's strong enough to handle a small power saw. And you were there when she shouted how she hated the old courthouse. Why not Helen? She always wanted it torn down. Always."

"Well, the sheriff doesn't agree with you." Maggie heard the hostility in her voice. But how *could* Lane? Helen was one of her best friends. Maybe that tumble into the well had jumbled Lane's brain. "Or he wouldn't have let Helen go."

"He might just need more proof. But I didn't say she did it, Maggie, so don't get all defensive on me. I just said she could have."

"So could more than fourteen thousand other people in Greene County. It wasn't Helen."

It did seem weird, Maggie thought as she hung up, that Helen had waited so long to admit that she knew Dante well. Just like Whit. Maybe that was why Helen had defended Whit's right to privacy. Maybe she was really talking about herself.

Maggie had half expected her mother to change her mind about canceling the committee's plans, but Sheila Keene was adamant. "No way. Absolutely not. I know a lost cause when I see one. We've already begun negotiations for that old warehouse downtown, and I have big plans for it. No, Otis Bransom can rest easy in his grave now. His old house is about to do the same."

I wish I could be sure that would make a difference, Maggie thought as she left her own house. But I don't. Not anymore. Whatever was going on in Felicity, it wasn't because Sheila Keene and her WOH had planned to restore the old Bransom place to its former glory. If that were the reason, Lane Bridgewater wouldn't have fallen into that well, because that had happened *after* the plans had already been canceled.

Then *what*?

Maggie knew the minute she arrived on campus that something was up. There were always a few kids lingering near the wide stone steps, reluctant to go inside. But on this gray, cool morning, there was a throng. As she parked the van, she could almost hear the buzz of gossip. She didn't think it could be about her. Her horror in the coal bin was two days old. Hardly news.

Something else was going on.

What *now*?

Her friends were already there, standing at the foot of the steps. Helen pushed her way through the crowd when she saw Maggie advancing. "You'll never guess!" she cried, grabbing Maggie's arm to pull her back toward the others. "You haven't heard or you'd have a different expression on your face. Maybe joy, although I guess that's kind of gross. But I wouldn't blame you."

"What? Helen, what's going on?"

Helen grabbed Maggie's hand and half dragged her back to the others. They looked up when Maggie squeezed through to stand with them. "Did you tell her?" Scout asked Helen.

"Nope. But I'm about to." She turned to Maggie, her eyes glinting. "Guess whose car went off Nestegg Road last night and landed upside down in that culvert along Hansen Creek? Which, by the way, was overflowing because of the rain."

"Oh, god, who?" Not someone she knew well or cared about a lot, Maggie guessed that much, or Helen's face would look pale and drawn instead of healthy with color.

"Chantilly Beckwith's. And James Keith was with her. They're in the hospital. Both of them."

Aware even in her shock that all eyes around her were watching to see how she reacted, Maggie sagged back against the black iron railing. Her voice, when it came, was husky with disbelief. "In the hospital? I thought they were in jail."

"They were. But they got out on bail. Anyway," Helen went on, "guess what they found in her car?"

"What?"

"Black construction paper. The kind someone used to make that blindfold on your creepy little doll. And rope, like the hangman's noose around its throat. And a saw. But," Helen added quickly, "not a power saw. Just an ordinary handsaw. Perfectly capable, though, of sawing that gavel into alphabet blocks."

"I heard," Alex said, "that they also found copies of diagrams of the old courthouse, including the grounds. They were wet, from the creek, so the sheriff won't know for sure until they dry out. Even then, he'll probably have to get an expert to look at them. But I'll bet that's what they were. That's how they knew about the well."

Maggie said nothing. She was picturing that white-faced, black-haired girl — the girl Helen claimed had been shy and quiet once upon a time — and burly, angry James Keith — who had hated the peer jury, especially its foreperson — upside down in an overflowing ditch of cold, muddy water. "Are they going to be okay?"

"I guess so. But if Whit hadn't come along and yanked them out of that ditch, it'd be all over for them."

"Whit saved them?"

"Yep. He's a hero." Helen made a face. "Sort of. I mean, it's not like we'd all be weeping buckets if they'd died, right?"

"Helen!"

"Well, it's true. Anyway," Helen declared triumphantly, "it's all over! The sheriff thinks they're responsible for all of it, everything, including the doll and the gavel and the scale. They were at the bazaar, both of them, and probably stole the scale then, after the explosion that *they* caused."

"Did he say why?" Maggie asked slowly, trying to think clearly.

"Why what?"

"Did he say why they would do all those things?"

Helen frowned, and exchanged a confused glance with Lane. "Because they were mad at the peer jury, Maggie, of course! They targeted you because you're foreperson, and they tried to get the rest of us in the basement. They saw us go down there, remember? One, or maybe both of them, followed us into the basement and kicked at that beam. James wouldn't have had to kick very hard. And the explosion was meant to take you out. If you ask me, they probably thought the rest of us would be working in the kitchen with you, too. Since we're your friends. And even if we weren't, we were sure to be around somewhere. They were probably hoping they'd get two or three of us instead of just you."

"And the well? What about the well?"

"Same deal. They knew we'd be there. Maybe one of us would fall in, maybe we wouldn't. But it was worth a try. And it worked, didn't it? They got Lane. Except they didn't know the well had been filled in, so she's okay. That must have really ticked them off."

"What happened out at Hansen Creek?"

"What do you mean, what happened?"

"I mean, how did the accident happen?"

"I guess they were going too fast. The road was wet, the car skidded, and ended up in the creek upside down. They were trapped inside, and would have drowned if it hadn't been for Whit."

A bell rang, and people began moving up the steps. "So," Helen added blithely, "you don't have to be afraid to go back inside that courthouse now, Maggie. James and Chantilly can't hurt us from their hospital beds. Alex and I have decided to help with the moving stuff now. Now that it's safe. Must be a big relief to you. You're the one they hated the most."

But, though Maggie waited for the news to wash over her and remove every last ounce of anxiety, it didn't happen.

Whit had just arrived, out of breath, his hair windblown, when Maggie stopped walking and turned to Helen to ask, "Okay, I get that Chantilly and James did the gavel and the doll and the scale. But the other stuff — the cave-in and the explosion and the well — that doesn't seem like their speed. I mean, it was sheer luck that no one died, and I never thought of those two as killers. Does the sheriff think they did those things, too?"

Helen looked baffled. "I don't know. But of course they did them. Who else?"

Maggie didn't know. "And none of it had any-thing to do with Dante Guardino?"

Lane gasped. "Dante?"

Scout put an arm around Maggie's shoulders and said, "You're just thinking that way because of what happened to you. I don't blame you. James and Chantilly chased you through that hall, and then you fell, and then there was Dante, in the coal bin. So it makes sense that you'd connect them with him. But that's silly, Maggie. James always lived in town. And he and Dante wouldn't have hung around together here at school. They weren't the same type at all."

"Maybe Alice Ann . . . Chantilly knew Dante."

"She didn't," Helen said. "She was never in 4-H. You're reaching, Maggie, and you know it. Why can't you just relax and be glad those two aren't in any shape to chase you down any more halls or send you nasty presents?"

"Anyway," Alex added, "that Dante thing, whatever it was, happened a long time ago, Maggie. It couldn't have anything to do with what's been going on in Felicity lately."

Maggie wasn't so sure. And when she glanced over at Whit, who hadn't seemed to notice Scout's arm draped across her, she knew he wasn't sure, either. He was frowning, and had the same faraway look she remembered from the night at Picadilly, when Christy Miller's name had come up. Was he thinking the same thing she was?

*You don't even know what that is,* her inner voice responded. *You don't know what you're thinking, so how could you talk to Whit about it? You'd sound stupid, so forget it.*

She tried. And through a day of classes and people coming up to her in the hall to commiserate with her about her gruesome experience in the coal bin, which Maggie refused to talk about, she managed to keep Dante Guardino off her mind. So that by the end of the day, when they had all changed into old sweats and sneakers and were on their way across the street to begin the moving process, she could actually look at the old courthouse building without her heart racing and her palms sweating. That . . . thing in the coal bin, which she refused to think of as ever having been a person, was gone. Nothing to fear there. And now there was no chance of James or Chantilly confronting her, threatening her in the hallways. For the first time in what seemed like a very long while, she could walk into the building thinking of it only as a tired old wreck long past its prime.

Maybe Helen was right. Though James and Chantilly hadn't seemed like killers, they had come at Maggie in that hallway with a board that had certainly looked lethal enough to her.

Deciding that Helen was right was comforting. Because if Helen was right about James and Chantilly, then she was also right about everything being okay now.

"It does deserve to be put to rest," Maggie commented calmly, her eyes regarding the building as they all trooped up the stone walkway to the front entrance. "It's been around a long time, and it's served Felicity well, I guess. I'm glad they're going to tear it down."

"Like who isn't?" Helen and Alex said at the same time.

"My mother, maybe," Maggie answered. "But she'll get over it. She's already got her eye on an old warehouse down here somewhere. Let's just hope no one objects to the WOH remodeling *that*."

It did feel different inside. Maybe because, with James and Chantilly in the hospital, there was no longer any reason to be afraid. Or maybe because the sun was shining so brightly outside, streaming in through the long, narrow windows upstairs in the law library, warming the huge, chilly room where they began working. Maggie, Alex, and

Helen climbed up tall, rolling library ladders to strip the shelves of thick, dusty volumes, dropping them into large, wheeled canvas bins that sat below them on the hardwood floor. Scout, Lane, and Whit manned the bins, and would wheel them out of the building and through the alleyway to the new courthouse, where everything was ready except the unfinished fourth floor. Since the third floor housing the new law library had been completed, they had been given the go-ahead to transport the books that hadn't been boxed already.

Alex had brought a portable CD player. He turned the music on, and they all got to work.

They had only intended to work for an hour or so. But they were making such steady progress, they lost sight of the time, until Maggie suddenly realized that the windows were darkening. The sun was disappearing, the light fading rapidly. She glanced at her watch. Five-thirty. It was getting dark. Safe or not, she really wasn't keen on being in this place at night.

When she pointed out the time and asked Helen to switch on the overhead light, Whit pointed to three full bins sitting at the foot of Maggie's ladder. "We'll take these over," he said, "and bring the empty carts back. Won't take more than half an hour to unload. Then we'll come back here and we can all go grab something to eat. My treat."

Everyone agreed to that plan. Even Scout, who didn't like being dictated to.

The trio was just about to leave with their carts

when the sheriff asked from the doorway, "Anyone know why someone might want to send Keith and his girlfriend into that culvert?"

Startled, their heads shot up to stare at him.

"Excuse me?" Maggie said, turning around on her ladder so that her back was to the rungs. "What did you say? Alex, turn the music down."

The room grew quiet.

The sheriff marched on into the room. "I asked you if you knew any reason why someone might want to kill those two."

"Kill?" Helen echoed. "It was an accident. And they didn't die."

"No, but they could have, if it hadn't been for Whittier. And there wasn't anything accidental about it. They were shoved into that culvert by another car. Maybe a truck. We're checkin' out the paint now. Black or dark blue, looks like. I figured, since those two been givin' all of you a hard time," glancing at Maggie and adding, " 'specially you, Maggie, you might know somethin' about how this happened."

"Well, we don't," Helen said tartly, "and frankly, Sheriff, I'm getting a little tired of being accused of things I didn't do."

He waved a hand. "Yeah, I know, Miss. But the thing is, what we've got here is attempted murder, pure and simple." He laughed shortly. "Not that there's ever anything pure *or* simple about most murders. But that's what this is, for sure." His eyes swept the group. "So none of you can help me out here?"

They all solemnly shook their heads.

He nodded. "Okay, then. I'll let you know what kind of car the culprit was driving."

When he had gone, the library echoed with a resounding silence. And Maggie knew why. It wasn't just the news that the two had been attacked deliberately, that it hadn't been an accident. It was that everything had changed again, so swiftly, when they least expected it. They had planned, as they would on any ordinary day, to finish up here and then go eat, probably pizza, just like they used to before all of this stuff began. Because they had thought it was all finished. Even she had finally decided that Helen was right, and they were safe now.

Wrong.

Someone had tried to kill Chantilly Beckwith and James Keith. They might have done the attacking before, with Maggie as their victim. But this time, *they'd* been the victims, which changed everything. It meant there was someone *else* out there who meant people harm. No one knew who that someone was, so that "someone" could walk freely about Felicity without anyone stopping them. No one was safe. No one at all.

# Chapter 36

"I don't know why you're all looking so surprised," Alex said into the silence. "Who had more enemies in this town than Chantilly and James? They were involved in a lot of things they shouldn't have been, and I'd bet they knew some pretty creepy characters. They made one of them mad, that's all. No surprise there."

Lane seized on that. "He's right. It doesn't have anything to do with us. The sheriff only asked us because those two had been bothering us lately, that's all. And whoever went after them is probably long gone by now, back to whatever grungy little hole they crawled out of."

Even Whit nodded. Looking up at Maggie, still on her ladder, he said, "I think they're right. It figures." He frowned then. "I just hope the sheriff doesn't take a good look at *my* car. It's in the parking lot outside. It's black. When I came up on that car in the ditch, I stopped too fast. The road was wet. I skidded and broadsided a tree. I haven't had time to take it to a body shop yet, so the scraped paint is still there."

"You didn't say anything about having an accident," Lane said.

"He didn't say anything about saving James and Chantilly, either," Maggie said defensively. "You already knew it when I got here. Someone else told you."

Whit sent her a grateful smile. "It wasn't an accident. I told you, I just skidded and scratched the car on a tree, that's all. But I'm not so sure the sheriff will see it that way."

"Did you file a report?" Scout asked.

Whit sighed. "How many times do I have to say it wasn't a big deal?"

"Okay," Scout said, turning to grip the canvas cart filled with books. "But the sheriff might make a big deal out of it." As he moved away, pushing the cart, he added over his shoulder, "Everyone knows you'd do anything to protect Maggie. And those two had threatened her."

Maggie was stunned for the second time in ten minutes. Scout's comment about Whit protecting Maggie had been said so matter-of-factly, as if Scout had completely accepted it. She hadn't even had a chance to talk to him yet, to explain that while he was still her good friend, what she felt for Whit was very different. She had meant to. It seemed only fair. But then, she'd been distracted lately. . . .

Scout must have figured it out for himself. He

wasn't stupid. And he sounded as if he were okay with it. That would be nice. One less thing to worry about. If there was one thing she didn't need right now, it was more bad stuff to worry about. She had plenty. Of course, so did Scout. Maybe that's why he wasn't willing to waste any more energy on her.

"I think," Helen said clearly, "that right now, we should just go ahead with what we were doing. Lane and Whit are right. What happened to James and Chantilly doesn't have anything to do with us. So I'm going to go wash up . . . Alex, you coming? Maggie? . . . and then when Lane and Whit and Scout come back from the new courthouse, I'm going to go stuff my face, because I deserve it after working this hard." And without waiting for Alex or Maggie, she left the room.

Maggie, still trying to comprehend how quickly she had lost the sense of safety she'd been feeling, said, "You can't take those carts over now. It's too dark out."

"We can see." Whit reached down to rearrange the top layer of books in his cart. "There's plenty of light from this building, and from the windows of the new building. Besides, we know our way through that alley by heart now, don't we, Lane? We could walk it in our sleep."

They wheeled their carts to the door. In the doorway, Whit turned to call to Maggie, "Aren't you going with Helen?"

Maggie had been repeating under her breath, "Helen's right, she's right, nothing to do with us, nothing, we're fine, we're fine . . . " To Whit, she said, "Sure. I will, in a sec. I just have another handful of books up here. I don't want to leave the shelf unfinished. But I'm going, I promise. Can't eat pizza with filthy hands."

"Alex, you stay with her until she leaves," Whit ordered. "Keep an eye on her, okay?"

Alex nodded. "Sure. Relax, Whit. Go, go! We can't eat until you get back." He turned the music on again, and went back to work on the bottom shelves.

Pushing his cart, Whit followed Lane out of the room.

Maggie turned around to reach for the last few books. "So," she called down to Alex, "you think James and Chantilly ticked off some bad characters?"

"Looks that way. And like I said, we shouldn't be surprised."

"Well, we weren't expecting the sheriff to come in and hit us with that news, Alex. I was just beginning to relax. Should have known better," she added.

"Quit worrying, Maggie. Your hair will turn gray."

They worked to music for a while, then Maggie called, "You said you weren't going to help with this, Alex, and I know it wasn't because you were afraid, the way Helen and I were. Why did you change your mind?"

Alex didn't answer her. She decided he couldn't hear her over the music and repeated her question, louder this time. He didn't answer.

"Alex? You still down there?"

Silence.

Maggie's hand, on its way to the shelf, paused in midair. "Alex?"

Before she could turn around to see where he was, the lights went out. Every light . . . the overhead light, the lights on the tables far below Maggie, the light in the glass display case.

The room was so dark, Maggie could no longer see her own hand.

Her voice rose as she called Alex's name again then again, and again, until she was shouting.

The music clicked off suddenly. And then, *"He's not he-ere!"* a falsetto voice sang out from far below Maggie. *"He had something really important to do. Wanta go for a ride?"*

Maggie clutched at the top rungs of the ladder. "No!" she shouted, "no!" Her heart skipped a beat.

But her cry went unheeded. The ladder shook slightly as hands far below Maggie seized it . . . and pushed . . . hard.

Maggie was nearly jolted off as the tall, wooden ladder flew from the middle of the wall to the far end, where it slammed with a thud into the corner bookshelves, empty now. An arrow of pain stabbed Maggie's left shoulder as it hit. Before she could recover, the ladder shook again, and this time it sailed from the left corner all the way down the long, shelf-lined wall to the opposite corner, slamming into the shelves there with a sharp, cracking sound. This time, her right side took the blow.

Maggie screamed Helen's name, then Alex's, then she screamed again, "Stop! Stop it!"

A falsetto laugh rang out below her. Then the ladder was in motion again, racing down the wall. It was going so fast, Maggie knew that when it hit, it would hit hard. She might not be able to hold on this time.

She was up too far. If she fell . . .

Her only chance was to move down the ladder, lessen the height from which she was almost certain to fall if her tormentor didn't stop. And she didn't think he planned to stop.

She tried. But descending a speeding ladder wasn't easy.

Where was Helen? Where was Alex?

She managed to lower herself by one rung before she hit the wall again, her shoulder and left side taking a brutal blow against the wooden shelves jutting forward.

*"Back and forth, back and forth,"* the falsetto voice sang, *"isn't this fun, Maggie?"*

It knew her name. It . . . that thing below . . . torturing her . . . making her dizzy and sick and certain that she was going to fall to her death any second now. It knew her name.

"Stop it!" Maggie screamed. "Just stop it! Why are you *doing* this?"

*"Because you were bad, Maggie. You were very, very bad. You spoiled everything for me. Now you have to be punished. Getting tired of holding on, are you? Of course you are. It's hard to keep holding on*

*when everything is going wrong, isn't it? Boy, don't I know it! Here we go, one more time . . . !"*

Maggie made it down another rung during the flight from one end of the wall to the other, but she was so sick and dizzy, she knew the evil voice below her was right. She couldn't hold on much longer.

This time, when she hit, the impact knocked her sideways, her feet, her legs leaving the ladder and swinging in midair above the floor. If her hands hadn't maintained their death grip on the third rung from the top, she'd have fallen. But her body weight was tugging on her arms, and her shoulders were on fire.

"Stop!" she gasped. "Stop, please!"

*"Can't,"* the falsetto voice answered. *"Can't do that. Why don't you just let go? I mean, I don't have a lot of time here, Maggie. I want this to end now, so I can split before it's too late. Come on,"* teasing, cajoling, *"just let go, okay?"*

"No!" she screamed. "No!" She couldn't see a thing. She was operating on instinct alone. She swung her legs to the left, got one foot back on the ladder, then the other. Pulled her body sideways, threw it against the ladder. She was back on. But she was still too high up.

A shout. No longer playful. Angry. *"Let go!"*

"Never!"

This time, the push alone took Maggie's breath away. Too exhausted to attempt climbing down one more rung, she braced herself instead for the blow.

"Maggie?" Lane's voice, from the doorway. "Why

are the lights out? Who's in here with you? What's going on?"

Then, though Maggie heard no footsteps, there was the sound of a door slamming shut off to her left. The side door. Someone had just left?

The lights went on just as Maggie slammed into the far wall. Because of the speed of the ladder, this was the harshest blow of all, and she screamed in pain as her body hit.

But the ladder stopped then.

Gasping with relief but determined not to cry, Maggie sagged against the ladder, her body trembling violently, her head against a rung.

Lane ran over to stand below her. "Maggie, where's Helen? And Alex? What's been going on in here? Are you okay? Should I come up and get you? Whit is going to *kill* Alex for leaving you in here alone."

Maggie lifted her head. "Please don't say *kill*," she said, almost laughing, but knowing that if she started, she wouldn't be able to stop. "I'm coming down now. I am coming down."

But she couldn't move. Her hands were frozen to the ladder rung, and refused to obey her command to let go.

Lane, understanding, was about to climb up to help her when Helen entered the room, and a second or two later, Whit and Scout. Though they had no idea what had happened, one look at Maggie was enough to realize that she was desperately in need of help.

"I'll go," Whit called. He sprinted the width of

the room and was halfway up the ladder before anyone could argue.

While Lane was filling Helen and Scout in on what little she knew, Whit stood just below Maggie, speaking in a quiet, reassuring voice, repeating over and over again, "You're okay, you're okay, just let go and start backing down. I'm right here, I won't let you fall. Trust me, Maggie."

And although the only thing her dazed mind was sure of was that she trusted *no one* and *nothing* at that moment, the voice worked its magic, and after what seemed to those waiting at the foot of the ladder to be a very long time, Maggie peeled her hands off the rung and began a long, painful descent. Whit stayed so close to her, they looked like one person climbing down.

The minute Maggie's feet hit the floor, her knees buckled. Whit caught her on one side, Scout on the other. Thus supported, Maggie gasped, "Where's Alex? He was here, and — " glancing around — "now he's not. Where *is* he?"

They found him beneath a long, rectangular wooden table against one wall. He was unconscious, but there was no blood. When he came to, a few minutes later, he rubbed the back of his head, but couldn't remember what had happened. "I never saw a thing," he said in a dazed voice.

Whit called an ambulance from the sheriff's office downstairs. Maggie had to tell her story three times before the sheriff and his deputy were certain of the details. She was careful to repeat her attacker's quote about "splitting." She thought it might be important. But as far as what had happened to Alex, she knew nothing.

"I didn't hear anything, I didn't see anything. I had my back turned away from Alex, and the music was loud. All I know is, when I called Alex, he didn't answer. And then I was off on my little ride," Maggie told her friends while they were on their way to the hospital.

"Goodman will be okay," Scout told her. "The paramedics said it didn't look like a fracture. Maybe a concussion. They probably won't even keep him overnight. He's going to feel really lousy, though, when he finds out what happened to you."

"Then let's not tell him."

"Have to," Whit said grimly. "He might have seen something, heard something . . . we have to know who did this, Maggie. And why."

"He said I was bad," she said quietly. "He had this funny, tinny, high falsetto voice, not his real voice, of course, and he told me he was doing it because I was bad."

"Did he say anything else?" Helen asked from the backseat of Scout's Jeep.

"Yes," Maggie answered after thinking for a minute. "He said he had to leave. To split, and that I was keeping him from doing that."

"You were keeping him from leaving the courthouse by not dying?" Scout asked angrily.

"I don't think that's what he meant. I think he meant leaving somewhere else. Like . . . leaving *here*. Felicity. That he wanted to leave Felicity, but he couldn't until I was dead."

# Chapter 37

Maggie had no intention of telling her parents about her ordeal in the library. She hadn't been hurt, not really, though she was bruised and sore, and she didn't want to scare them. If they heard about Alex, who was going to be fine and would probably be discharged the following day, she would have to make up something.

She wasn't going to volunteer anything. Her parents knew and liked Alex. Unless they heard about his visit to the emergency room through the small-town rumor mill, always in operation, they didn't need to know. It wouldn't be on the news. No one had been killed. And the sheriff wouldn't be keen on spreading any more bad news. Greene County residents were already upset about the discovery of the . . . of Dante.

She came home to an empty house, and hadn't been lying on the couch more than ten minutes before the doorbell rang. When she opened the door, the sheriff was standing there, saying he had a few follow-up questions to ask her.

He also had a few things to tell her. Things she really didn't want to hear.

"It turns out," he said, "that Dante Guardino was murdered."

Maggie gasped. "Murdered? I heard he fell and hit his head."

"Oh, he hit his head, alright. Truth is, someone hit it *for* him. With a blunt object. Don't know exactly what. Then buried him in that coal bin."

"And no one ever knew?" Maggie found that incredible. Four years, and no one ever knew?

"Nope. And I know what you're thinkin'. But it was February when it happened. Pretty darn close to freezing in that unheated coal bin. Didn't really warm up much that year until the end of July. By that time, it didn't matter much."

Maggie sank back against the couch. Murdered? Dante Guardino had been murdered? "Do you know who did it?" she asked, her voice husky with shock.

"I got an idea. Seems to me the boy was innocent all along. Only thing that makes sense. I feel real bad about that. Too late now, though. He was innocent, and maybe the real killer had an attack of conscience — we figure it had to be a friend of his and the girl's — and came that night to get Guardino out of jail. And *did*, that's clear enough. But something went wrong at the last minute, seems to me. Maybe Guardino, once he was free, said he was gonna tell. At any rate, he ended up in the coal bin, his skull fractured just like the girl's. And the killer got off scot-free. Till now, anyway."

Maggie couldn't think straight. Dante hadn't murdered anyone, but *he* had been murdered? By a friend?

"Well, the jig's up now," the sheriff continued. "And our killer knows it. You findin' Guardino's remains, that's probably what he'd been afraid of all along, and why he tried to stop the restoration project. He wanted that building *gone*."

"You think this . . . person . . . caused the cave-in, and the explosion, and sawed through the cover of the well?"

"You betcha. Tryin' to make everyone think that building was a real hazard, and the grounds, too. By the way," he added casually, pulling a folded piece of paper out of his breast pocket, "I guess you already know a lot of your friends knew the dead girl?"

Maggie had been thinking of Dante, and was taken aback by the switch. "What dead girl?"

"Christy Miller. Turns out you know a lot of her friends."

"No, I don't."

"Yeah, you do." He unfolded the paper and began reading off names. "Paul Batcheler, Mary Linda Myers, Helen Morgan . . . "

Paul and Mindy were on the peer jury. And Helen had already admitted to Maggie that she knew Dante *and* Christy better than she'd let anyone think. No big deal.

"Tanya Frye, Lane Bridgewater, Benita Sawyer . . . "

Tanya and Bennie? They'd never said anything. Neither had Lane, not really. But then, like Helen said, who wanted to admit they'd been friends with either the victim or the killer?

"Lucas Broom, Alex Goodman, Tyler Smith."

Maggie didn't know Lucas Broom or Tyler Smith. But she knew Alex.

"Scout Redfern, Timothy Dwyer, Alice Ann Beckwith." The sheriff refolded the piece of paper and stuck it back in his shirt pocket.

Didn't know Timothy what's-his-name, either. And Chantilly, that was no surprise. She'd lived out that way. If she hadn't already been in the hospital, Maggie would have been certain it was Chantilly who had attacked her in the law library. She hadn't been in 4-H. But she still could have known Christy. "Not Scout," she said firmly. "Scout didn't know that girl."

"His mother said he did."

His mother. His mother hardly knew what day it was anymore. "Well, he didn't." Scout had said very clearly that he hadn't known Christy. "*I never met her,*" he'd said.

"But they all went to different schools," she protested. "And lived in different communities."

"They don't go to school in the summer. They get together, out there in the country. I know, 'cause I lived all my life out there in Nestegg. Don't matter which little spot they live in. They meet at swimming holes, at the Dairy Queen, at fairs and carnivals, community picnics. So how come you didn't know your friends knew that girl?"

"Nobody wants to talk about it," she said, using Helen's excuse. "And I don't blame them. I wouldn't talk about it, either. It's too creepy." Then, hoping she'd misunderstood, Maggie pressed, "Are you saying that these are the people who knew Christy? Or who knew Dante? Because I already knew Scout and Alex knew Dante. Helen and Lane, too. Through 4-H."

The sheriff shook his head. "Nope. Not talking about Dante. Just the girl. These are people who knew the girl . . . some better than others. And, by the way, Whittier's boy came by my office and said he knew them, too. And that his car was scratched up the other night when he pulled those two out of that ditch. Told me like he thought he might be a suspect. Tell the truth, he is."

"So you're saying that girl and Dante were both killed by the same person?"

"Looks that way." The sheriff glanced around the room. "Your mom or dad home?"

"No. And you haven't caught that person?"

"Well, now, we can't very well apprehend someone when we don't know who to apprehend, can we? That's what we're tryin' to find out now. And," looking at Maggie again, "what I want to know is, can you tell me anything about the person in the law library? 'Cause I would guess that's our guilty party. And he's bound to be real mad at you, Maggie. You spoiled it all for him. That building was about to be torn down, cemented over, and a new building put on top of what was left. Hadn't been for *you*, nobody would ever have known Guardino was in there, and our boy would have committed the perfect crime. You ruined all that. I imagine he's just about as mad at you as a person can get."

"Well, it wasn't *my* fault. It was because of James and Chantilly . . . " Maggie's voice faded, and her face drained of color. "Oh, god. That's why they were sent into that ditch, isn't it? He was mad at *them*, too. Because they chased me into that bin. He must have heard it on the news, the whole story. And then he went after them, shoved their car into that culvert!" She fixed apprehensive eyes on the sheriff.

"Listen, you told me he said something about splitting. And you didn't think he meant the law library?"

"No, he didn't. He meant Felicity, I'm positive. Like . . . like he wanted to leave here, but he couldn't until I was . . . until he punished me." She let that sink in, then added slowly, fearfully, "So I guess that means he's in a hurry, right?"

"Oh, he's in a hurry, all right," the sheriff said, standing up. "He knows his days are numbered. He *could* give up and just leave, right now, but I really don't want him doin' that. He's got a lot to answer for, this one." The sheriff sighed. "And me, I got a lot to make up for. Some I can't, but some I can. But first, I gotta get my hands on this bad number."

As he was leaving, he warned, "If I were you, I'd stay put for a day or two. Let you know as soon as we've got him. But like I said, it's *you* he's mad at. No point in makin' it easy for him."

The minute he was out the door, Maggie swiftly

closed and locked it. Like the sheriff said, no point in making things easy for a killer.

At first, she huddled on the couch, under an afghan, trying to digest everything the sheriff had said. Killer . . . Chantilly and James in that ditch . . . would have died if it hadn't been for Whit . . . not much time . . . mad at *her* for ruining things . . . not much time . . .

But slowly, very slowly, the terror began to ebb, and the more she thought about the position she seemed to be in, the angrier she got. "The sheriff said to stay put," she said aloud to the empty room. "Why do *I* have to stay put?"

*Because someone wants to kill you, dummy,* her inner voice answered.

"That doesn't mean that he *can,*" Maggie's voice rose. "If that creep thinks," she said aloud, "that he's going to make me a prisoner in my own home, he can just think again! *I* haven't done anything wrong."

*Sure you have. You screwed things up for him. He's really pissed, Maggie, and may I just remind you that he's already killed twice? And he did his best to kill James and Chantilly. What's one more corpse to him?*

Maggie's jaw tightened. "I am *not* going to be locked up like those prisoners in the basement cells!" she shouted. "I'm not giving *anyone* that much power over me. I can take care of myself."

*Oh, yeah, like you did on the ladder?*

"I held on, didn't I? I am *going* to school tomorrow, and I am going to the peer jury hearings in the morning . . . only," her voice weakening slightly, "I don't think I'll be helping with the moving tomorrow. There's brave, and then there's stupid. Going anywhere near the old courthouse would be truly stupid. I'll be safe at school."

That plan, of course, would only work if her parents didn't find out what was going on. If they did, her mother would lock her in her room and hire a twenty-four-hour security guard to make sure she stayed put. But they were both so busy . . . unless the sheriff talked to them, they might not find out about the ladder incident, or that Dante had been murdered, or that someone wanted their daughter dead.

They didn't, at least not by the following morning, when Maggie got up and dressed in a denim miniskirt and a red sweater, her hands not shaking in the least as she zipped the skirt or pulled on her boots or picked at her hair and fastened it back with combs, and went downstairs where she pretended to eat breakfast.

They did talk about Dante, but they believed his death had been accidental. "That poor Mrs. Guardino, this must be awful for her," and, "Hard to believe no one knew anything for four whole years."

Oh, but someone did, Maggie thought, pretending to swallow a bite of toast. Someone knew *everything*. Only they weren't telling.

She had one really bad moment when she opened the front door and realized that out there, somewhere, in spite of the warm breeze and the bright sunshine, someone wanted to take her life away from her . . . and as soon as possible.

I am crazy, she told herself as she climbed into the van and started the engine. I've lost it. Maybe being terrified on that ladder unhinged me. I could stay home today. I could hide in my room with all the doors and windows locked, and I'd be safe. I could stay there until the doorbell rings and it's the sheriff and he's smiling and he says, "Well, Maggie, you can relax now! We caught our guy and he's safely behind bars."

But if I did that, she thought, backing down the driveway, *I* might as well be behind bars. That would be so unfair. And so spineless.

Besides, she already knew that the sheriff was wrong about her friends. They shouldn't be on that list of suspects. Not even Whit, whom she really hadn't known that long. It had to be someone else, maybe that Timothy Dwyer person, or Lucas-somebody. The only reason Scout and Alex, Lane and Helen hadn't told her how well they knew that girl, Christy Miller, was what Helen had said: They didn't want to talk about it. They weren't guilty of anything except, like Whit, keeping a little, tiny secret. And that was not a crime.

She would be safe at school.

# Chapter 38

What struck Maggie as really odd when she walked into the gym for the peer jury hearing was how *unsafe* she suddenly felt. Alex, Helen, Lane, Whit, and Scout were already seated when she hurried in, as were the other jury members. They all looked up and said hi and asked her if she'd had any after-effects from her wild ride in the law library. Whit smiled at her, and Scout got up to take her back-pack and dump it on the bench with the others, and Helen and Lane said they weren't going to the game that night because they didn't feel safe enough to, considering . . .

Maggie said she wasn't going, either. School was safe. But a stadium with hundreds of people in it wouldn't be.

Susan was already seated behind the judge's desk, and the defendant, a boy who had cursed out the coach for not giving him more playing time in last week's game, was in place, along with Ralph

Santini. Everything was ready for the trial.

Maggie couldn't concentrate. She found herself picturing the faces of all of her best friends and wondering, though she didn't want to, if any one of them could have grabbed hold of that ladder and sent her flying along the wall, slamming into the corner shelves. Who had been in the building when that happened? Besides her, Helen, and Alex?

Lane, Scout, and Whit had been transporting bins of books to the new courthouse. Or so they'd said.

That thought shocked Maggie, and when she took her seat, her face felt hot. What was the matter with her? Of course they'd been out of the building.

The sheriff's talk yesterday was getting to her.

If any one of them had attacked her yesterday, wanted to kill her now, they wouldn't have called her last night, every single one of them, to see how she was. She'd talked to Whit the longest, but she'd talked to Helen and Lane a long time, too. And to Scout, who had seemed really worried about her, asking her if she was sure she was all right, and didn't she think she should see a doctor?

She hadn't told any of them except Helen what the sheriff had said. She'd told Helen because Helen was the only one who had admitted that she had known Christy Miller and Dante Guardino. That kind of honesty deserved more honesty. So she'd told Helen.

Who had been predictably shocked. And who had promptly warned her best friend to stay home until the killer had been caught. When Maggie had argued for her independence, Helen had cried in anguish, "Maggie, you're my best friend! If anything happened to you, I don't know what I'd do!"

As much as her concern had touched Maggie, she'd decided, after she'd thought it over, that she couldn't let Helen make her decisions for her. Maybe Helen would stay home if she were threatened. And that was fine. For Helen. But not for Maggie Keene.

"You are so arrogant!" Helen had shouted into the telephone. "Anyone else would be sensible. But you just can't stand having anyone tell you what to do, can you?"

"I can't stand having a *criminal* tell me what to do," Maggie had said then.

Helen had sighed and given up. And Maggie had made her promise not to tell the others what the sheriff had said. Some of it, they would already have heard. The part about Dante being innocent, and about him being murdered. But maybe not the part about the killer being furious with Maggie Keene, and in a hurry to do something about that fury, because he had to leave town quickly.

She was right. She could tell by their faces that they hadn't heard that part. Good.

Warning Helen with her eyes to keep her mouth shut, Maggie opened her notebook to begin taking notes.

The boy received one week of detention for his foul mouth. He was angry, and stayed in his seat arguing with Ralph after the sentence had been announced.

Bored, all of the peer jury but Maggie went to get their backpacks.

But the boy was so angry, as he left, he gave the bench a hefty kick, spilling out notebooks and hairbrushes and pens and textbooks and paperback novels and schedules on Post-It notes and tissues and combs and even a clean pair of white socks. A handful of objects skidded across the hardwood floor to Maggie's feet.

She bent to pick them up.

A packet of tissue. A roll of breath mints. A small, silver key. And a bus ticket. Maggie had no idea whose backpack it had spilled out of, but assumed it was Scout's because he had gone to the bus station. The ticket was for his mother's trip to rehab. She glanced up to wave at him, but he wasn't looking in her direction. No one was. They were all crouched, their backs to her, scrambling to retrieve their belongings.

Maggie looked at the ticket again. There was something not quite right about it. Its destination wasn't California, where Scout said his mother was going. It was Phoenix, Arizona. So maybe it wasn't Scout's. Maggie pursed her lips. Which of her friends, the only people left in this room, was planning a bus trip to Phoenix, Arizona?

The school year had just begun. Traveling from Ohio to Arizona by bus took a while. You couldn't go there and return in just one weekend. Which one of her friends was planning to take time off from school to go to Arizona? And why would they?

Maggie looked at the ticket again. Something else was wrong with it. It was a one-way ticket. The person who had bought it wasn't planning to return any time soon.

She heard again the eerie, falsetto voice in the law library saying, *"I want this to end now, so I can split before it's too late!"* Split. As in depart, exit, leave town.

Someone on the peer jury was planning to leave town. And they were not planning to come back.

Scout had gone to the bus station. And Scout had said he never knew Christy Miller, but his mother and the sheriff said he had. Scout didn't like cheats, and rumor had it that Christy had definitely cheated. How many times had Scout said, "Three is a crowd"? Three . . . as in Scout, Christy, and Dante? Scout was possessive, even jealous.

And he had gone to the bus station.

He had been in the basement when the beam collapsed, and he had been at the bazaar where the stove blew up. And he knew how to handle a small power saw. Maggie knew that because he had worked on a construction crew headed by Lane's father the summer he turned sixteen.

Everyone was stooping, laughing, wailing over the mess.

She bent to pick up the small, silver key. She knew what it was immediately. The key to a locker at the bus station. She knew that's what it was because it had been lying right there with the ticket, and because if you were planning a really quick getaway, you would stash your packed stuff in a bus station locker so that it would be right there, ready to go, when the right moment came.

Phoenix was a good-sized city. You could probably hide there fairly easily. And the climate was supposed to be nice. If you were planning to get away with murder and escape, you might as well choose someplace with a nice climate.

The bus ticket was in her hand. Without even thinking about it, she scooped up the key, too. Then without even grabbing her own backpack, only her shoulder bag, and without saying good-bye, she ran from the gym, expecting at any moment to hear Scout shout, "Hey, come back here with my bus ticket!"

But he didn't.

Maggie went straight to the bus station, on foot.

"How would I know who I sold it to?" the clerk, a middle-aged woman in a lime-green pantsuit, her hair long, gray, and straight, said irritably. "Coulda been anybody. I don't keep track."

And although Maggie pressed, the woman was adamant. She had, she said, better things to do with her time than memorize every single person who bought every single ticket.

Giving up on that, telling herself the sheriff might have better luck because he had a badge and a uniform, Maggie went to the pay telephone and called Scout's house. She could tell by his mother's voice when she answered that she had been asleep.

"Phoenix?" she repeated in answer to Maggie's question. "I'm not going to Phoenix. Why would I be going there? I'm not going anywhere. I loathe traveling. Did Scout tell you I was going somewhere? Well, I'm *not*. He lies, you know. He always has. He tells people things about me that aren't true."

"Did he know Christy Miller?" Maggie demanded.

"Of course he knew her. Scout knows everybody. And everybody loves him. He's just like his father," she added bitterly, and then she hung up.

Next, Maggie slid the small, silver key out of her skirt pocket, and went straight to the wall of metal lockers, murmuring, "Sixty-two, sixty-two, sixty-two . . . "

The locker opened by the key contained only three things.

A gray tweed suitcase, bulging at the seams. An athletic jacket, Bransom's blue-and-white, neatly folded and perched on top of the suitcase. And on top of the jacket, a baseball cap. Cleveland Indians, just as Whit had said.

Maggie reached in and located the label on the inside back of the jacket.

Dante's name on the label, in black felt pen: GUARDINO.

How foolish, how stupid, to keep the jacket of a person you'd murdered. And Helen thought *Maggie* was arrogant!

Other than Dante's name, she found no other identification in the locker. There were no name tags on the suitcase.

But Scout's mother wasn't planning a trip. She had said so. Not to California, and not to Phoenix. *Scout* was. Because he needed to leave town.

You just never really know people, do you, Maggie thought, an incredible sadness filling her. He'd been in love with Christy Miller at thirteen, the way Maggie had been with him? And Dante had got in the way?

Maggie glanced up just then, and drew in her breath sharply. Scout. Approaching at a rapid pace, his face dark with anger.

Of course. He knew she'd taken the ticket, and he was furious.

"Is there a back door?" she called to the clerk.

The clerk waved, and Maggie jumped up and ran to the left and out a side door just as Scout came in the front entrance.

She ran through the alleyways from Second Street to Fourth, avoiding the main streets where she would be an open target.

At the last minute, she veered into a drugstore, grabbed a quarter out of her shoulder bag, and called the sheriff's office. No way was she going anywhere near the old courthouse, not now, not ever.

"He's not here," the deputy told her. "He's over at the new courthouse. Third floor. They're bringing his desk in today. Can't call him there, though, phone's not in. Want me to try his pager?"

She wasn't afraid of the new courthouse. And it would be better to show him the ticket and the key in person. "No. I'll go on over there. Thanks."

Lady Justice was lying on her back on the unseeded lawn beside the new building. If she hadn't been blindfolded, she would have been staring up at the bright blue sky, or perhaps at the top of the building, her next destination. The scale in her hands spilled over to one side, the scoops lying facing up, as if waiting for something to drop into them. Maggie couldn't imagine what it would take to get that gigantic thing all the way up to the top of a four-story building. But she couldn't worry about that.

Inside, the building was so different from the old courthouse. So fresh and bright inside, everything so clean and new. The black-and-white tile on the floors sparkled under the faint carpet of dust created by moving things in, sunshine streamed in through the wide windows, the walls had been newly painted white, and where there was paneling, it was rich, dark wood. The paint smell was still pretty pungent, but Maggie loved the newness of it all and puzzled again over her mother's attachment to things old and decaying.

The building seemed to be empty, which surprised her. Where was everyone? Shouldn't there be work crews in here?

Her footsteps echoed like gunshots as she hurried across the tile and up the stairs.

The sheriff wasn't on the third floor, although the huge, wooden desk was already in place in his new office.

Maggie glanced around the hallway fearfully. The sheriff was *supposed* to be here. She should have had him paged, if only to find out exactly where in the building he might be.

She hadn't seen him on the first or second floors while she was climbing the wide, curving staircases. In fact, she hadn't seen anyone. It wasn't lunchtime yet, not even close. Where *was* everyone?

Couldn't that ticket have fallen out of someone else's backpack, not Scout's?

But Scout had been to the bus station. And he had lied about knowing Christy.

Besides, she didn't want the killer to be any of her other friends, either.

If the sheriff wasn't on the first or second floor, and he wasn't here on the third, that only left the fourth floor. What would she do if he wasn't up there?

She was running up the last flight of stairs to the fourth floor when she first heard the foot steps. Coming up the stairs. *Clickety-clack, clickety-clack.*

Maggie stopped, held her breath. It could be anyone. A secretary, a member of the work crew, the sheriff . . .

The sheriff's footsteps wouldn't *clickety-clack.*

She leaned over the thick, wooden railing to look, but saw nothing. If it was someone who could help . . . she should call out, tell them to hurry, hurry up here and tell her how to find the sheriff without going near the old courthouse.

"Maggie? Are you up there?" Lane's voice. "Wait up! What are you doing in here?"

Maggie heaved a sigh of relief. "Up here! Fourth floor." Then, "Are you alone?"

"Yep. Wait for me. I know about Scout, Maggie. And it's worse than you think."

Worse? How could it be worse? Maggie leaned against the railing and waited for Lane.

Lane continued calling out to Maggie as she climbed the steep stairs from floor to floor. "I know you're upset, we all are. But at least the truth is out."

"How did you know?" Maggie called down over the railing.

"I've always suspected it was him." *Clickety-clack* on the stairs. "I knew how he felt about Christy. I never told you because he made me promise not to. But I knew."

Maggie stood very still at the railing, but her mind was racing. "Has Scout been arrested?" If he had, she'd be safe now. But she'd hurt inside, a lot.

"No. Not yet. But he will be as soon as the sheriff has that bus ticket and the locker key. You *do* still have them, don't you?"

"Yes. They're in my purse."

A laugh, the sound closer now. "Can you imagine someone picking Phoenix to run to? Yuk! So dry and dusty and hot! Why not New York City? Lots more fun."

"Phoenix?" Maggie's palms on the railing felt clammy, as if the wood were wet. But it wasn't. She heard birds cackling outside and remembered that the walls on this floor weren't finished. They were open to the outside, with only sheets of plastic as protection from the elements. "How did you know it was Phoenix?"

"What?"

Maggie took a step backward, letting go of the railing, the heel of her boot on the top step. "How

305

did you know Scout was planning to go to Phoenix?" Lane hadn't seen the ticket. She couldn't have. Her back had been turned when the ticket skidded across the hardwood floor and landed at Maggie's feet. And Lane had been searching frantically among the mess, as if she were missing something valuable. Something like . . . a bus ticket? One-way? To Arizona?

Lane's *clickety-clacking* footsteps stopped on the stairs. "Oh. Well, I . . . I saw it. I saw it fall out of Scout's backpack."

Not a chance.

Maggie went up another step.

Lane, too, had been in that basement, been at the bazaar, could even have come back to the law library instead of coming to this building. Could have struck Alex on the head, sent that ladder flying, then shouted from the doorway as if she'd just arrived. Could have then quickly run across the room in the dark, slammed a door as if someone were leaving, and then flown back to the door to turn on the lights. Could have done all of that.

But . . . *Lane* was the one who had fallen into the well.

Maggie remembered then why Dante Guardino's picture in the paper had seemed so familiar. She *had* seen that face before, and she wasn't remembering it from years ago when he'd been on trial. She was remembering it from Lane's wallet. That was *his* picture in there. Lane hadn't actually shown her the picture. Maggie had happened to notice it when Lane was paying for something at the mall. And then she had said it was a college boy she was dating, someone named Scoop.

But it wasn't. It was Dante Guardino.

How foolish, how arrogant, to carry around with you the picture of a boy you'd killed. Almost as foolish as keeping his jacket and baseball cap.

Lane's father drove a black truck. Much bigger and heavier than Chantilly's old blue sedan. It wouldn't have been much of a contest on a dirt road slick with recent rain.

Maggie fought her thoughts. Lane was her close friend. They'd had sleepovers, they'd talked about boys and hairstyles and clothes and books they'd read. They'd gone through freshman and sophomore years together, and sometimes they'd even cried on each other's shoulders when life seemed to really stink.

But . . . Lane couldn't possibly have known that ticket was for Phoenix unless she had bought it herself. She was the one planning to leave town. Because she *had* to. Because Maggie Keene had discovered the boy Lane had killed in the coal bin of the old courthouse.

It wasn't Scout. The person who had killed that girl, and then Dante, the person who had driven James and Chantilly into that culvert, the same person who intended to kill Maggie Keene because she'd found that body and ruined everything, was Lane Bridgewater.

And Lane and Maggie were, at this very moment, the only two people in the new courthouse.

# Chapter 39

Lane was here to tie up one last loose end. No one had to tell Maggie that. Lane was, this very second, climbing the stairs of the new courthouse in pursuit of one last prey.

She had killed before. She wouldn't hesitate to kill now.

There was nowhere to go but up. Maggie ran.

In the silent, white-walled corridor on the fourth floor, she glanced around wildly for someplace to hide. The wall on this floor on the right side of the building, where she'd come in, wasn't finished. From far below, she had noticed the huge sheet of plastic used as protection against the elements flapping in the breeze. She could go into one of the offices and scream for help through that opening. If there was anyone at all around, they'd hear her and come to help her. Before it was too late.

*Clickety-clack, clickety-clack.* "Maggie? Where are you? Why didn't you wait for me?" A low chuckle. "Why, you little scamp, you! You *know*, don't you? You figured it out, all by your little self. Congratulations. Not that it makes any difference. We're the only people in this building, Maggie. I phoned in a bomb threat to the high school. The police are there, waiting for it to blow up. And all of the men working in here went over there to see what was up."

Out of breath, her heart hammering in her chest, Maggie stood in the middle of the empty, unfinished office, shaking. The floor was bare, the boards she was standing on wobbly, clearly not nailed in place yet, and there were tools everywhere. Directly in front of the plastic, two sawhorses faced each other, as if they were carrying on a conversation. A long, loose board two inches thick rested at a slant against the sawhorse facing Maggie. A hammer, a saw, and a box of nails sat on the other.

Someone was working up here, she told herself in an effort to calm herself. They'll be back. Any minute now, they'll be back.

There was no place to hide, none at all. No desk, no file cabinet, not even a potted plant. And no place to run to.

"Sheriff?" she shouted desperately. "Sheriff Donovan, are you up here?"

No answer.

She moved swiftly to the plastic curtain and would have pulled a loose edge aside to scream for help, if there hadn't been a sudden whoosh of air behind her. She hadn't heard a thing until then, hadn't realized that she had no more time left.

Something thick and black slipped over her eyes, and a voice whispered in her ear, "I took my shoes off so you wouldn't hear me, just like I did in the law library. Wasn't that clever of me?" Then strong hands whirled Maggie around, grabbed both of her hands at the same time, and roughly wound a rope around her wrists, tying her hands in front of her. "I have just picked up a large hammer. If you make one sound, just one, I'm going to bash your brains in."

Terrifyingly conscious of the four-story drop to the ground directly at her back, Maggie made no move to resist. One gentle shove and she'd fall to her death.

The hands that led her, then, away from the opening were not rough. They walked a few feet, and then she was gently pushed into a sitting position on what she realized was the sawhorse facing the door. When Lane spoke next, Maggie could tell that she was seated, too, on the opposite sawhorse, facing Maggie.

"We have plenty of time," Lane said, in a normal, rather friendly voice. "Felicity doesn't have bomb-sniffing dogs. Doesn't even have a bomb squad, can you believe that? So it'll take a while for them to figure out there's no bomb over at the high school." Her voice hardened. "Where's my ticket? And my key?"

"In my purse." Maggie let herself feel relief that it wasn't Scout. His mother must not have been told yet that she was being sent to California. Or maybe she just hadn't wanted to admit it. They really should tell her soon.

Maggie could feel the edge of the board that rested at a slant against the sawhorse digging into her left hip. It felt oddly comforting, as if it meant she wasn't completely alone. "You saw me pick up the ticket?"

"Nope. But I couldn't find it, and then you flew out of the room. Wasn't hard to figure out. I knew you'd think it was Scout, because he'd been to the bus station. And I knew that, as much as you'd hate to, you'd go straight to the sheriff even though Scout is one of your best friends. Everyone knows how fair you are. That's why you're foreperson. So I called the sheriff's office to find out where he was, and they said he was here. I knew you'd come here looking for him. Then I called in the bomb threat."

"I get it about the beam collapsing . . . you were there . . . and the explosion, which probably wasn't hard. What I don't get is the well. *You* fell in."

"Yep. I did. Saw the well on the diagrams at the WOH. I was afraid your mother was going to change her mind about canceling the plans, and I couldn't let that happen. When I went over there to find the well, some old guy came along, showed me where it was, and told me it was pretty well filled in. I knew I wouldn't get hurt. But I wore the sweatsuit for added protection." Lane laughed. "Those diagrams they found in Chantilly's car don't have anything to do with the old courthouse. James takes drafting class. That was his homework."

Maggie, loathing the blindfold, nodded. "I knew that sweatsuit wasn't the kind of outfit you usually wear in public. But . . . why Helen's hankie, if you were trying to make it look like an accident, like the cover had just given way?"

"The sweatsuit helped, you know," Lane said. "The doctor said so. As for the hankie, I was afraid the sheriff would notice the boards had been sawed through. I'd had that hankie for a long time. Took it from Helen's room before I'd even thought of any of this stuff. It was pretty, and I wanted it. I figured, if he *did* notice the boards hadn't just given way, he'd suspect Helen, which would buy me some time. So I took the hankie with me when I dove into that hole in the ground. Good thing, too, because that sheriff isn't as dumb as he looks."

"Well, you just think of everything, don't you?"

"Don't be cute. Okay, here's the deal. You, Magdalene Jaye Keene, have been convicted of destroying my life. By finding Dante when no one else had."

"That wasn't my fault."

"Well, yeah, I know that. But the other two have already been taken care of, and you *do* bear *some* responsibility, you know. Anyway," continuing blithely, "I've appointed myself your executioner. Any last wishes?"

"Sure. Don't kill me. Like you did the others."

"I'm not *going* to kill you like I did the others. I'm going to kill you in an entirely different way." Low, cold laughter. Not maniacal, but still, insane in its own way.

Maggie's blood froze. Lane *was* insane, though few people would have guessed it. But you couldn't kill two people and try to kill three more without losing your sanity, could you? Or did the sanity go *first*, and then the deaths?

Why hadn't she guessed? Why hadn't anyone?

"Actually, I'm not going to kill you at all."

Maggie held her breath.

"I'm just going to make you take a little walk, that's all. Right through that opening over there. Blindfolded, of course. You're going to walk the plank, just like pirates did once upon a time." Lane sighed heavily. "Anyway, that's an unacceptable last wish, asking for a reprieve. No reprieves. Got another wish?"

When the nervous tapping sound began, Maggie wasn't sure at first what it was, and a tiny sprig of hope arose within her . . . someone might be coming up the stairs? Then she realized, with bitter disappointment, that Lane had put her shoes back on and was tapping the heels of her black flats against the slanted board resting at her feet.

Maggie shifted imperceptibly closer to the board beside her. The bottom edge was resting on the floor, the upper half directly adjacent to Maggie's left shoulder. Being blindfolded seemed to have improved her hearing. If Lane continued tapping her feet . . .

But with her hands tied, and her eyes covered . . . impossible to save herself.

"Yes. I do have another last wish. Tell me why you did it. Tell me *what* you did." Maybe the sheriff would come. Maybe a worker. Someone. How long did it take to discover that a bomb scare had been a hoax, without bomb-sniffing dogs or a bomb squad?

"Sure. Why not? But just in case you get any dumb ideas, remember the hammer in my hand."

Maggie felt sick. "Just tell me."

She felt even sicker as the story of Christy's death and Dante's imprisonment unfolded.

"All I wanted him to do was leave town. I even gave him money. And I got him out of his cell and up the chute. But once we got outside, Dante changed his mind. He said why should he leave Felicity when I was the one who had killed Christy? He said he wouldn't go, that I had to go to the authorities and confess. Right. Like I was stupid enough to do that. So I pushed him. Hard. He fell, landing on his back on the parking lot, with his head facing the open chute window. He was sort of stunned, so I grabbed his feet and pushed again, harder this time. Pushed him into the chute. He slid down backward, and I heard the crack when his skull slammed into the wooden railroad ties holding the coal in the bin."

The voice paused, and Maggie said, "I guess you didn't call for help."

"Very funny. I slid back down the coal chute. I knew right away that Dante was dead. His face looked peaceful. I thought that was nice. I figured I'd probably saved him a lot of heartache, you know? I mean, no one would ever have believed that I killed Christy instead of him, and that would have been really hard on him. He'd have felt persecuted all of his life," a giggle, "not to mention *prosecuted*."

The casual way Lane spoke of murder, even if it

had been involuntary in the beginning, at least, turned Maggie's entire body icy cold. Lane could just as easily have been discussing a football game, or shopping at the mall, or a movie.

"I couldn't leave him there for someone to find. And I couldn't carry him out of there. The bin was half-full of coal that no one ever bothered to remove, so I used my hands to scoop out a kind of well. Sort of like a grave, you might say. It took forever, and I was scared to death someone would hear me. Then I took off his jacket and cap, because *he* certainly wasn't going to need them and I'd always liked them. I thought it would be nice to have something to remind me of him. Then I put him in there and covered him up. Then I went home. The next day, I sent a letter to the newspaper, saying I'd seen rats coming out of the coal chute window and urging parents to keep their kids out of that cellar. Signed it with a fake name, of course. And it worked, as far as I knew. If any kids did sneak down there after that, they never found Dante. But then, why would they? No one ever played in the coal pile itself. Too dirty."

The wind at Maggie's back was stronger now, whistling like a teakettle, tugging at the plastic flap. If only she could see. She was as helpless as she had ever been. And so scared, her teeth were beginning to chatter. She clamped them together fiercely, biting her tongue in the process, but refusing to cry out with the sudden pain. "You saw the renovation plans during P.E.?" she asked. "That's how you knew about the beam?"

"Good guess. But it was James who locked you in that coal bin. I saw him do it. I was pretty sure then he'd be blamed for anything I did. I wasn't trying to hurt anyone. I just wanted to push home the point that the building was a wreck, that's all. So your mother would stop. But," she said hastily, "James and Chantilly did all the other stuff. The gavel, the bloody scale, the doll." Contempt laced the words, "I would never bother with that kind of adolescent stuff."

"No, just murder," Maggie mumbled.

"I'm still holding this hammer, Maggie. So I'd watch my mouth if I were you."

"You turned the gas on in the kitchen at the bazaar?"

"Of course. That was so easy! I could have thrown a flaming log in through that window, and no one would have noticed. All they cared about was filling their stomachs with barbecue. Anyway, it was just a match. A fireplace match. Not that big. But it did the trick. I *did* wait until I saw you leave the kitchen, Maggie. Give me credit."

"You must have really loved him," Maggie said quietly. "To do all that for him."

"I didn't blame Dante for picking Christy. Any guy would have. And by the way, Maggie, Scout wasn't lying. He never knew Christy."

Well, that was something. Scout hadn't lied. His mother was wrong.

"But I blamed *her* for the way she treated him. It was awful, horrible. She deserved to die! If someone treated Whit like that, you'd hate her, wouldn't you?"

"No. I'd hate *him* for letting her. And maybe you hated Dante, too, Lane. Maybe you just don't want to admit it." Maggie thought, just for a second, that she heard voices. Distant voices, but still . . . maybe help was on its way.

They'd better hurry.

"Maggie, we have to get this over with. You have to stand up now."

"Why did you stop in the law library? Why did you quit pushing the ladder?"

"Because *you* wouldn't give up! When I saw that you weren't going to let go, I knew I would have to quit before the others came back. You are *so* stubborn!"

It might be okay if Lane stood up, too. It might help. Crazy thought, crazy . . . but she was *not* going to just sit here and let herself be pushed from the fourth floor.

"What if someone else had fallen into the well? Instead of you?"

She could almost hear the shrug. "That would have worked, too. But I really *didn't* want anyone else to get hurt. So I made sure I got there first, knowing I wouldn't get hurt."

"This from someone who's killed two people and is about to kill a third," Maggie said acidly. If she could just time this perfectly . . . no, no, it would never work, crazy, crazy . . . But it was something. "Do you really expect to get out of town before anyone sees or hears me fall screaming to my death? What makes you think you'll even get out of the building?"

"This building has sixty zillion entrances. I'm going out the one that's farthest from where you'll be . . . landing. Everyone will be on that side, where you hit. Not anywhere near the exit I'm using. Now, I want that bus ticket and my key. Then you're taking a walk, like I promised."

"I can't take my shoulder bag off, not with my hands tied in front of me. You'll have to come over here and get what you want." *Stand up*, Maggie urged silently, *go ahead, stand up*, feeling with her left shoulder for the board. It was still there, still resting beside her, like a teeter-totter, with her at the high end and Lane at the low end. She strained to hear the slightest sound, the tiniest whisper of fabric that would mean Lane was rising from the sawhorse.

She heard it. The sound of Lane's brown corduroy skirt rubbing against the sawhorse as Lane got to her feet.

So fast it took her own breath away, Maggie whirled to her left and pounded down with her bound, fisted hands on the top of the loose, seesaw board.

And a hot, triumphant surge of satisfaction rushed through her as the next sound she heard was the clicking together of Lane's teeth and a pained grunt when the board flew up and caught her under the chin. The sound that followed immediately was that of a body flying backward, tumbling over a sawhorse, and hitting the bare floor with a thud.

With the hammer no longer an immediate threat,

Maggie reached up with her bound hands to rip the blindfold from her eyes. Being able to see again made her weak with gratitude.

Lane was on the floor, on the other side of the sawhorse, blood dripping from her mouth. She wasn't unconscious. Her eyes were open. But she was clearly stunned.

The saw . . . where was the saw? Maggie needed it. Fast! There . . . it had fallen to the floor when Lane hit the sawhorse.

Maggie knelt, brought the rope around her wrists up against the edge of the saw, ripped it back and forth rapidly three, four times, until the rope gave. Glancing over her right shoulder to see Lane struggling to get to her feet, Maggie ran to the plastic flap to scream for help.

Lane got up. Swayed dizzily. Reached down blindly for the hammer. Grasped it, picked it up.

Maggie screamed. Far below her, like ants at a picnic, she saw workmen walking slowly toward the building from the direction of the high school. She screamed again, then looked fearfully over her shoulder.

Lane, swaying precariously, blood dripping steadily downward from her chin, creating a ribbon of red on the front of her white blouse, took a staggering step toward Maggie, hammer raised high.

"Lane, don't . . . don't," Maggie said softly. "You know it's over. It *is*."

The beautiful eyes blinked once, twice. "It's over?" she asked. "It's all over?"

"Yes," Maggie said gently. "Put the hammer

down, Lane. The sheriff is coming." And that was true. Maggie had seen him heading for the same door she'd come in, the one directly opposite the giant statue.

And for one quiet, peaceful minute, she thought Lane had accepted that. That she was going to put the hammer down and then maybe sink down to the floor or sit on the sawhorse and just wait for whatever was going to happen next.

And then Lane's pretty face twisted, and her bleeding mouth opened, and out of it came a scream of raw, pure, animal rage that filled the empty room. Maggie thought that even the blank, white walls shuddered in fear, hearing that sound.

Lane lifted the hammer. Still screaming that terrible sound, she rushed at Maggie, who stood beside the opening, clutching an open edge of the plastic in terror.

At the very last second, with the hammer only inches from her forehead, Maggie threw herself to one side, crying out Lane's name as she fell to the floor.

She stayed there, her face in her hands, as Lane went through the plastic and out into nothingness.

She screamed all the way down.

Maggie lay unmoving on the unfinished floor for what seemed like a very long time. She could hear distant voices outside. Maybe they were shouting. Maybe they were just talking. She couldn't be sure. It didn't seem to matter.

The next thing she was aware of, was a closer voice. Right there beside her, in fact, which surprised her. She hadn't heard footsteps coming up the stairs. Hadn't heard anything, only the steady *flap-flap* of the plastic wall that hadn't kept Lane from falling.

But there it was, a voice, asking her something. Scout. And then another voice . . . Helen's? . . . and a third . . . Whit's. They wanted her to get up. They were telling her it was okay.

She had told Lane that. Only it hadn't been true. Maybe it wasn't true now. Maybe she shouldn't get up.

But she did, finally. And then she walked, as unsteadily as Lane had, pulled aside the flap, and looked down.

And there was Lane, lying on her back in the scoop on the left side of the scales in the hands of Lady Justice. Even from four floors up, since Lane wasn't wearing a blindfold like the statue, Maggie could see that her eyes were wide open. But she looked quite comfortable, as if she were only resting, and would get up in just a minute, when she felt better.

It seemed so perfectly ironic. Lane hadn't trusted the criminal justice system. Her sick and twisted mind had created a system of her own. And it had brought her here, where she rested in the scales of justice, after all.

"I'd like to go home now," Maggie said to her friends.

They took her home.

# Epilogue

The party was going well, in spite of the recent tragedy. The new courthouse, the last set of hinges fastened, the last coat of paint applied, the last desk in place, was resplendent with red, white, and blue crepe paper streaming from its pillars, and huge pots of red geraniums dotting the front veranda. High above the ground, at the very top of the building, the statue was firmly fastened in place. Lady Justice stood unseeing, towering over the town of Felicity, balancing the set of scales in her hands.

It seemed to Maggie that everyone in town, maybe everyone in the county, had turned out. Even James and Chantilly were there, their faces scratched and bruised and a lot of their usual swagger missing. Maggie thought that maybe their brush with death had drained some of the fight out of them. When they passed Maggie and Whit, they each actually raised a hand in acknowledgment. The gesture seemed to say, *I still don't like you very much, but one of you* did *drag us out of that ditch.* They were still facing charges of malicious mischief, but probably would get probation. It wasn't as if they'd *killed* anyone.

There had been talk, upon Lane's death, of canceling the party. But the consensus of opinion was, considering the pain and heartache Lane Bridgewater had caused the town, that wasn't necessary.

There hadn't been many people at her funeral. No one was especially eager to be known as her friend. Whit came, and Helen, Scout, Alex, and Maggie. And Ms. Gross, and most of Lane's teachers. Although Lane had been popular, few of her other classmates attended. One of them told Maggie, when asked later why she hadn't attended, that her parents wouldn't let her.

"Right," Maggie said curtly, and walked away.

Scout's mother wasn't at the party. Saying that she was not about to travel all the way to California alone, she had insisted that Scout return the California ticket, which was what Scout had been about to do when Maggie saw him approaching the bus station looking so angry. He *had* been angry. And disappointed. But after some negotiations, Mrs. Redfern had agreed to attend rehab in Cincinnati, and Scout and his father were driving her there. She would get the help she needed.

Maggie hadn't seen any need to tell Scout that she had, even for a little while, suspected him of committing horrendous deeds. He had accepted, with grudgingly good spirits, the fact that she was with Whit now. The least she could do in return was keep her big, fat mouth shut about thinking him a murderer.

With his mother about to leave for twenty-one days, and one of his closest friends, Lane, gone, Scout might have looked a little more forlorn if it hadn't been for Bennie Sawyer, who was doing her very best to cheer him up. Bennie was good at that. It seemed to be working.

Helen and Alex were playing Ping-Pong, and even laughed once in a while, though Helen, especially, had taken the news of Lane's death (and what she had done) hard. But Helen was looking forward to helping Maggie's mother restore the old warehouse and turn it into a children's museum. Sheila Keene had called it "therapy" when she talked them all into volunteering.

"She never stops, does she?" Helen had asked Maggie as they filled paper plates at a buffet table set up on the new lawn.

"Nope."

"You don't, either," Helen said with admiration. "Like mother, like daughter, I guess."

Maggie took that as a compliment.

She had looked, just once, at the old courthouse as they'd passed it, and felt a pang of remorse for Otis Bransom and the beautiful mansion he'd built. But it was time now for the building to pass on into history, time to move on to something new. The new courthouse would serve Greene County well. And there were no dark secrets hidden inside.

Whit had repeatedly asked her if she was still going to the party. She had said yes, of course she was going. And he'd repeated something he'd said to her earlier, a long, long time ago. "You don't scare easily, do you?"

She hoped not. Being scared was not a good way to live.

Now, he came up to her with a cup in each hand, handed her one, and asked her for the second time that afternoon if she was okay being here after what had happened.

No, of course she wasn't okay. She had lost a best friend, in a horrible way. And in spite of everything that Lane had done, Maggie would miss her fiercely for a very long time. Then there was the pain of thinking she knew someone so well and finding out she hadn't known Lane at all. That was scary. Then there was the matter of visiting Felicity even after she'd left for good. Every time she passed the new courthouse, she would remember, and she would feel sick, remembering.

But . . .

She had lost Lane, but she still had good friends. More important, she still had her life. Lane hadn't taken that from her.

And she was Maggie Keene. Who didn't quit.

The first time Whit had asked her if she was okay being here after what had happened, she had answered, "I don't know."

This time, she forced a smile, tilted her head to look directly up at him, and answered, "Something happened here?"

And he laughed.

# THRILLERS

## D.E. Athkins
- ❏ MC25490-1 The Bride . . . . . . . . $3.99
- ❏ MC45349-1 The Ripper . . . . . . . $3.50

## A. Bates
- ❏ MC45829-9 The Dead Game . . . $3.99
- ❏ MC43291-5 Final Exam . . . . . . . $3.50
- ❏ MC44582-0 Mother's Helper . . . . $3.99
- ❏ MC44238-4 Party Line . . . . . . . $3.99
- ❏ MC50951-9 Krazy 4 U . . . . . . . $3.99

## Caroline B. Cooney
- ❏ MC44316-X The Cheerleader . . . $3.50
- ❏ MC45402-1 The Perfume . . . . . . $3.50
- ❏ MC45680-6 The Stranger . . . . . $4.50
- ❏ MC45682-2 The Vampire's Promise . . . . . . . . . $3.50

## Richie Tankersley Cusick
- ❏ MC43114-5 Teacher's Pet . . . . . $3.50
- ❏ MC44235-X Trick or Treat . . . . . $3.50

## Carol Ellis
- ❏ MC44768-8 My Secret Admirer . $3.50

- ❏ MC44916-8 The Window . . . . . . $3.50
- ❏ MC46411-6 Camp Fear . . . . . . . $3.50
- ❏ MC25520-7 The Stalker . . . . . . . $3.99

## Peter Lerangis
- ❏ MC46678-X The Yearbook . . . . . $3.50

## Lael Littke
- ❏ MC44237-6 Prom Dress . . . . . . $3.50

## Christopher Pike
- ❏ MC43014-9 Slumber Party . . . . $3.50
- ❏ MC44256-2 Weekend . . . . . . . $3.99
- ❏ MC43014-9 Slumber Party . . . . $3.50

## Edited by Tonya Pines
- ❏ MC45256-8 Thirteen . . . . . . . . . $3.99

## Sinclair Smith
- ❏ MC46126-5 Dream Date . . . . . . $3.99
- ❏ MC45063-8 The Waitress . . . . . $3.99

## Barbara Steiner
- ❏ MC54419-5 Spring Break . . . . . $3.99
- ❏ MC67449-8 Sweet Sixteen . . . . $3.99

**Available wherever you buy books, or use this order form.**

# CAROLINE B. COONEY

## Caroline B. Cooney — Takes You To The Edge Of Your Seat!

| | | |
|---|---|---|
| BCE98849-2 | **Wanted!** | $4.50 |
| BCE45680-6 | **The Stranger** | $4.50 |
| BCE45740-3 | **Emergency Room** | $4.50 |
| BCE44479-4 | **Flight #116 Is Down** | $4.50 |
| BCE47478-2 | **Twins** | $4.50 |

Available wherever you buy books, or use this order form.